I0547946

THE AQUITAINE DECEPTION

THE AQUITAINE DECEPTION

Copyright ©2014 Paul Bourdon

All Rights Reserved. No part of this publication may be reproduced, distributed or transmitted in any form or by any means, electronic, mechanical, photocopying, recording or stored in any database or retrieval system without prior written permission of the publisher except in the case of brief quotations embodied in critical articles and reviews.

ISBN: 978-0-9960789-4-8

WHAT PEOPLE ARE SAYING ABOUT
THE AQUITAINE DECEPTION...

"The story was fast paced and interesting, it also ties in with his previous novel "Trojan Horse" but you don't have to have read it to like this book...though there's an enjoyable plot twist near the end which may be more meaningful for those of us who have."

— GABE HERNANDEZ

"I like that the author's characters are credible, without some of the "super agent" abilities that require you to suspend belief to get past seemingly impossible outcomes. The storylines seem like they were pulled from today's headlines which makes me think that either Paul Bourdon is a damn good guesser or can write a really decent book in a week!"

— MIKE STAHLMAN

"A fast moving and interesting plot — now I'm looking forward to reading his other books. I liked it enough that it felt like it ended too soon. That doesn't happen nearly enough for me."

— LINDA M.

"If you're into covert op's type stories you should read it. Though it's fiction, it offers more realism in how an operations officer goes about collecting information to infiltrate America's enemies and uncover terrorist plots."

— ADAM MCPHERSON

Paul Bourdon

THE AQUITAINE DECEPTION

CHAPTER 1

TO THE CASUAL OBSERVER, SVETLANA GORENKOV WOULD pass for an American exchange student. To others, she was a target.

Her light grey hoodie draped over her tight-fitting jeans that pegged down to her running shoes. The Ralph Lauren logo on her pale denim sailing cap was barely legible and the adjustable strap allowed her chestnut ponytail to swing to and fro in a Western look, which was her trademark.

In spite of an exhausting day, she scaled the outside stairs of her apartment building two steps at a time, a habit sprung from her endless energy and charge-ahead personality. Her apartment was one of thousands of postwar buildings that received minimal updating every thirty years from the benevolence of some bureaucratic apparatchik. She stopped just long enough to unlock her worn, brass-faced mailbox and remove the day's post. Turning the key to relock her box, Svetlana's hand froze; her senses heightened. A woman that lives alone soon learns that every door has its own signature sound, and she was sure that the creaking sound she heard was her apartment door slowly closing. Someone had either just entered or left her home and was trying to be quiet.

Svetlana was Russian to her core, and couldn't let go of the need that haunted her; the need for a free and honest Russia that she first dreamed about while attending grad school in America. Because her passions ran so deep, she was drawn back to the land of her birth and became an investigative journalist, one who had a knack for exposing corrupt government officials—especially those whose lips were soiled by kissing the tar baby called the Russian Mafia. She had a gift for digging deep and getting results and was no stranger to harassment or death threats. Her friends whispered that perhaps she had a death wish, but at age twenty-eight, she was more of an anomaly of beauty and intelligence, coupled with an absolute lack of fear.

This latest apartment was her third in two years and was small enough to know like the back of her hand. The creaking noise bespoke her door, and she was determined to find out what was rotten in Denmark. She carried no weapon, yet she turned on her heels and dashed up the flight of stairs. Reaching her door, she paused to listen for any sound—either inside or outside her unit. Everything around her was silent. Dropping to one knee, she checked the lower corner of the door. The strand of hair that she had applied across the doorjamb with saliva was gone. Someone either has been or is still in my apartment, she thought.

She rose, took a deep breath, and unlocked the door. Entering, her nose was assaulted by the smell of natural gas. She grabbed the waist pocket of her hoodie and pulled it up over her nose. Making her way inward, she paused at her dining table and felt the top of her laptop. Room temperature, she thought. It hasn't been turned on.

She turned toward the kitchen and froze. She heard a tick, tick, tick…Her heart stopped; it felt as if it had leapt into her throat. She knew death could be seconds away. Spinning on her feet, she ripped her computer from its power unit and bolted for the open door. As her foot hit the tiled hall floor, a massive explosion of light, fire, and smoke blew out the windows, raining debris everywhere, its percussion hurtling her against the opposite wall. Enormous heat followed, scorching the side of her face. Her body sagged to the floor.

She struggled to open her eyelids—her world was disoriented. Where am I? What happened? Svetlana tried to regain her senses, to shake the cloud from her head; her ears were deafened by a shrill, discordant ringing. She struggled to get up; her hands slapped at the wall—there was nothing to grab hold of. Wobbling, she raised the laptop on her shoulder, pressed it to the side of her head, pushed off the wall, and rocking from side to side, negotiated her way down the steep flight of stairs. The sound of her erratic steps, awkward and echoing, made her head feel like it was trapped in a sealed, steel drum. Everything around her seemed to move and drift; nothing appeared solid.

Outside, she spotted her car and tried to run toward it, but her equilibrium failed and she fell to her knees. She shook her head, stood up, and stumbled her way toward it, crashing into its door. She fumbled through her pockets and found the keys. She slid in and her shaking hand struggled to push the key into its slot. The fog in her head lifted enough for an alarm to scream in her mind. She stopped and backed her hand away, as if the key was toxic. Why was the door unlocked? She looked across and down the street. There—a man, sitting alone in a car: His head turned—he's staring at me! she thought.

She spotted a bicycle in a rack. Within seconds, she was on it, one hand holding the computer under her arm, the other steering the bike. The car started up, but Svetlana took off in the opposite direction. The car faced the wrong way and couldn't break traffic to turn around in chase. Several times more the driver tried to force his BMW out, only to get edged back by the unyielding cars. Each time he looked, Svetlana was further away. He slammed the car into park, jumped out, and attempted to cross the boulevard in pursuit. By the time he reached the other side, Svetlana was halfway down a narrow side street, struggling to gain speed and keep her balance as she skidded along the raised curb. The assassin stopped and drew a bead on her with his silenced pistol. He spit off two rounds, which spattered into the cobblestone pavers to the left of her. He squeezed off two more rounds; this time he aimed higher—they landed well behind her. He pulled his weapon up, bent over, and took a deep breath of failure. He knew she was out of range and could not be caught.

Svetlana at last gained control of the bike. As she approached a cross street, she turned down its narrow, one-way divide, and wobbly disappeared into the fading light of the cool evening.

CHAPTER 2

AARON COHEN SAT IN HIS CHAIR WITH HIS BACK TO THE door, staring out the window of his small office and robotically twirling a rubber band around his fingers. He was in deep mental weeds and struggling. At The Agency, it was unheard of for someone his age to have his own office with a window. After his success in the Trojan Horse mission, he was taken under the director's wing and encouraged to just let his mind wander—wherever it took him. For whatever reason, the backwoods-raised director saw something special in the West Coast Jewish geek. Their close relationship was a study in contrast that was all the talk at The Agency's water coolers—all of which bred contempt and jealousy, sprinkled with an undercurrent of WASPish anti-Semitism.

Aaron's face and eyes registered nothing and he appeared a thousand miles away. This wasn't unusual; he would often sojourn into an intellectual wilderness. Most people who knew him called him "Mr. What-if."

He hadn't had a breakthrough on his latest algorithm and wasn't even thinking about it when CIA Director Ernest Hatcher stepped in unnoticed and slapped him on his back. Aaron nearly jumped out of his skin, tilting backward and grabbing his desk for support.

"What's going on, Cohen? Not making any progress on that Chinese population theory of yours? Maybe you need to take a break and get on up to Alaska and see that McKenzie guy. You two girls should be able to work that idea out together."

Aaron had heard the "you two girls" line once too often. He bristled as he drawled out Hatcher's well-worn expression in an almost perfect impression of the director. "I know, sir, 'Good God! What's this world coming to?'"

"Listen, Cohen, you may think I'm busting your chops, but I actually like your idea; I think it has merit. Now, *how* many Chinese boys are never going to find a wife?"

Aaron turned and stood to face his director. "Sorry, sir, I meant no disrespect. In any normal society, there are one hundred and three boys for every one hundred girls. Because China aborts girls but keeps boys, their rate is one hundred twenty-eight to one hundred. This aberration has produced a surplus of seventy million young men with deep sexual frustration and a lot of resentment toward this government-fostered situation. In addition, China has just forced five hundred million people from rural areas into cities to work in manufacturing. The problem is exacerbated when the global economy heads into a long-term recession because of debt, and China's manufacturing is already showing signs of slowing. They *must* have ever-increasing manufacturing to provide jobs for this massive influx of relocated people, which they don't. God knows what will happen if a global recession becomes a depression, because there isn't any economic model that shows a country how to feed, clothe, and house two hundred and fifty to five hundred million people suddenly out of work.

"Compounding the matter are our old pals, the Russians. Their birth rate is so skewed that by 2040, their population will be lower than, say, a third-world country like Yemen. You can't control a land mass that is one sixth of the planet with a population of that size. What are they going to do when the Chinese generals look northward to a mineral-rich, underpopulated Siberia and recognize the overwhelming population disparity? How could Russia possibly defend its borders, when we can't defend our own?"

"Hell's fire, Cohen, I don't know. The last time the world dealt with something even near that was in the late thirties…and that led to a world war. Remember, that's why The Agency hires young brainiacs. We're hoping forward-thinking people like you are going to keep us out in front of the curve. Hopefully we won't see another world war. So when do I get your report on this?"

"Sir, I don't mean to cut your question short, but something else is bothering me and consuming my thoughts right now."

"Is it more important than this Chinese thing?"

"It might be. On the Internet, I came across an obscure article whose authorship is none other than the Russian Northern Fleet. It—"

"Did you say the Russian Northern Fleet?" interrupted Hatcher.

"Yes. The story laid out a compelling case that the BP Deepwater Horizon platform disaster was caused by a submarine attack—a *North Korean* submarine attack. As I said, this intel was put out on the Internet, but here's the kicker—it had an ether-life of less than one day. Then it was gone; the Internet was scrubbed of its contents, and there's been a total blackout on this report ever since. I've never seen anything like this!"

Director Hatcher gave Aaron Cohen a frowned look, turned, and stared out the window. After thinking it through, he turned around and said, "If you're telling me that the Russian Northern Fleet has written a paper that connects North Korea to the BP gulf disaster, then you best get your pampered ass on the next flight to Fairbanks, son."

"Sir, you seem intent on getting me and Devon McKenzie together. Can I ask why?"

"Let's just say that if anyone knows those bastards in the Ruskie navy, it's him. Besides, I'm sure that McKenzie fellow is chomping at the bit to wrestle with one of your…you know…al-go-rithms."

Aaron half laughed and then opened both palms in acknowledgement of the obvious.

Before Hatcher went out the door, he paused and faced his subordinate once more. "One more thing, Cohen, before you fly out, I want a detailed report of this Russian article on my desk—my eyes only."

"Understood, sir, but is going to Alaska an order?"

"Does a flat-faced possum hang in a tree?"

CHAPTER 3

ABOUT TWO HOURS HAD PASSED SINCE DIRECTOR HATCHER left Cohen's office, and Aaron was struggling with the order to fly to Anchorage. Working with Devon McKenzie excited him on his cerebral side, and he knew that Devon could be of great help, but the downside was the weather. Alaska's freezing temperatures were a complete turnoff.

Aaron admitted to being a strange package. Growing up in Malibu, he was a tall, lanky kid with buzzed blondish hair and tanned skin. He should have been attractive to the opposite sex; however, the intellectual Jewish geek always took over as he walked his high school halls Monday through Friday. But when the weekend came and the surf was up, he led a different life. On those days, he was the consummate "surfer dude." Riding the board gave him personal confidence, but that confidence never really rolled over to his social life off the water. When Stanford offered a full-ride scholarship, he stowed the board in his garage and never looked back. He completed his degree in mathematical science with a second degree in computer science in record time. After completing his master's program, CalSci beckoned for his PhD.

He had been planning to take a real vacation back in California, where he still had visions of himself as some sort of Big Kahuna. But Anchorage was where his intellectual equal was, and the order to go had come from Hatcher.

As he rose from his desk, a ping sounded as an encrypted icon of a Russian bear popped up in the lower right-hand corner of his computer screen. No text accompanied the icon, for it wasn't necessary. This was a distress call—a call he couldn't walk away from.

CHAPTER 4

AARON FIRST MET SVETLANA GORENKOV SEVERAL YEARS earlier as he was getting a snack in the student union at Stanford. For him, it was love at first sight. The problem was that he was years removed from his Malibu surfer dude persona. When he arrived at Stanford, he returned to being an intellectual geek. Mittyesque confusion came over him and he believed the only way to approach her was to act like someone he really wasn't. Each attempt was a valiant try, but she continually brushed him off as if he were a gnat. Aaron was deflated, but found himself returning to the student union every day at the same time for a month. Then he hit pay dirt. This time, there was no dude facade... just Aaron Cohen.

He had misread her initial brush-off. Svetlana was an exchange student on a scholarship to earn her master's degree in journalism. She wasn't a Crusader Rabbit because she chose journalism. To the contrary, she chose journalism because she *was* a Crusader Rabbit by her very nature. As such, she had no time for silly things like romance. Her Mother Russia had transitioned from inept corruption under Communism to sophisticated, yet thuggish corruption under so-called capitalism. Hers was a country of extremes. In its history, there never seemed to have been any middle ground. Russia needed cleaning and Svetlana was ready to roll up her sleeves, pick up the broom, and take on the task.

It took several "chance encounters," but Aaron hung in and after a long while, Svetlana relented or at least grew weary of the constant rejections and granted the forlorn suitor a date. To her surprise, she found that she enjoyed herself. That first date led to others, and after many months, Aaron began thinking that a life without Svetlana Gorenkov could never be possible. As graduation came closer for both of them, their weekly outings slowed down to every other week and then little by little, became seldom. Aaron felt the pain of the dilemma, but hoped the drop-off in their relationship was because of the stress of finals. Svetlana knew the truth, though, which had never changed from what she had always told him. After graduation, she would go back to the country she loved and he would remain in the United States. Then one day, she was gone; however, she never left his mind. Aaron didn't even have a "Dear John" letter to console him.

Two years later, he read articles written by her on the mysterious poisoning of the democratically elected president of Ukraine, Victor Yushchenko. On the eve of victory for his Orange Revolution, Yushchenko attended a dinner with the Ukrainian Secret Service chief, Ihor Smeshko, and his deputy, Volodymyr Satsyuk. The gala was set to perfection; the restaurant was bright and festooned with orange-colored decorations and flowers; the orchestra was lively and entertained everyone with traditional, pre-Communist Ukrainian songs. Glasses could be heard clinking in anticipation of the soon-to-be announced victory. In retrospect, two glaring omissions occurred: No one from Yushchenko's inner team was invited to the dinner, which in itself should have caused suspicion, nor had the food been inspected. Three hours later, the duly elected president, suffering from a massive headache, fell violently sick. Victor's condition deteriorated and it seemed that his prospect for a long life was not in the cards. His health was in free fall.

Svetlana was in Ukraine covering the ramifications of the Orange Revolution and her instincts smelled a rat. She was the first journalist to broach the possibility of an attempted political assassination by former Ukrainian communists unwilling to relinquish power. Three weeks later, Yushchenko developed severe facial disfigurement, which was a sign of dioxin poisoning. Studies of his blood proved that it contained over 100,000 units of TCCD, the key ingredient of Agent Orange. Because he had visited the nuclear site of Chernobyl several times, the state-controlled media insisted that Yushchenko must have been exposed there.

Svetlana bought none of that and began digging. The poison was not a mix; it was a highly developed toxin that was so pure, it could only have come from a technologically sophisticated laboratory. Ukraine had no such lab, but Russia did. After her stories began targeting them, three opposition members who had attended the dinner fled to Russia. Her continued digging ultimately began penetrating the inner sanctum of the Kremlin; it was then that her harassment began. The shadows closed in, the threats became real, and her nights became long and sleepless.

She contacted Aaron and poured out her fears. The two agreed on an encrypted icon that meant one thing—trouble was dangerously close and her life was at imminent risk. In five years, Aaron had never seen the icon posted...until now.

CHAPTER 5

One Year Earlier

NORMALLY, A FINANCIAL MEETING OF THIS MAGNITUDE would be held at a capital city in North America, Europe, or Asia, where the comings and goings of the heavy hitters of the industrial world would make international news, resplendent with an army of worldwide media and the usual demonstrations in the streets. News coverage would be twenty-four seven, with world leaders craning their necks and preening at every photo op. This gathering, however, was different.

Collapsing the U.S. dollar in favor of a world currency required complete privacy—as only a secure chateau in the French countryside of Aquitaine could provide. Security was handled by one of the best paramilitary companies to come out of the Iraq War. The chateau was swept on a continual routine for bugs and no expense was spared installing sophisticated devices to block electronic eavesdropping. Armed guards swept black limos as they arrived and more were stationed at every vulnerable point in and out of the compound, including a mile radius around the chateau. Even the chateau's regular servants were sent home and military-trained regulars were brought in from the United States.

Seated around the gilded Rococo table were representatives of the world's six largest banking families, with two empty seats for their special North Korean guests. A previous meeting of these same families had taken place in 1910 at Jekyll Island, off the coast of Georgia. From that gathering, the Federal Reserve of the United States was born. Many believe that was the first step on a forced journey leading to a financial oligarchy that would transcend national boundaries and ultimately control the world. Others believe that journey had already been in place for centuries, even before the founding of the Illuminati in 1776 in

Bavaria. They also believe that these families directly trace their lineage to the Khazars, who came out of the Caucasus, and today are one in the same. However their pedigrees are traced is not important. Underlying this all is a fundamental truth; the world's supply of money is finite and controlled. It is controlled by a small number of mega-banks, which in turn are held by a small number of families that are related by birth, marriage, or social invitation. In short, these families control the money supply of the globe.

***

When World War II crushed the British pound sterling, a new standard for the exchange of currencies had to be established. In 1944, at the Mount Washington Hotel in Bretton Woods, New Hampshire, delegates from the Allied countries gathered to create financial order while the war was still raging, its final outcome not yet determined—at least by eyes that were not part of this oligarchy. That standard was thereafter called the Bretton Woods System. Because it was backed by both gold and a reconstructed British pound sterling, the U.S. dollar was chosen as the world's standard and the International Monetary Fund (IMF) was set up as a monitor. The world's financial families nodded their collective blessing. They believed this was a temporary solution.

Then, on August 15, 1971, for reasons known only to the global financiers, the United States unilaterally ended its ability to convert its dollar to gold. The U.S. paper dollar became the sole backer of international currency. The Bretton Woods System came to an end and the dollar became nothing more than a fiat currency supported by the hollow promise of the U.S. federal government to pay.

A nation is no different than a human being. When it loses its ability to pay its debts, it inherently falls under the control of its lender. In order for the world's financiers to maintain control of the United States, massive consumer debt in the range of twenty trillion dollars had to be implemented. This was accomplished through a series of bubbles and busts that lasted for over forty years. Because of the exploding strength of the newly created Chinese economy and the projected rise of India, the time had come to break the back of the dollar and move to an international currency that would bring all emerging countries under the control of this amoral, corrupt, financial octopus; hence, the call for another clandestine meeting.

The meeting at Chateau d'Arbonne began with the serving of the finest blends of coffee and exotic teas, mounds of fresh fruit from around the world, and the most delectable pastries made by a local patisserie; the food was monitored and tasted, of course, by the security company. Four massive, cut-crystal Italian chandeliers hung from a complex, vaulted ceiling resplendent with cherubs in a cloud-filled sky, providing an ambience of diamonds pouring forth from heaven. The irony of cherubs looking down and almost blessing this corrupt group was lost on its attendees. They were either lost in their own self-aggrandizement or absorbed by the golden hue that played on the four-hundred-year-old tapestries that adorned the chateau's gilded walls.

Although all family representatives were well known to each other, names were never used and conversation between them was kept to a minimum. Acknowledgements among themselves were made with tight handshakes accompanied by terse smiles.

When the pastries and fruit had been consumed, the representative of the wealthiest and most influential family took control of the meeting and asked a series of prearranged questions. Members responded to his questions in a pecking order of wealth and power, which also dictated the assignment of their individual responsibilities.

His first question was dry and without emotion, "Will the destruction of one oil rig in the Gulf of Mexico accomplish a large enough ecological hazard to shut down U.S. offshore drilling for years?"

The second family member in line responded, "Our projections say yes—although we certainly need to inflame the media to continue making doomsday predictions. We control enough talking heads who are at the ready to confirm those predictions."

"We need a total ban on Gulf of Mexico drilling for at least three years," the first asserted.

"Our handpicked people control the American EPA. We will have our ban, but it will be only on new permits."

"Is three years long enough to force the current oil platforms to relocate elsewhere?"

"Two years alone moves out fifty percent of the rigs. By the end of the third year, Petrobraz of Brazil will make an offer that the remaining oil companies won't refuse. The American president has already signaled to the Brazilians that the U.S. is committed to buying their oil."

"Oil *must* spike to over one hundred dollars per barrel and stay there for at least two years. That will shock all other commodities, which will immediately follow."

"Yes, even the vilest of commodities, humans, will follow suit," said the third family member, as he leaned forward to present a mordant smile to all members at the table. "The Middle East will explode, just as we have projected. We have sent out the directive to call it an 'Arab Spring,' and our 'friends' in the world's news services will follow our lead."

"The funds are in place to foment the demonstrations—weapons as well?"

"Yes, the Iranian Twelvers will both foment and keep tight control over the events. Those in the West have been instructed to hail it as a blossoming of democracy, but in truth, the Muslim Brotherhood will succeed and the Twelvers will have their caliphate, as is our intention."

"Tunisia across to Syria?"

"Yes, and far beyond that as well. We project that Iraq will fall into total disarray within one year. America is in full retreat and chaos will fill their leadership void. The exception, of course, is Israel. But Iran will arm Hamas in Gaza with enough rockets to keep them occupied. Do not fear, though; the United States will not defend Israel when it becomes apparent that there is no other way, short of a nuclear exchange."

"The Saudi royal family?"

"Our projections indicate that it will take oil remaining at one hundred and fifty dollars per barrel to accomplish their downfall."

"The Saudi royals must fall to produce enough chaos to establish a single world currency."

"For that to happen, the Alaskan oil fields must be disrupted for at least one year," said the fourth family member.

The second member looked right, then left with his beady eyes and said, "Then we are left with no alternative but to destroy the pipeline."

"And there must be an ecological disaster that accompanies it!" exclaimed the fourth member.

"Do we use the North Koreans for that also?" asked the third.

Participant number four responded with his usual ice-cold demeanor. "Of course. Kim Jong-un is easily purchased. And if discovered, he is expendable and will be terminated. The NK generals are always looking for an excuse."

The first family member's eyes turned as he raised his arm and snapped his fingers. The side door opened and two North Koreans were escorted in. When they reached their empty chairs, they bowed left and right and took their seats.

The first family member said, "Let's get back to the business of destroying the Trans-Oceanic oil platform. I trust the miniature submarine has been armed."

Chin-Hae Kwon, the North Korean admiral, spoke for the two. "Yes, the sub, an SSC Sang-O Yugo class, has in fact been armed with Russian 53-65 KE torpedoes. We have handpicked the crew and they are ready to martyr themselves for the greater glory of North Korea."

"The sub's transport ship—I take it all arrangements have been secured?"

"Yes, after they release the sub, the Dai Hong Dan and its crew will be lost at sea before they reach their destination of Venezuela. An explosive device is sized to take the ship and its entire crew quickly to the bottom of the sea. There will be no trace of their existence."

"Could this explosive device be found before it is set to go off?"

"Not a chance. It has been welded into a blind bulkhead and set for the timing of our plan. If something should change, we can redirect a satellite and reprogram its timing. It is failsafe."

"Tell me about the Cubans. Are they ready to receive the transport ship and facilitate the necessary refueling?"

"Yes. The transport ship is scheduled to dock at Cuba's Empresa Terminales Mambisas de La Habana on fifteen April. The crew for the final destination will board the ship while the transport is refueled. Its shipping manifest is set to leave on eighteen April, bound for Venezuela's Puerto Cabello. Right now, everything appears as any normal shipping passage."

"And what happens to the original crew?"

"They have passage back to North Korea on another of our ships...but that ship will never return either."

"Back to the submarine crew...have they been properly drilled on where to attack the structure? I cannot overemphasize the importance of this appearing as an accident spawned of negligence."

"I repeat, this crew has been handpicked for their devotion to North Korea. They are all members of the 17th Sniper Corps—suicide troops. For safety measures, they have been informed that their family members will suffer the consequences of their failure. They will use two incendiary torpedoes to cause a massive explosion. Two days later, they will explode the minisub and themselves below the Deepwater Horizon platform, causing it to sink beneath the Gulf waters."

"Fine." He paused, then said, "Let us move on to topic two. Are your preparations complete to launch the intermediate range ballistic Rodong missile off the coast of Los Angeles?"

"We are ready. The Chinese cargo ship that we purchased has been retrofitted with the launching system. The sales transaction went through the black market and is untraceable."

"Will the ship be able to get to deep enough waters when it is scuttled?"

"Yes. The ship will, at all times, be in international waters and has been, let us say, outfitted the same as the freighter that carries the minisub. The missile's vapor trail will be visible to all, and we will explode it in the middle of the Pacific Ocean. There will be no tracing this back to North Korea or anywhere else."

The financier zeroed his eyes in on the North Korean admiral and asked, "The crew members involved...?"

"Their fate will be the same as the others."

"Good. This will further heighten fear and instability in the international markets."

"Very well, the attack on the Deepwater Horizon platform is set to commence twenty April. The ICBM launch will commence on ten November."

He looked at the other North Korean and said, "I want a plan drawn up to sabotage the Alaskan oil fields. The plan must inflict sufficient damage to render the pipeline inoperable for a period of at least one year. I want this plan sent to me in the usual encrypted way and I want it within two weeks. I will critique it and send the redacted version to the other family members for their review. We meet again in three months. This meeting is adjourned. Please deposit your programs on the desk by the door."

CHAPTER 6

Present Day

BOREDOM HAD CREPT IN AND WAS TAKING OVER DEVON McKenzie's life. At least when he was the hunted ex-agent known as Trojan Horse, daily life was perilous and lonely, but never boring. Living on the edge of death may have been exhausting, but it kept his adrenaline flowing. Now, his life was staid and challenges were hard to find.

As compensation for his four years of being hunted by the CIA, Devon received all his back pay and was reinstated as a field agent at full pay. However, The Agency hadn't given him any field assignments or taken advantage of his intellect. Julie had inherited her father's house, so there wasn't even a financial struggle. Julie ran the household like a well-oiled machine, leaving him feeling somewhat out of place. As much as he loved his wife, something was missing.

Sitting in a chair with his feet up on their back porch railing, Devon often replayed in his mind his mission to disarm the Russian nuclear sub, Yuriy Dolgorukiy. With that came the remembrance of the sacrifice of the Russian seaman, Feodor Strivnych. While it brought him sadness, the heroism of the sailor who gave his life to save a Navy Seal inspired him. Devon had no desire to die for his country, but his idea of patriotism did require sacrifice. That sense of sacrifice was the void in his life, the five-hundred-pound gorilla sitting in the corner, staring at him.

Along with the nostalgia of that mission, Devon often thought of Aaron Cohen and the pure genius of his mind. Over time, he was honest with himself and admitted that without Aaron's help, the mission to the North Sea may not have been successful. He had only known Aaron for the ten-hour flight to Norway, but that was long enough for him to take measure of the man. He was a square guy who could be trusted, much like the man who had sacrificed his life for him five years earlier,

Tim Daniels.

The cell phone in Devon's pocket vibrated and rang. He jumped up, scrambling to fetch the ringing object, as if it were a lifeline that had been thrown to a drowning victim. The caller ID showed it to be Aaron Cohen.

Devon cleared his throat and tried to answer with a calm demeanor. "Hello?"

"Devon? This is Aaron...Aaron Cohen. Do you have a minute?"

"Do I? I've got all the time in the world for a CalSci man. What have you been up to, Aaron?"

"More than I can handle myself. I could use your help, Devon—outside The Agency."

"Sounds serious. Does our buddy Hatcher know that 'us two girls' are talking about this?"

"That's a yes and a no. He did tell me to come up and solicit your help on an 'al-go-rithm' issue that I've been trying to sort out, but something has come up that I don't want to talk about over an unsecure line."

"Well, you know that I would do anything for you, Aaron. When can you fly up?"

There was a pause before Aaron responded. Devon wondered if the connection had been lost.

"Could...could you meet me in Moscow—no questions asked?" Aaron asked.

Devon turned his head around and looked into the window behind him. Julie was curled up on the sofa, reading a book. "When?" Devon whispered, forgetting that he needn't be quiet.

"Could you fly out tomorrow...say, at two p.m.? I have this friend in Moscow...her life may be on the line. I wouldn't ask if it were otherwise. Devon, you're the only person that I trust, the only one I can turn to."

"Tomorrow? I'm not sure, Aaron. I mean...I don't know if I can book a flight by then."

"I...took the liberty of booking you on KLM—first class, of course. You can pick up your tickets at the airport. They're already paid for," he added.

"I owe you this much, Aaron. Alright, I'll be there."

"Somehow, I knew you would. I'll be waiting for you at Domodedovo Airport in Moscow. And thanks, Devon."

Ringing off, Devon turned around and looked again through the window at Julie. I might be in trouble for this, he thought. He went in to face the music.

As he entered the house, he looked at Julie and said, "I…uh, was just on the, uh, telephone with Aaron Cohen."

"Really? How's he doing?"

"He…he's doing fine, but he has this, uh, small problem in Moscow."

Julie glanced up at Devon and asked, "Is this small problem for the CIA?"

"No. It's outside work…gratis for Aaron."

"Dangerous?"

Devon answered, "I don't know; it could be. Well actually, I'm not sure. Aaron couldn't give me any real details because we weren't on a secure line."

"Let me see…he can't discuss any details over an unsecure line and you don't know if danger is involved? How long will you be gone?"

"To be honest, it's hard to say—I guess maybe a few days…could be a week at the most."

"Right. When do you leave?"

"Well, I guess that would be tomorrow."

"Tomorrow is it? Best hurry," she said with a knowing smile.

CHAPTER 7

SVETLANA GORENKOV SAT ON THE EDGE OF AN UNMADE bed in the Hotel Tsarina. The hotel was a dump in the worst section of town that housed the dregs of Russian society. Nevertheless, she deemed it safe, or at least prayed that it would be. It was her second day in the same clothes after fleeing her exploding apartment. Her head hung low and she stared at her clasped hands in her lap. She pondered her life and where it had taken her. Had she really chosen this solitary life over one that might have included Aaron Cohen? He loved her, of that she was sure, but would he react to the icon she sent, begging his help?

They had set up the encrypted icon five years ago when the FSB harassment came to a boiling point over the Yushchenko poisoning. Back then, she had backed off her accusations of involvement by the Russian president and began investigating the subsidized sale of Russian submarines to North Korea. Aaron's plan had been simple enough: Send the icon and he would meet her two days later, midday, at the Krymskaya public park. Svetlana had recommended the park, as it was primarily used by native Muscovites.

Midday was two hours away. Would he come? And what would he be able to do for her? The questions had been torturing her ever since she sent the distress signal. Now she had to summon the courage to exit her safe haven and do what she hadn't done in two days—venture outside where there were those who wanted her silenced.

***

Trying to blend in, Svetlana wrapped her head in a babushka and kept her eyes lowered during the three bus changes it took to get to the park. She passed myriads of people, and if she was being trailed, she had no way of being sure. Shaken as she was, she had to keep moving forward. During her whole adult life, she had been fearless, but the near-death explosion in her apartment changed all that. Never-ending thugs tailing and harassing her was one thing, but knowing that someone wanted her dead and was both capable and willing to do so, was another. She would be just one more name on a long list of dead Russian journalists.

As she reached the designated park bench, her heart began to race. It was empty. She looked around, but there was no sign of Aaron. Beads of sweat appeared on her forehead. She felt nauseous. He's not coming, she thought. Oh God, I'm all alone. Did he even see the icon? She rose to walk away and then sat back down. Two burly men in black suits and ties approached her. With her nerves frayed, she looked up and saw that they were looking at her. Oh God, are they Mafia or the FSB? Does it even matter? She dropped her head and watched their feet as they appeared to walk away in slow motion. When their feet disappeared from sight, Svetlana covered her face with her hands and began plotting her exit from the park. She was in such deep thought that she never noticed that someone had sat down on the bench beside her.

As Aaron gently put his arm around her shoulder, Svetlana let out a short scream and jumped to her feet. The only thing she saw was a man standing near her with a scar that ran from his left eye to his ear. In a flash she ran, clutching the rucksack that held her computer. Aaron stood and gave immediate pursuit. As he got closer to the terrified journalist, he let out a muffled plea, "Lana! It's me, Aaron."

She recognized the soothing sound of Aaron's voice. She slowed and turned. "It's you! You came!" Tears welled up and streamed down her cheeks.

He came up to her and embraced her, as only a lover could. "Lana, I've been a basket case since you sent the icon. Are you all right?"

"Yes, yes," she said through streaming tears. "Oh Aaron, I've been such a fool. Why did I let you go?" she mumbled, while clutching him tighter.

Devon McKenzie slowed his own run and came to a stop beside them; Aaron pulled away and made the introductions. Devon noticed that she couldn't pull her eyes away from his scar. His instincts knew what was frightening her. "You'll have to excuse the scar, Ms. Gorenkov; it was from an auto accident…many years ago."

Svetlana was embarrassed; she lowered her eyes to the ground and whispered, "I'm so sorry."

Devon scanned the area around them. Memories of his days with the CIA in Moscow came flooding back. He saw himself as he found the message from the dissident Georgian scientist, Batu Sigua. He shook off the pain it caused and said, "It's okay, ma'am. I get that reaction all the time. We need to move on. Someone may be watching."

Svetlana's refocused her eyes on Devon. "There were two men that passed in front of me minutes before you sat down. I'm positive they were either Mafia or FSB."

Aaron pulled the rucksack from her shoulders and placed his hand under her arm for emotional support. Svetlana's body jerked and reacted by hanging on to her pack. She realized the foolishness of her angst and said, "I'm sorry, Aaron. Please, let's go."

As Devon took the lead, his mind processed the environment around them like a computer. Every person was scanned and assessed for danger. Devon was amazed at the ease of how everything he remembered about Moscow came back to him.

"We need to get to a CIA safe house, Aaron."

"For right now, Devon, I'd rather not. Hatcher doesn't know anything about me coming for Lana—we're supposed to be in Anchorage, remember? I booked us at the Hotel Slavia. I checked them out before I left Langley. The owners are not antigovernment, but they do loathe President Bukin—it should be okay." Svetlana nodded her approval and the three headed for Aaron's rental car.

As they approached the car, Svetlana stopped in her tracks and tugged on Aaron's hand. Devon looked over and saw the raw fear in her eyes.

"Lana, what is it?" Aaron asked.

Her whole body began to shake. "My apartment—they tried to blow me up in my apartment, and they also wired my car to explode. You don't understand, Aaron...they want me dead." With that, she burst into tears.

Aaron nodded to Devon to hold her back. Without hesitation, he got on his knees and inspected under the car. When he knew it was clear, he unlocked the door, hopped in, and with trepidation, turned on the ignition. The car started right up and Aaron breathed a sigh of relief.

Svetlana looked at Aaron in the car and gave a heartfelt smile. She was beginning to see him in a different light.

CHAPTER 8

PYONGYANG, NORTH KOREA

HIS OFFICE WAS STARK. NONE OF THE TRAPPINGS OF POWER or prestige were present. There was no décor that even hinted of Korean patriotism. Plain, off-white walls, no photographs, and a simple, functional desk constituted his workplace. His surroundings spoke of nothing and gave no clue to a persona that was void of feeling…unless he was double-crossed or under attack.

The North Korean drew a heavy drag on his Russian cigarette and exhaled slowly before speaking into the phone. The Russian smokes were harsh, but they soothed his nerves and satisfied his craving for nicotine. He would have preferred using fellow Koreans to do his dirty work, but it was too risky to use them inside Russia. The brutes he was forced to hire were not actual Mafia hit men; they were freelancers who contracted with anyone that would pay their killing fare. It didn't matter what you wanted done—murder, torture, stakeout, security—all were on their resume. To this Korean, a killer was a killer; his uneasiness came from his lack of total control—plain and simple.

"I don't like it when people to I pay a lot of money to let me down," he hissed. "You screwed up the apartment bombing, you let her and her computer get away, and now I find out that you let her escape from the park. Worse, she is now in the protection of two unknown males."

"I can assure you that the two men will die with her. We're trailing them now, and when they arrive at their destination, we will eliminate all three of them."

"Where are they going?"

"We don't know, but that is of no concern. We'll take them out in Red Square, if necessary."

"Of course you will, because you will not get one more ruble if you don't. I want her terminated and her computer either in my hands or destroyed. Now get the job done!"

CHAPTER 9

AARON DROVE AND DEVON SAT IN THE BACK, BOTH NAVI-gating and watching for anyone following them. Svetlana sat clutching her rucksack in the front seat of the Lada Kalina, which had been rented at the airport. Like all Russian cars, it was as compact as it was sparse.

Devon reached forward and tapped Aaron on his shoulder. "At the next street, turn left, go two blocks, and then right at the first opening. It'll be a narrow alley that allows for just one car to navigate between trash dumpsters. Go to the other end and stop. If we're being followed, we'll know it there."

When they arrived at the end of the alley, Aaron put the vehicle in park. Svetlana looked forward while Devon and Aaron watched behind them. Svetlana raised the first alarm.

"Aaron! Look out!"

Aaron and Devon looked forward to where the alley met the next street. A man in a dark suit reached into his coat and pulled a weapon out of a shoulder holster. Devon first processed the shooter and then he turned his head and saw a black Mercedes roaring at them from the rear. He jumped out of the car and positioned himself between the closest dumpster and a wall. He pushed the container to the center of the alley. Two muffled shots hit the wall inches from his head, spraying shards of brick onto his face. He looked again at the Mercedes—its brakes couldn't stop its forward trajectory. It slammed into the garbage container—its occupants slumped over the dashboard.

Devon ducked low and ran to the Lada. As he jumped in, he shouted a warning to Svetlana, then reached over the front seat and gave her head a large push downward. A bullet burst through the windshield, barely missing her. Devon heard the whiz as it shot past, grazing his ear. "Go! Go!" he shouted. Aaron stepped on the gas and the Lada leapt forward.

The assassin on the street drew a bead on Aaron and managed to get off three rounds before the surging car hit his hip, sending him sprawling and unconscious.

"Stop!" Devon shouted. Before Aaron came to a halt, Devon flew out of the car and pulled the assassin's silenced Makarov from his hand. He searched the man's pockets and retrieved two loaded clips for the automatic pistol.

Jumping back into the car, he shouted, "It's one-way! Turn left—against traffic."

Aaron obeyed and within seconds was dodging cars as they veered out of his way, horns blaring. Devon and Svetlana rolled from side to side as Aaron negotiated the oncoming traffic.

"Quick! Take the next right!" Devon shouted.

The Lada nearly flipped as Aaron cut the wheel sharply.

"Where to?" he asked.

Devon, whose head was now up and looking left, right, and forward, took a deep breath and said in a calm voice, "Two more blocks, then right three blocks, then turn left onto Smolenskaya Boulevard. Look on the right for the Lubyanka Restaurant—it won't be fancy, but it's a drop site for The Agency."

He reached over the front seat and displayed the gun he had pulled from the would-be assassin. He slapped Aaron on the shoulder, smiled, and said, "Don't worry—I'll see if I can get one for you in the restaurant."

Aaron followed directions and within minutes, pulled the car to a stop in front of the Lubyanka. Devon told them to wait before getting out. Once more he did a 360-degree search. Satisfied the street was clean, he held up his hand, indicating Aaron and Lana were to wait in the car. Devon went in and paused as his eyes adjusted to the lower level of light. His eyes locked on the owner behind the bar. "Sergei," he said, announcing his presence.

Devon saw Sergei Belova look up, pause and recognize his trademark scar. "Ah, it is my old friend, Devonovich." Sergei opened and raised his arms and said with a sincere smile of welcome, "Please come into my humble abode."

Devon raised one finger, indicating that he would be right back. Within seconds he returned, with Aaron and Lana in tow. After introductions, Sergei grabbed four shot glasses and a bottle of Stoli, showed them to a table, and joined them. When he had filled the glasses, he raised his own in toast and said, "To an old friend and new friends… and to my favorite company."

With that, Devon got down to the business at hand. "Sergei, can you get rid of our car and get us a new one?"

"My cousin runs the best chop shop this side of L.A. Consider it done. Is tonight soon enough?"

"That would be fine. Now, what about two rooms?"

"Best security in Moscow—my home. You're lucky my kids are grown and out of the house. I'll call my wife. How many days did you say?"

Devon looked over to Aaron who, without hesitation, held up two fingers.

Sergei smiled like a Cheshire cat and asked, "Agency pay rate?"

Aaron feigned a pained look and answered, "Agency rate, just don't screw us without a kiss."

Tongue in cheek, Sergei shot Svetlana an amorous look, smiled, and whispered, "I'll lower the price if the kiss is on this beauty's lips."

"Steady, Sergei. Oh yeah, two more things," Devon said. "I need a silenced Glock, two additional clips, and the name of someone to whip up a passport for the young lady."

"Come back tonight, ten o'clock. I'll have the car, the heat, and the name of the forger waiting. Don't be late—I like to kick the last customers out early if I can."

"Ten it is."

***

Sergei Belova's wife welcomed the strangers into her house as if they were long lost friends. She knew from past experience that the pay would be good and, frankly, they needed the money. They were in their sixties and Sergei wanted out. She led them up the stairs to the second floor, where she stopped in front of two doors that were opposite each other. Devon and Aaron shared one room and Lana took the other. Satisfied that the social mores were in order, Sergei's wife bade them well and returned to the first floor.

After they cleaned up, the men knocked on and opened the door to Lana's bedroom. Aaron saw that she had her laptop already open on the desk.

"Is this where the briefing starts?" he said with a smile. "You never change, do you, Lana?"

Svetlana returned a cursory smile, sat down, and fired up her laptop. Aaron was astonished to see the same Russian Northern Fleet report that had been scrubbed from the Internet. Huddling and looking over her shoulder, he let out a whistle, which caught Devon's attention.

Scrolling down the first few pages, she paused as she came to the photographs. "This is what came across the Internet," she said. "I was able to download it before it was cleansed."

Devon was dumbfounded. Aaron was not. Aaron had seen this report before. Its implications were so fantastic, it was hardly believable. When they had reread the report, Devon spoke first.

"I don't know…how can we be sure of its validity? I mean, the North Koreans for God's sake! If this is true, and I do mean if, our president would have no recourse but to declare war. This destruction is an act of terror."

Lana looked up and saw Aaron nodding in agreement. "I'm sorry, but I've got more—and it gets worse. You're forgetting that I *am* an investigative journalist—and a damn good one. I have sources in the Northern Fleet that have verified the original existence of this report and the facts contained herein."

Aaron asked in astonishment, "Knowing you, Lana, I'm sure your sources are good, but do you have any sources outside the Northern Fleet?"

"Of course I have other sources," Svetlana said, giving Aaron a look that found irritation in what she presumed was condescension. "Here!" she said, scrolling down to her notes on the computer. "How about Evgeny Zakorov, Minister of Transportation, or Arkady Banketik of the Ministry of Trade and Economy, or Viktor Chortina of the Ministry of Emergency Situations? Or here! How about Sergei Diemchuk of the Ministry of Justice? Just where would you like me to start?" Svetlana's voice reached a controlled crescendo, and it was obvious to both men that the danger of the last two days was taking its toll.

"You have to excuse us, Lana," Devon said, "but we have been trained to pore over details and never take anything as it appears. We are taught to dig for the truth. Period. I can assure you that we mean no offense. To the contrary, we're impressed with what you have accomplished."

"I, too, am sorry, but you should know that I've also been detail trained in the same way, and I have a good nose for the truth. So good, that people are trying to kill me because of my discoveries." Lana rose and arched her back. "I'm sorry, but I think I've hit a brick wall. I'm exhausted and not in a very good mood. Perhaps a night's sleep will help."

Aaron stood up and guided Lana into his arms. After a minute, he motioned Devon to read her computer notes as he led her to sit down next to him. Devon decided to wait and instead went to get them a drink. The effects of the alcohol eased in, taking the edge off their tense emotions. After a while, they returned to business.

After he finished reading Lana's notes, Devon looked over to Aaron, pursed his lips, and nodded his head in approval of the veracity of her work. Aaron eased Lana's head down on to a pillow and after she dozed off, followed Devon back to their room with her computer in tow.

CHAPTER 10

CHATEAU D'ARBONNE
FRENCH COUNTRYSIDE OF AQUITAINE

Nine Months Earlier

THE INTERNATIONAL FINANCIERS HAD GROWN NERVOUS. They knew that the latest decision on which they were about to vote was going to be another momentous gamble. Blowing up an oil rig in the middle of the Gulf of Mexico was dangerous enough and firing an ICBM in international waters off the California coast was high stakes, but these acts that they had already voted on had not been directed against the sovereign property of the United States. Sabotaging the Alaska Pipeline was a direct threat that could not be mistaken. As weak as the American president was, no one on either side of the political aisle would consider this new action to be anything but an act of war. The North Koreans insisted they would leave enough evidence to make it appear as another act of terrorism perpetrated by al-Qaeda, and that seemed to give the membership enough of a comfort level to move forward.

When the cognac was served and the attendants vacated the room, the head of the largest family again chaired the meeting and brought it to order. "Alright, you have the North Korean report on the sabotaging of the Alaska Pipeline. Same rules apply; the shredder is to the left of the door. Nothing leaves this room. As always, the remains will be taken to the incinerator behind the chateau. I will personally oversee the burning. Once an agreement is reached, no one will make any further contact until our next meeting. You will be notified in the usual manner of the date and time. He nodded to the second family spokesman to continue.

"Gentlemen, as you can see in the North Korean report, should we decide to proceed with this next phase of the mission, they are prepared to commence activities without further delay. As always, we are open for comments."

"I have read the report," said another family member, "but I do have concern about the assurances that al-Qaeda will be the ultimate and only target of blame."

The North Korean raised his hand and was given the nod to speak.

"We have gone to extraordinary lengths to assure this. All the tools, all the explosives were made in Iran. We have lifted fingerprints from a well-known terrorist in Yemen and one homegrown U.S. terrorist. Those prints will be left on several pipe shards at the crime scene. We will make the FBI work hard to find this evidence, but as we all know, they are the best in the world and they will find it. The homegrown and one Yemeni will be ordered by a fake Imam in Philadelphia to drive to Seattle. There, they will be given orders to drive to Anchorage, where they will be told to wait eight days and then return to Seattle. Their vehicle will be seen crossing into Canada, then in and out of Alaska, returning to Seattle. At that time, they will be drugged and an anonymous call will be made to the motel owner. He, in turn, will call the local FBI. The homegrown will awaken to an FBI swat team standing over him. The Yemeni will have died of an overdose and his body will carry traces of explosive residue.

"This, of course, is only the beginning. All of the demolition will be handled by us. The same type of Sang-O submarine that destroyed the Gulf oil platform will make a long trek off the coast of Russia and cross to Alaska's Norton Sound. There, a demolition team will come ashore west of Kotlik. We will use another old Chinese oil tanker to refuel the Sang-O sub. The equipment for their trip inland is already in place. We will kidnap three additional Yemenis who will be transported on the submarine and taken ashore. They will be taken to separate sites and blown up with the pipeline. Thus, ample evidence will make it crystal clear as to who was responsible. If the Americans choose to pull another George Bush-type maneuver and invade Yemen...so be it."

Another family head interrupted the North Korean. "My concern is that the Americans could make repairs to the pipeline in short order. They could be back in business within weeks."

The head of the largest family clasped his hands behind his head and leaned backward in his chair. His eyes were fixed on the ceiling, but he had paused only for dramatic effect. He abruptly sat upright and, pausing once more for emphasis, said, "You all must remember our ultimate goal. We are not trying to permanently shut down the ability of the

Alaska Pipeline to deliver oil. Stay focused! It is all about toppling the U.S. dollar. Yes, these breeches can be repaired, but this will *also* be a major ecological disaster, and we have quietly pumped millions into a whole raft of green organizations who are ready to protest and take to the streets, burning and looting on our orders. We will cause total chaos. The president will react and put further oil flow on hold. It is only the disruption of that oil flow that we need. In case anyone hasn't paid attention, crude oil has just fallen back under one hundred dollars per barrel. This disruption, along with the disruption of Libyan oil, will spike it to possibly two hundred dollars per barrel. That will cause a major Western backlash, and with monies paid to the Islamic Brotherhood, we have funded a new group of young, Sunni extremists called Da'ish, or more commonly referred to as ISIS, who want to topple the old, Sunni Wahhabis in Riyadh, Saudi Arabia, because they are not radical enough. They have promised massive demonstrations to go along with a military march across Iraq. They will be armed with American armaments that they will capture from the fleeing Iraqi army. Iraq will explode in chaos, the Saudi royal family will fall, the U.S. dollar will crash, and we will be there to pick up the pieces with a new world currency. Remember, it is all about perception. When the world looks at an international financial disaster that could cause Weimar-like inflation, it will demand we create a new world currency. This is and has always been our ultimate goal. Anything less is simply unacceptable." He held his stare at the group for emphasis.

The room fell silent. "Are there any more questions? If not, then I call for a vote to proceed with the mission. All those who dissent, raise your hands."

No hands were raised. "The motion is carried unanimously." He looked at the North Koreans and said, "Proceed with the plans for the destruction of the Alaska Pipeline!"

CHAPTER 11

Present Day

AARON AND DEVON CONTINUED TO STUDY SVETLANA'S notes on her laptop. Her first source was Evgeny Zakorov, the Minister of Transportation. His people in North Korea had uncovered the retrofitting of a merchant marine vessel, the Dai Hong Dan, to accept and carry an SSC Sang-O Yugo class minisubmarine. As they scrolled down, the photographs were grainy and of poor quality, yet were able to show the ship's modification and the ultimate loading of the sub.

Next were notes from Arkady Banketik of the Ministry of Trade and Economy. The photos verified the Dai Hong Dan in dockage at Cuba's Empresa Terminales Mambisas de La Habana; the second photo showed the modification of its hull. Subsequent copies of documents showed the ship's registered maritime schedule, which included dockage in Cuba and Venezuela's Puerto Cabello plus the notation that the ship never reached Venezuela. It concluded with the memo: Presumed lost at sea.

Continuing to scroll down, they stopped when they came to the report of Viktor Chortina of the Ministry of Emergency Situations. His report was extensive and technical. It documented, with the addition of digital photographs, that the American government's story to the media was a complete fabrication. It could only have been caused by sabotage; that is, either by direct application of explosives to the platform's substructure or, on a more realistic basis, by assault from a submarine. The report didn't rule out direct application, as saboteurs and their explosives could have come in on one of the many supply ships that attended the platform's needs on a regular basis. This approach was deemed unrealistic, as the logistics and secrecy that would have been required were herculean in scope, thus leaving the submarine scenario as the only viable cause.

The author admitted that a potential difficulty with the submarine scenario was in regard to the second explosion that occurred two days later and ultimately made environmental containment near impossible. The stumbling block in this line of thought was that a minisub would have had to cause this explosion also, but did not have the range for its own escape. A suicide crew was discussed as a possible solution to the dilemma.

Then they arrived at the name Admiral Boris Sobchak. His information seemed to be an amalgamation of all the other data, but Aaron swore it read exactly like the Russian Northern Fleet report that had been posted briefly on the Internet. Admiral Sobchak was the ranking admiral in the Northern Fleet—until he died mysteriously three days after the disappearance of that very report.

After they finished reading all of Svetlana's notes, Devon checked his watch. "Damn!" he exclaimed. "I've only got fifteen minutes to get to Sergei's restaurant. Listen, when it's time to wake Lana, have her cut her hair short and dye it with that stuff Sergei's wife purchased." With that, he was out the door and on his way to the Lubyanka Restaurant.

Winded after running the distance to the restaurant, Devon slowed to a walk as he passed the front windows. The lights were on, but the sign on the door read: Closed. He peered through the windows, seeing no one. He tried to open the door, but it was locked, so he knocked hard on its surface. No response. A sick feeling began roiling in his stomach. This was not right. Sergei had said to come at ten o'clock and he was only a few minutes late.

As Devon went around to a small parking lot at the rear of the restaurant, he turned sideways and made himself as invisible as possible by keeping his back to the rear wall. His hand squeezed the lock, but it didn't yield. He knelt down and picked the lock open within seconds. Rusty hinges creaked, announcing his arrival. He pulled out his silenced Makarov, slid in, and began inching toward the dining area. No signs of any activity. The dining area was dark and added to Devon's tension. The only light came from a flickering street lamp outside. He scanned the room from right to left and he saw an overturned table. A man and a woman lay on the floor. Light reflected off the pool of blood that oozed away from their heads. Ten feet away, two men lay together on the floor in the corner, their blood-soaked faces spoke of the accuracy of the shots.

The scene was ghoulish. In the pit of his stomach, Devon knew that his old friend was dead. Feelings that had haunted him his entire career in service to the CIA came rushing back. Visions of people who died because of his presence flashed across his consciousness. His head grew hot; he became flushed and wiped his brow with his sleeve. Where is Sergei? With his gun extended in a two-fisted grip, he made his way to the side of the bar. Barely visible, Sergei was sprawled on the floor. He had been beaten about the face so savagely that Devon barely recognized him. When he was of no more use, they had shot him in the back of his head.

Devon ran his fingers through his hair trying to clear his thoughts. He stood up and opened the cash register. No money seemed to be missing. He pulled the cash tray out and saw a folded piece of paper. It contained a single telephone number. Devon assumed it was the number of the passport forger. He searched for the guns and car keys near the bar, but found nothing. He looked over at the two men lying on the floor. They look street savvy, he thought. Could they be the chop-shop men? He made his way over and searched their pockets. A set of car keys with an attached entry fob was found on each. He took them both. As he pulled the set off the second man, his hand brushed against something solid and hard. The dead man's holster held a Glock semiautomatic pistol. He grabbed it, then reached into the man's jacket pocket and pulled out two loaded clips and a silencer. Devon stood up and attempted to think it out. He had to stay calm and reason it through.

"Aaron and Lana!" he said in a loud whisper. He knew they would be next—Sergei's torture may have forced him into giving up their location.

He flew out the rear door and onto the street in front of the Lubyanka. He clicked the first fob, then the second. Both a BMW and Mercedes lit up. Devon decided that the Mercedes was the private car of the chop shop and could be traced. He hopped into the Beamer and sped the short distance to Sergei's house.

CHAPTER 12

DEVON PARKED SHORT OF THE HOUSE, TURNED OFF THE ignition and lights, and without making a sound, slid out of the car. Hunched over, he crept around to the rear kitchen door. It was unlocked, so he eased his way in. The house was dark, and as he moved past the table, his foot bumped into something soft, causing him to stumble. His hand hit the wall, but he was able to catch his balance without making a sound. Kneeling down, he groped in the dark until his hands felt a mass—it was the body of Sergei's wife. His fingers slid up to her neck—no pulse. As he removed his fingers, he felt a wet sensation—her blood was warm. His next action was a result of rage trumping his training and instinct.

Devon bolted to the top of the stairs. Two men were standing outside of the bedroom doors. Their entry had been delayed by the sound of Devon storming the stairs. They knelt and drew a bead on their would-be assailant. At that moment, Aaron flew through the door and slammed into the body of the closest killer. Devon squeezed off his first shot, hitting the second assassin in the side of the head, causing him to fall backward. The other recovered from Aaron's body slam and rose to one knee, trying to get a shot off in desperation. Devon's next shot caught him before he was able to take aim. The assassin's lifeless body keeled over on top of Aaron, who was sprawled on the floor.

Devon pulled the fallen assassin off Aaron and said, "Lana okay?"

Aaron took Devon's hand and righted himself, but his eyes never left the floor. Devon knew Aaron felt as if he hadn't helped. "Yeah, she's in the bathroom. She was finishing her hair color. I told her to lock the door—like that would've helped."

"Hey, wait a minute. You did great, Aaron. Without you, brother, we'd all be dead. Now we gotta go—and fast. Sergei's dead, his wife is dead downstairs, and the chop-shoppers are dead. This is getting ugly, Aaron. You and I were looking for proof that Lana was onto something.

Well, here it is. We don't need any more proof. C'mon, we're out of here. Apologies to Lana can come later!"

***

As the Beamer raced out of Moscow, Devon turned his phone on and dialed the number written on Sergei's note. He was correct in thinking that the telephone number from the cash register was that of the forger. With the directions and address locked in his head, he patted Aaron on the shoulder and said, "Take the MKAD outer ring to the Leningradsky exit. Turn right and go about a mile till we see a street called Petrovskiy Pereulok. Look for an old, postwar apartment building, number twelve sixteen. Our forger is waiting. When we get there, Aaron, I'll take Lana in and you call Langley. I think it's time Hatcher finds out what the hell we're up to. Just don't get lost in your conversation with Hatcher; we could've been followed."

Devon felt Aaron's hand reach back over the seat and catch his shoulder as he was about to get out of the car. He paused to see a serious look in Aaron's eyes as he said, "You're right about being followed. Maybe you should give me one of those pistols you're carrying—I do know how to use one. Even a pencil-pushing, geek analyst has to go through basic training at The Farm."

Devon nodded at Aaron, slapped the Makarov into his palm, and exited the Beemer without a word. Bit by bit, Aaron was growing in his eyes, and he liked it.

CHAPTER 13

CIA DIRECTOR HATCHER WAS ON HIS WAY TO A BRIEFING at the White House. As he closed the door of his Suburban SUV, his secure phone buzzed. With his mind deep in thought, his body jumped, as if someone had poked him with an electrical wire.

"Goll dang it!" he shouted, as he fumbled to get the phone out of its holder. He was heading to a meeting in the White House Conference Room regarding chatter that had been picked up by Homeland Security about a possible terrorist attack on the Alaska Pipeline. The chatter was vague at best, and everyone was in agreement that to raise it to the level of a planned attack may be premature. But the possibility of any attack against the homeland required all agencies to share any intel, real or otherwise.

He looked at the caller ID and saw that it was Aaron Cohen. Irritation flared up. He paused, debating whether to answer the call. Why in blue blazes did I give that al-go-rithm geek my number? he thought. But Aaron had never called him on his private phone—not ever.

"Cohen, you'd better have a good reason to call me on this line. May I remind you that I said to call only in the direst of emergencies? To a deer standing in the road at night, only headlights are the direst of emergencies."

"Yes, sir, I do understand. And yes, sir, I think this is that dire."

"What kind of emergency can crop up at that McKenzie fellow's house in Fairbanks—you two girls running out of topics to talk about?"

There was a noticeable pause. "You *are* with McKenzie, right?"

"Yes, sir, but there is one complication—and it is an emergency… you see, we're in Moscow."

"Moscow? What in all that is holy are the two of you doing in Russia? Who authorized this?"

"You told me to get with McKenzie over the BP Deepwater Horizon issue. Well, Russia is where we needed to go."

"Cohen, I didn't authorize that and you know it. Somehow, I get the feeling you think I was born on some sort of a mayonnaise farm. You better come up with one hell of a good reason why you two are there, and you only have thirty seconds to do that."

***

MOSCOW, RUSSIA

As Devon and Lana climbed the stairs to the third floor of the shabby apartment building, Devon was reminded of some slum building in the bowels of New York City. "What a dump!" he whispered.

Lana replied, "In the old Soviet days, people would have waited three years to get a place like this and would have been grateful for it. Then, their married children would have moved in while they, in turn, waited for their own place, sometimes for years. Even now, I'm sure there are no vacancies, in particular for more than one family."

Devon nodded to acknowledge her point and then gave a soft knock on the door. When no one answered, he knocked harder. They saw the peephole go dark as the forger peered through from the other side. From top to bottom, they heard the succession of multiple locks releasing. The door creaked ajar and a scraggly-haired old man with a long, pointed nose and small, dark eyes peered out from behind.

"You the American?" he whispered, opening the door another half inch.

"Yes," replied Devon. "If you want the money, let us in."

A wrinkled hand reached out, grabbed Devon's shirt, and began pulling him in. "Well then—get in—and be quick about it. I only take cash—in advance. Come back in four hours and I'll have everything ready. If you're late, it'll be daylight and I swear I won't answer the door."

The old man looked over at Svetlana and gave a top-to-bottom stare that only an old, filthy pervert could render. His appearance was like some throwback to a Dickens novel. She felt as if she was being undressed by a sick deviate and without a pause, grabbed her blouse above her breasts to cut off the ogling.

"You're too late, little sweetheart, I've already had you...and might I say, you were good, very good. Now, sit down over there and let's get this

— 38 —

over with." Lana felt his sliminess rub off on her, but sat down anyway.

***

WASHINGTON, DC

"What did you say, Cohen? You have proof positive it was a North Korean minisub that took that platform down?"

"Sir, it's as close to positive as possible. I received the intel from a close friend of mine who's an investigative journalist in Moscow. I've examined all of her sources and the sources' own reports. In my opinion, the proof is as solid as it gets."

"Cohen, I'm like Br'er Rabbit. I want some questions answered before I kiss any so-called Tar Baby. What about that Trojan Horse jackal? Is he with you on this?"

"One hundred percent, sir."

"How would a minisub get away without being spotted? It's got no range, man."

"The Russian reporters struggled with that also—they referred to it as an enigma. Their best supposition, and I concur, is that it was a suicide mission. Elite members of the 17th Sniper Corps were transferred to their navy and taught to operate the minisub, which has been documented flat out, *and* here's the kicker—the 17th is famous for the suicide oaths that they take."

"It sounds like you need to get your ass back to Langley, Cohen—and I mean faster 'n a pig slidin' down a mud trough."

"We've got one issue, sir. We…I mean, I've got to bring the journalist with us. They've already tried to kill her, and us I might add. We're securing a passport for her as we speak."

"No, Cohen. I'm ordering you and that other rogue agent to get back here now—without that damn journalist. Hell, she was probably in a heap of trouble before you even got there."

"No, sir. She is the only reason I came here and I *will not* leave without her."

"Damn you, Cohen, I need that intel! I'm on my way to a meeting at the White House and I never like surprises."

"Sir, we'll send you the intel—look for a walking bear icon within the next few hours. The encryption is rosebud. That's r-o-s-e—"

"Damn it, you idiot; I know how to spell rosebud."

Aaron tried to stay calm and speak with a steady voice. "Sir, leaving ASAP without the girl is a no-can-do. We've also got one more lead to follow; the journalist told us about a North Korean that appears to be the ringleader. My bet is that he'll be in Moscow tomorrow."

"How do you know?"

"Science, sir, science."

"Cohen—" Hatcher heard the phone go dead. "Damn! One more geek wanting to be 007! What's this world coming to?"

CHAPTER 14

AARON SAW HEADLIGHTS BEHIND HIM AND SLID DOWN IN his seat. He hated hanging up on the director, but time was short. The headlights turned off and the vehicle parked about five hundred feet away. This was no ordinary visit. He sensed that trouble had arrived. He picked up the Makarov, rolled down the window, and slithered out through the opening.

Crawling across the pavement to a stand of bushes, Aaron heard what sounded like two men getting out and approaching. They hadn't been followed, of this he was sure.

He saw the two assassins walk up to his car—for whatever reason, they weren't concerned. Their guns were drawn and silenced, but they never crouched or aimed their weapons. Aaron breathed a sigh of relief. He hoped that maybe the B-team was sent. They searched his car and then made their way toward the apartment building. After they entered, Aaron rose and followed, careful not to be seen. With his back to the wall, he waited until he thought they would be climbing the stairs. He took a deep breath and opened the door. As expected, he could hear their whispers one floor up. The scratching sound from their hard-soled shoes telegraphed they were climbing. Aaron's black sneakers allowed him to proceed undetected.

When he came to a middle tread on the third staircase, Aaron heard one man whisper in Russian, "On ready...Kick!" Aaron lunged forward, scrambling up the last steps before reaching the top. He heard the door crash open. They were now in the apartment. Two muffled shots went off. His heart paused.

Opening the door, he was greeted by Devon's Glock aimed at his head. He froze in his tracks. Lying on the floor were two dead assassins. Devon raised the barrel of his gun and motioned with his head for Aaron to go to Lana.

Pointing the Glock at the forger, Devon said, "Picture's been taken, now let's finish the job. You've got two hours, not four."

"But they will come back and kill me," the forger whined.

"If the passport's not finished in two hours, I'll be the one to kill you. If you finish, you'll have the time and money to disappear. Choice is yours. Best get on it."

Aaron stared at the dead gunmen with a dumbfounded look. All he could muster was, "How?"

"Years of living as a marked man in the wilds of Alaska. There's an invisible line between hunter and prey, a sixth sense if you will. Believe me, it never goes away."

Devon paused while he collected his thoughts and then asked, "Lana, so far our choice of accommodations hasn't worked out. Be thinking about where we can crash till daylight—low-rent district will be fine."

CHAPTER 15

THE NORTH KOREAN POUNDED BOTH FISTS ONTO HIS DESK in an explosion of rage. With one giant sweep of his arm, Kyong Ran sent the contents of his desktop hurtling to the floor. Sitting in his chair, his head dropped to his chest as he again felt the pangs of failure. These feelings were new to him. In fact, until this Russian woman and those two Americans came along, he couldn't remember when he had ever been beaten. Looking at the mess on the floor, Ran realized that his reaction was that of a loser. He couldn't tolerate this behavior and vowed it would never happen again.

As he stood to massage the back of his neck, it was apparent what years of heavy smoking had done to him. His waistline was abnormally sucked in and the constant phlegm in his throat gurgled when he spoke or coughed through his deeply yellowed teeth. At three packs of Russian cigarettes a day, emphysema was either near or had already started to take its insidious toll. A classic Type A personality, he lived by an obsessive-compulsive schedule that cut him no quarter.

Why do I have to deal with these miserable Russians? he thought. I can't seem to buy one that is capable of killing a lousy journalist—and a woman at that! Kyong Ran put his hands on his hips and leaned backward to invert his spine. He closed his eyes and made the decision he had dreaded since coming back to his office. With great reluctance, he pulled his smartphone out of his pocket and dialed a number. He had to fly in North Koreans—he had no choice. He couldn't get it done with the inept, corrupt Russians.

"I need four of your best men," he said.

"Where will they be going?"

"Moscow. Have them at the Gulfstream by five a.m. We take off at six o'clock sharp."

"I trust it's the usual business delegation wardrobes?"

"Yes. Their equipment will be provided upon arrival."

As soon as he rang off, Ran began questioning the call he had just made. Bringing in this group carries the risk of linking the hit to me, he thought. If any of these four North Koreans ends up dead or kills some FSB trash, then an investigation could compromise my mission. Are four men enough? I don't know…so far it's only been Russians killing Russians, so the police would write it off as Mafia activity and shrug their shoulders. His mind was a swirl of activity. That's it! I'll pick up two more Russians. I'll have them go in first and we'll kill them and leave *their* bodies to be found. There can't be any connection to North Korea—I've got to be careful…very careful.

His phone rang. Looking at the ID, he cringed. "Yes?"

"The journalist—she is dead, yes?"

"Not yet. We ran into more opposition than anticipated."

"I don't want any more of your bullshit. I want to know when that bitch is dead. Do you understand what the word dead means?"

"Yes. It will be finished tomorrow."

"What about her computer?"

"She always keeps it with her. Don't worry; when we take her out, we *will* get her computer."

"When will you make the move on Transportation Minister Zakorov?"

"If not tomorrow, then the next day."

"Every day that goes by with the two of them alive jeopardizes our plans. We have invested a massive amount of money to scrub the Internet, let alone pay you more than you are apparently worth. Will you get your hands on the balance of Zakorov's photos?"

"I am sure we will."

"Why do I get the feeling that you are holding something back from me?"

Kyong Ran wiped the sweat from his forehead. He hoped they had not heard about the two men from the CIA. "I don't know, because there is nothing more to tell you."

Ran heard the connection go silent. He coughed and lit another cigarette. By the second heavy drag, the nicotine began to steady his frayed nerves.

CHAPTER 16

DIRECTOR HATCHER BIDED HIS TIME WHILE THE SKETCHY intel on the pipeline plot was laid out. All Homeland Security had to go on were two intercepted phone calls and an encrypted Internet message. The first call came from a black Muslim American named Qasim Ali and emanated out of Philadelphia to a mosque in New York. He inquired about a van delivery and whether it would be reliable enough to make a long drive. Given his answer, the connection was broken. The second intercepted call came out of the docks in Newark, New Jersey. It was sent to the same mosque in New York. The call was simple, "The Yeminis are ready to transport." One day earlier, an encrypted message had come over the Internet from Pyongyang to a Yemeni site. It was comprised of two words: Pipeline ready.

FBI Director Kearns reported that Qasim Ali's apartment had been scoured, but nothing was found. Ali had disappeared into thin air. The FBI had monitored the New York mosque and combed the Newark docks—there was simply nothing more to go on. What they didn't know was that the body of Qasim Ali was rotting in a shipping container in the port of Jacksonville.

President Coleridge raised his hand for quiet. "I can't argue that the pipeline mentioned could be the Alaska Pipeline, but it also could be any pipeline, anywhere in the world. A van was mentioned, but without another tie-in, we're left hanging. We need more information, so Hatcher, keep checking your foreign sources. Now, let's move on to the next situation until something more connective turns up."

As was his usual manner, Hatcher waited to the last moment. "Excuse me, sir, but I have some intel coming in later this evening that may shed some light on all this." He paused to gain full attention. "There is a possibility that the Deepwater Horizon platform was sabotaged by a North Korean minisub."

The conference room went stone-cold silent. All eyes riveted on Hatcher. His eyes, however, were focused on the president's, who looked at his NSA director,

Jim LaSpesa. Their stare remained strangely fixed on each other. Hatcher frowned as an uneasy feeling came over the old country boy. That's the look that a rooster gives the fox as he guides him out of the coop with a chicken in his mouth, he thought.

"Ernie, you can't be serious," LaSpesa said, breaking the silence.

"As serious as Bobby Lee when he rode to Appomattox. I'm sure everyone in this room remembers the CIA agent called Trojan Horse. Well, he's the one that's on it, along with one of the best minds in the CIA—Agent Aaron Cohen. I will receive more intel in about two hours. We won't be sure until then."

"How do we know that this isn't some Internet hoax?" asked LaSpesa.

Hatcher was stunned. "I never said a word about the Internet, Jim," he said, staring at the NSA director.

President Coleridge shot a look at LaSpesa and said, "Gentlemen, this meeting's adjourned. We'll reconvene on this matter tomorrow at eight thirty a.m. In the meantime, put the pipeline on high alert. Ernie—full report for my review by seven a.m."

"Yes, Mr. President."

The president addressed his NSA director. "Jim, meet me in the Oval Office."

As Hatcher exited the conference room, his thoughts were fixed on LaSpesa's comment about the Internet. He whispered to himself, "Something stinks in the sty, and it ain't pigshit."

***

LaSpesa followed Coleridge into the Oval Office and took a seat on the couch. "Sir, I'm sorry that I slipped on that Internet crap with Hatcher. Do you think he's on to anything?"

"Is he on to anything?" Coleridge's words dripped with angry sarcasm. "Just what the hell do you think he is—an idiot? That man was running coon traps in the backwoods of Tennessee while you were still in diapers with a silver spoon hanging out of your mouth. Of course he suspects something! Couldn't you see it? It was written all over his face.

You and the rest of your Ivy Leaguers at NSA may not think much of the CIA, but they're still the largest and best spy network in the world. Yes, we need to worry about Hatcher! If you recall, I brought him in to clean up that organization and he's done one hell of a job."

"The odds of—"

"The odds of what, Jim? Listen, you're the one who talked me into helping scrub that story from the Internet. This is *my* ass that's on the firing line and someone just took aim."

"But the South Koreans begged us to—"

"Screw the Koreans!"

"It was more than that. You remember the pressure from BP and from England itself! Hell, they were willing to accept responsibility. They just wanted to keep a lid on it, that's all."

"I know, I know—we could ride out the environmental disaster, we could ride out the spike in oil, but we couldn't afford to blow up a conflict with North Korea. Well, maybe the way we covered it up was a colossal mistake."

"Let's not forget the advice from the money men."

"Damn it, Jim, I'm sick and tired of kowtowing to those egomaniacal financial families. I'm the damn president of the United States!"

"Please remember how much your reelection will cost. Every president since TR has dropped to one knee for these people. You're no different," LaSpesa coldly answered.

"Alright, alright…I need some time to myself. Be here at seven a.m., and you'd better pray that this doesn't come to light."

CHAPTER 17

THE QATAR AIRWAYS FLIGHT FROM SANA'A, YEMEN RAN about thirty minutes late. Waled al-Ashbot was tired, but as the plane touched ground at Dulles International, the reality of landing on American soil gave him a rush of adrenaline that pumped through his whole body. His mission was simple and well defined. He was to pick up a navy blue van in long-term parking, drive to a prearranged address in Philadelphia, pick up an American-born Muslim named Ishaq Shabazz, and drive to Seattle. No problem, he thought. At least I'm not being shot at, or worse, being asked to strap on a suicide vest.

When first recruited, he jumped at the chance to become a suicide bomber. Then after two years of terrorist training and fighting in Yemen, that dream had waned. He wasn't afraid of death, but he found greater appeal in dying with an AK-47 in his hands rather than having his body blown to a million pieces. Besides, could he be sure that Allah would put the million pieces of his body back together so he could enjoy the promised seventy-two virgins in paradise?

The light-brown business suit that was provided fit him well and the passport documentation was of the finest quality, which allowed him to breeze through customs. What fools these Americans are, he thought. Because these clown princes are so obsessed with being fair, grandmothers get patted down, but terrorists are allowed to pass. Yes, it is only a matter of time until we have this Satan-nation completely under Allah's sword.

He picked up his bags, pulled out the keys, and headed to long-term parking. A bounce was in his step. Praise be to Allah, he thought. This apple is ripe for picking and soon will be ours.

CHAPTER 18

THE NIGHTTIME SKY WAS FILLED WITH A LIGHT RAIN FROM heavy, low-lying cirrus clouds. The Sang-O class submarine stayed twenty miles off the coastline of Siberia, but used the calm waters of the Gulf of Anadyr to refuel itself for the second time. All hands on board the sub and the tanker were nervous. Calm waters or not, the task was so risky that one spark from a lightning bolt would send them all to kingdom come.

Standing on the deck of his sub, the North Korean captain looked up at the sky and then over at his exec, saying, "The skies are with us, tonight, Mr. Ryu. Neither the American satellites nor the Russian radar stations will be able to pick us up."

"Yes, Captain, let us hope these waters allow our refueling to go smoothly."

"If only we had a submarine fleet capable of longer destinations. Wouldn't you love to be on an American Ohio class sub…even for just one tour at sea?"

"It is truly a beautiful thought, Captain, but I'm afraid we will never even get an outdated Akula class boat. The size of our divided nation chains us like slaves to a navy of mediocrity."

"Yes, Mr. Ryu, and what's worse is that even when our exploits are successful, they are kept under a basket of secrecy, never to see the light of day."

Behind them wobbled the lead saboteur, Captain Dong of the 17th Sniper Corps. He never could get used to the rolling motion of the sea, especially when standing on the narrow plank of this small submarine. Even so, the cold wind that bit at his face was better than the claustrophobic confines below. The minisub normally carried a crew of nineteen sailors plus six divers. Adding Captain Dong, five saboteurs, and three Yemini hostages meant that three crewmen had to stay behind. To accomplish this, three of the Sniper Corps members had received special training to handle the lesser operations of the sub. In addition, no Russian type 53-56 torpedoes were carried, allowing room for demolition equipment.

"When will we be under way, Captain?" Dae Dong asked.

"We should be done in about an hour. You seem anxious, my friend," said the captain. "Perhaps you don't get enough of the cold in our homeland? Your journey through Alaska is not to be envied."

"It is not the cold, Captain, just the opportunity to strike a blow against these arrogant American bastards. Let's just say that sixty years of denying us our prize to the south has created a hatred that consumes my life."

"And mine as well, Captain Dong."

The exec, Ryu, looked at the demolition leader. Yes, he thought, it is also your ilk that would gladly commit suicide when asked, just like your sniper corps did in the Gulf of Mexico. Then he remembered that only half that crew was made up of the 17th Sniper Corps. The main part of the crew was, in fact, submariners. Did they volunteer to drink the Kool-Aid or were they murdered? Remembering other stories of mass suicide when captured by South Koreans, Ryu looked at his own captain and wondered if he too was a zealot, like Dae Dong. Without a sound, he turned away in disgust to finish watching the refueling.

Dae Dong gently slapped Ryu on the back and asked, "Mr. Ryu, do you not share the hatred of the Americans as your captain and I?"

"I have never met an American, Captain, so I can only say that I see the United States as an enemy. As to its people, I have no feelings."

The sniper captain frowned and looked at the submarine captain. "I wonder how your exec feels about the succession of our former leader's son to the presidency?" he asked.

As the captain opened his mouth to speak, the exec jumped to his own defense. "I am perfectly capable of stating that myself, Captain Dong. I never met President Kim Jong-il, nor have I met his son. My loyalty to the People's Democratic Republic is not in question. I will support whoever is our leader, and my orders are always obeyed."

"Even to death?" asked Dae Dong.

"I said, to the completion of my orders."

As the EO turned away to go back into the submarine, Dae Dong watched him with an evil eye. *When I get back to Korea, I will make life hell for that bilge rat,* he thought. *The man who has no fervor to die for his country, has no spine.*

"You may not like my exec, Captain Dong, but he is fully capable and will be there for us when the chips are down."

"In the Navy, I can see where special attachments are made between a captain and his men. In our 17th Sniper Corps, I make no friendships. My men are here to fight, sacrifice, and die. The triumph of our nation over the money-obsessed weaklings to the south is our only goal. To that end, everything is expendable—including our lives."

CHAPTER 19

WHITE HOUSE CONFERENCE ROOM
WASHINGTON, DC

DIRECTOR HATCHER SAT ALONE AT THE CONFERENCE TABLE with his completed report on the Gulf of Mexico oil rig explosion in front of him. Copies of the report lay in front of empty chairs, as he was the first to arrive. As a rule, he liked being first in; it gave him a moment to clear his head, whether he was to be in the hot seat or not. Opening the report one more time, he flipped forward to the photographs that were taken before the second attack. He had always been suspicious of the pictures that were released to the public. The angle of the shots was always one that showed the least. As he took a closer look at the photographs, he had to admit that the photo of the final position of the chopper platform did not coincide with the government's story of how the initial explosion occurred.

By instinct, Hatcher knew that Svetlana Gorenkov had done her homework. The fact that this story had been wiped clean from the Internet was incriminating enough, and the necessity for people to eliminate her was gasoline on the fire. However, LaSpesa's slip on the Internet comment had raised the largest red flag, one that he couldn't ignore. If I allow it, this meeting could turn ugly, he thought. But I still don't have concrete proof of anything—at least not yet. And dad gum it, Coleridge is still the president. I need those two mavericks to get their asses back here with something I can sink my teeth into. Damn it!

As the other participants filed in and took their seats, most picked up and scanned Hatcher's report. President Coleridge came in last and gave it the longest perusal, then closed the file and asked Director Hatcher for his overview.

"Mr. President, this intel is frightening. It's either an elaborate hoax or we have had an act of war perpetrated on us by the Democratic People's Republic of Korea; and as far as I can see, we have done nothing to answer this aggression."

With that statement, a pall hung over the conference room. Coleridge looked nervous and shifted in his chair, finally clearing his throat to speak. "Ernie, let's presume it's not a hoax. Are you prepared to state it's true beyond a shadow of a doubt? Because if it is, then are we in this room not required—no—*obligated* to the American people to ask for a declaration of war against the DPRK?"

Before Hatcher could respond, General Belden interrupted with his own question. "Before you answer that, perhaps you would consider, which *is* stated in the report, that the disappearance of the sub could not be, without a doubt, attributed to suicide. I believe 'an enigma' is what they called it."

"Mr. President…General, let me answer both questions at the same time. First, in regard to the suicide issue, I would like to point out that North Korean soldiers are taught to fight to the bitter end. In September 1996, a North Korean submarine got stranded at Kangrung, South Korea, and its crew abandoned the ship. Eleven of the crew committed suicide and the rest fought to the last man, with one exception, who was captured. In June 1998, another submarine got caught in fishing nets at Sokcho and its crew committed mass suicide, rather than be captured by the South Koreans. So yes, they may have committed suicide by blowing themselves up.

"Second, it is not my intent to grind for a declaration of war, even if it was directed against 'The Little Sisters of the Poor.' My question is: Does this intel rise to a credible level of possibility? It does not have to be provable in every detail, but it should be believable. If it is, every person in this room will have a lot of explaining to do regarding why we did nothing about a naked act of aggression. It could be one of the largest scandals in American history. We can't change what was already done in the Gulf of Mexico nor do I think it prudent to take on another war at this moment in our nation's history—especially one that involves the DPRK. In light of all this, the new chatter we're picking up on a possible pipeline attack needs to be addressed as credible and all our efforts going forth must be directed at preventing a second act of terrorism."

NSA Director LaSpesa chimed in, "Ernie, I think your report is well laid out and, Mr. President, I think his council is wise indeed. Even though this report does not definitively tie the North Koreans to the oil rig disaster, I think we need to take this pipeline threat with the utmost seriousness and move forward, redoubling our efforts as necessary."

A hog would gag on that mouthful, Hatcher thought.

Coleridge paused and rubbed his closed eyelids, appearing relieved. "Alright, Ernie, thank you for a most timely report. Now, I want Homeland and FBI's efforts redoubled and I want daily status reports by seven thirty a.m. until we have this under control. Ernie, are the two agents on their way back?"

"No, Mr. President, they still have some leads to wrap up in Russia."

"Leads regarding this report?"

"Yes."

Coleridge fidgeted as he glanced at LaSpesa and said, "Well, bring them back as soon as possible. I'd like to personally congratulate them both. You know…good for morale."

"Well, Mr. President, we have an old saying in Tennessee: You climb and climb to reach the top of the mountain where you can look down on everyone else, but no one can stay up there very long."

Coleridge paused, appearing to freeze as he realized Hatcher had just insulted him. Hatcher rose and grabbed his folder. He knew the president got the message. Yep, he thought, I've seen that same look on a flat-faced possum in a tree.

CHAPTER 20

AARON AND LANA AGREED THAT THE ONLY GOOD THING about their morning was that it wasn't the previous night. It had been the worst night of sleep they had ever encountered. Devon smiled. The countless lonely nights he had spent under the fear of being killed made this last night seem like a walk in the park.

Sliding behind the wheel of their car, Aaron looked over at Lana and asked, "I didn't want to push you last night, but why all the secrecy about where we're going?"

"The person we're going to visit is my friend who first received the Northern Fleet paper and put it out on the Internet. Don't forget, that report was leaked—it was never meant to see the light of day. I couldn't tell you last night because I didn't know if we were going to be attacked again or not. This man, kid really, lives in desperate fear of his life. The Koreans and the Russian mob want him silenced—forever. What I'm saying, Aaron, is that, just like me, they have a target on his back—they want him dead."

Driving up to an abandoned warehouse, Devon whistled and said, "Good Lord, I think even the rats gave up on this place."

"Sorry, Devon, rats and pigeon droppings are what we're about to go through. It shows how desperate Yakov Isroel truly is."

Pointing, she said, "Aaron, pull up and park by that opening over there."

"What was this place?" Devon asked.

"An old munitions plant from World War II. It's been abandoned for decades—no money to tear it down…no money to clean it up either. Remember, we have no real green movement in Russia, and even if we did, it would take a hundred years to clean up all the toxic dumps left from the old Soviet days."

"How are we going to get in?" Aaron asked.

Svetlana pulled her sleeve back and looked at her watch. "I sent him an encrypted message from that Internet café an hour ago. I told him we would be here at exactly this time." She knocked twice, picked up a rock, and scratched the surface of the steel door.

One by one, the latches from the inside began releasing. There were six in all. The door creaked open and Yakov Isroel poked his head out, squinting as the direct sunlight hit his face. He smiled at the sight of Svetlana and bolted forward to give her a hug.

"Thank God you're still alive. I read that your apartment had a gas leak and exploded. They said there were no fatalities, but I didn't believe them. I wept for my friend and figured that I would be next. When you contacted me this morning, I wasn't a hundred percent sure that it was you. But when you scratched the door with the rock, I tell you…" He paused, trying to talk through his emotions. "My…my heart, Lana… it exploded."

Yakov came to his senses, looked over their shoulders, and pulled at Lana's sleeve. "Come in—hurry!"

He slammed the door and reset all the locks. "Follow me," he said. "We'll make our introductions upstairs where it's nice and safe."

Yakov led them through a labyrinth of rusted steel halls and stairs until they reached his living quarters. Devon took note of the elaborate security cameras that overlapped each other, leaving no area unseen. He also took note of all the rats and climbed the stairs without touching the handrails, which were laden with pigeon droppings. The stench of that, the rats, and the leftover munitions sulfur made his eyes water. I'd take my one-room cabin with an outhouse in the snow over this. Then again, the constant fear of death is a strange bedfellow and does weird things to the mind, he thought.

When they reached Yakov's living quarters, Aaron and Devon stood dumbfounded at what they saw. Opening a rusted steel door exposed a long workbench with at least a dozen main frame computers that were supporting six monitors streaming data. Above them on a rack were a series of two dozen smaller screens displaying live feed from his security cameras. Aaron was quick to recognize that Yakov was not only a microcosm of the NSA, but possibly a geek of his own stature. He liked the guy straight off.

Yakov left to start a fresh pot of coffee. The three visitors took close examination of his equipment while he was gone. They were astounded at the technology that this single individual had not only acquired, but had improvised into a state-of-the-art information and security station. What he was working on was pure genius.

"Mind boggling," said Devon.

"Must've been a CalSci man," replied Aaron, jabbing Devon in the ribs with his elbow.

When Yakov returned with coffee on a silver tray laden with ornate Russian cups and saucers, the three looked at each other in bewilderment. Svetlana led with the first question, while a sly smile appeared on her lips.

"Yakov, there's a strange dichotomy going on here, I mean…"

"What? A geek can't have culture? Besides, they belonged to my wealthy mother, God rest her soul. Without her, I wouldn't have this luxurious lifestyle."

All four broke into laughter. When the humorous banter subsided, it was Svetlana that got down to business. "Yakov, we need to know who ordered the removal of the Northern Navy report. If we know that, we might be able to zero in on who's trying to kill us and what they're trying to hide."

"It's interesting you should ask—tracking this down is all I've worked on since it happened." He reached over and with great affection, tapped the computer to his left. "With this baby, I've been able to listen in on all calls emanating from North Korea to Moscow. Filtering out the garbage with that box over there, I've zeroed in on the calls from one, let's see, yes, a man named Kyong Ran, who very well could be your assassin. Because no calls were recorded prior to the scrubbing, I've had to put the pieces together. I can play the recordings if you like, but here is my list: He placed a call to a Russian hit man the night before your apartment blew up. I didn't know the target, Svetlana; otherwise, I would have warned you…I'm so sorry."

"I understand, Yakov, please continue."

"He placed another call to the same man the next day. He was furious when he was told the target had escaped and disappeared. The assassin called him the following day and told him the target had been found and was about to be taken out at the Krymskaya Park."

"Those must have been the two men that passed in front of you just before we got there," said Aaron.

"Oh my God, Lana! To think that *you* are the target that I have been tracking! All these calls are about my best friend—it breaks my heart."

"I know. Please, Yakov…"

"Later that afternoon, the North Korean was called again to inform him they had followed you to the Lubyanka Restaurant and you would be eliminated before midnight. Then after midnight, the Korean called and was told you escaped, but they would get you at the apartment of a passport forger."

"I guess you could say that we've had a busy two days," said Devon. "Anything else?"

"The North Korean received a call from a man who chewed him out for failing to assassinate you."

"Where did that call come from?"

"I've got it logged in, but haven't tracked it down yet. It came from southwest France, in the Aquitaine area. Oh yes, he also made a call to someone unidentified in Pyong Yang. He wanted four men to meet him the next morning to travel on a Gulf Stream to Moscow. They were to depart at six a.m. today—North Korean time."

Yakov looked up at his large world time clock hanging on the wall beside him. "They should have landed two hours ago."

CHAPTER 21

INTERMITTENT BUZZING SCREAMED IN YAKOV'S OFFICE, sounding an alarm that the gate of his perimeter fence had been breached. All eyes zeroed in on the series of security cameras as three vehicles smashed through the locked gates, roaring to a sudden stop at the entrance to the warehouse.

Devon and Aaron pulled out their weapons. Yakov continued to sip at his coffee. "Relax, my friends, we have plenty of time."

"Uh, judging by the assault rifles they're carrying, I think we'd better do something fast," said Aaron.

"First they have to find their way up here." Yakov took one last sip and then placed his cup on the saucer as gently as if he were handling a fine museum piece. He patted his lips with a linen napkin and stood up. "Now, if you will please follow me, we will begin our exit. It's all a matter of exact timing, so listen to every word and do exactly as I say."

Yakov led them down a narrow hall and motioned for them to enter a dark room. In the total darkness, the three visitors groped for each other and tripped over their feet. Yakov, however, was like a cat in the dark, having practiced this drill many times.

"The darkness will not protect us," Devon whispered.

Just then, he heard the creaking of a steel door. "Over this way," Yakov said, without the protection of a whisper, "through this door." The three felt around until they found his guiding arm.

Yakov stepped in behind them, locking the latches of the door. Another creaking sound, as Yakov lifted a steel hatch built into the floor.

"Please pay attention," he said. "I just opened a one-meter by one-meter hatch in the floor. Below is a chute that is at a sixty-degree angle. We are going to go down one at a time. We will fall three floors, dumping into a well-padded bin in the basement. When you land in the bin, climb out as fast as you can, because the next person will be right behind you. Wait for me there, as I have to wait for the right moment to set the delayed explosion. We will have only thirty seconds to enter an exit tunnel before the whole building comes down. Okay, Devon, you first. Reach for my hand to guide you."

As Devon moved forward, Yakov stopped him. "Kneel down and feel for the edge of the hatch. Then put your legs in, fold your arms across your chest, and pull the rest of you in with your feet—go!"

Devon did and straight away felt the racing plunge downward. Thinking it would never end, he was spit out and landed in a bin filled with bedding on mattresses. As quick as he could, he climbed out as Svetlana followed behind. He helped her out just as Aaron plunged into the bin behind her.

Yakov felt his way back to the door and ran his fingers down the latch side of the door. They bumped hard into the box that was mounted on the wall. Like a blind man feeling the face of his lover, he caressed the box until he felt the lower right button. He pushed it and a black-and-white screen lit up. Now visible were the eight commandos coming down the hall toward his quarters. He knew the time had arrived and they were in perfect position. He reached above the screen to a smaller box and pushed its only button. The button began to flash a silent red signal—the detonator had been set. He turned and made his way back to the hatch. With great effort, he pulled the latch over and toward his head in one motion, beginning his slide down the shaft.

Yakov landed with a thud. In a matter of two seconds, he was out and groping the short, outer side of the bin. There! He found the flashlight and turned it on.

"This way," he said, pointing with his flashlight to the open entrance of an underground rail tunnel. As he led the way in, he paused and found a second flashlight mounted by the entrance. He threw it to Devon and said, "You're last—let's go—run—run!"

The sound of the explosion was horrific. Kyong Ran was sitting in his Mercedes when the top floor of the warehouse burst into a flaming mass. By the time the second explosion blew, he had already reversed his car and skidded to a stop. He slammed the gearshift into drive and the Mercedes leapt forward toward the gate as the third explosion momentarily deafened him, raining debris over his car.

As the four made their frantic way through the tunnel, they felt the second and third explosions. Yakov was concerned, but not panicked. He wasn't worried about the flames, only the force of the blast of two floors imploding into the basement. Did he allow enough of a delay for them to get out? He couldn't be sure. Then he saw the faint outline of light that surrounded the outer entrance of the tunnel.

As his hand grabbed the latch, he gave a sharp turn of his wrist and released it. At that moment, the blast percussion hit the backs of Devon, Svetlana, and Aaron. They were pummeled forward and strewn on their stomachs. The wave proceeded until it hit Yakov and the unlatched door. It blew the door off its hinges. Yakov was thrust into the air and landed with the heavy steel door on top of him. Blood began pouring from his mouth and the back of his head.

Within seconds, the other three were back on their feet, wobbling back and forth while clearing their heads. Covered in dust, they coughed as they staggered in different directions, one not aware of the other, trying to gain their bearings. Svetlana was the first to come to her senses and spot Yakov under the blown door. She ran to him and in an adrenaline-filled moment, she pulled the two-hundred-pound door off his body. Shocked at what she saw, she knelt down and felt the vein in his neck.

"He's alive," she screamed. "Help!"

With both hands, Devon grabbed Aaron by the hair on the sides of his head. His face was covered with soot and dust. Looking into his eyes, he could tell that Aaron was all right. "Aaron! Go and get the car and pull it up here next to Yakov. Go—quick!" he shouted.

Devon could barely hear what he had said to Aaron over the ringing in his ears. He staggered back to Svetlana and dropped to his knees. Her eyes met his and told him everything he needed to know...Yakov was not going to make it.

When Aaron brought their car to a stop, he hopped out and saw Devon motioning him to help get Yakov into the backseat. When this was done, Devon raised Yakov's head up, allowing Aaron to slide in. He gently rested Yakov's head onto Aaron's lap.

As they sped off, Yakov opened his eyes and tugged at Aaron's shirt to bring him close. "Follow the Korean—pipeline is target...then follow...money," he gasped, spitting out the blood in his mouth. "Sholem, mayn bruder."

Aaron felt Yakov's body sag as it ceased to function. With a gentle touch, he closed Yakov's eyes, kissed his forehead, and whispered, "Shalom."

CHAPTER 22

THE BODY OF WATER THAT WAS THE BERING STRAIT WAS choppy, but once the minisub neared the territorial limits of St. Lawrence Island, the water calmed and the sub slowed to a minimum speed. So far, everything had gone better than expected, but the mission had reached another of its critical points. The sub would be at its most vulnerable point for detection once it entered Norton Sound. Both the boat's captain and the leader of the commandos knew that if they were detected, blowing up and scuttling the minisub was their only option. All hands would have to be sacrificed.

In the cramped conning tower, the leader of the commandos, Captain Dong, stood at the map station with the captain of the minisub. Dae Dong was more than confused; he was irritated to a point of exploding. "I don't understand why you cannot bring this submarine to this point in Norton Sound," he said, tapping the map with his index finger. "This clearly gives us the shortest distance to shore, and the water has more than sufficient depth for you to maneuver this boat. I insist, Captain, that you drop us off there."

"I am sorry, Captain Dong, but that point takes us within the territorial waters of the United States. My orders are very specific that we do not encroach that limit."

"But that is eighteen miles off the coastal area where we must land. That's six more miles for us to travel in the water." He paused, drew a deep breath, and hissed in a voice so low that he was barely audible, "You don't seem to understand our logistics. Our timing is critical."

The boat's captain blanched at Dae Dong's tone, but knew he had to follow his own orders. "You are not taking into account that we will be intruding on the *southern* shoreline. If you want to reduce your distance and time in the water, I suggest that you make landfall on the southern shore—here," he said, his finger pointing to a spot on the map.

"Do you take me for a fool? That point adds another thirty miles that we will have to travel on land—by foot."

"If this were wartime, we would have the opportunity to do as we wish. However, it is not, and I regret that I cannot be more helpful, but I have my orders. You are in charge of your men when you are on land. On sea, I am in charge of this boat, which includes you and your men while you are on board—no exceptions."

"Damn it! Don't give me that 'if it were wartime' garbage. No armistice was ever signed in the fifties. We have continued to be in a de facto war with the United States and South Korea ever since."

"That is true, but my orders are my orders."

Dae Dong exploded, pounding his fist on the table. He spun around and, while looking at the floor, pondered his next move. As he looked up, he detected what he thought was the trace of a sarcastic smile on the EO's face. His rage boiled over and he clenched his fist to hit the EO. In a lightning move, the captain slammed his hand down, locking a vice-like grip on the commando's wrist.

"Perhaps, Captain Dong, I might consider your request as we move into place in the Norton Sound—if it appears that we can do it undetected." With his grip firmly holding Dae Dong's wrist, he leaned over and whispered, "That is, if I have your assurance as an officer that you will get off my EO's back and that there will be no further animosity toward him. Am I understood?"

"Understood," hissed Dae Dong.

"Mr. Ryu, set course for the coordinates that Captain Dong requests. The bridge is yours...I am going to my quarters. Notify me when we are twenty-five miles from the target location. Captain Dong, I think it wise for you to return to your men and get them ready. The time is near."

CHAPTER 23

WALED AL-ASHBOT FELT GOOD BEHIND THE WHEEL OF THE navy blue van. In my whole life, I have never experienced a vehicle such as this, he thought. He marveled at the all the gauges and the built-in navigation system. He even liked the sound of the female navigation voice as she told him when to turn—her silky, commanding voice aroused him. Waled had no experience with the opposite sex, and as a twenty-year-old male, his hormones were not only raging, but were backed up and in severe need of relief. As he drove on I95 north to Philadelphia, his mind drifted to the XXX sex shops his friends had told him would be available in America.

"Be careful," they warned him. "You'll mess your pants before you finish reading even one magazine."

He hated America; that was for sure. Their society is decadent and weak, he mused. They let women dominate their society, and other than their military, their men have become craven sissies. But, they do have everything in life to give a man pleasure. Ah, yes, the sex shops! He felt the heat in his crotch grow and began rubbing himself as he drove.

"Turn right at the next exit to 495 north," interrupted the navigation voice.

"Damn," shouted Waled. He was all the way over in the left lane and had only had a quarter mile to make his exit. His heat vanished as he had little time to veer right, changing two lanes at a time. The honking was nonstop, but he liked giving the American gesture of sticking his middle finger up in the air. He liked doing it so much that it caused the van to rock from right to left with each lane he changed.

After several minutes, he saw a billboard that advertised an XXX adult shop at a truck stop. His mind told him to drive on, but his hormones commanded the driver's seat and he pulled off. He decided he would pick up the homegrown terrorist in Philadelphia after he got a small amount of relief.

***

The burly man behind the counter looked at his swarthy customer and curled his upper lip. Yeah, another 'A-rab' that wants to keep his own women in some kind of ugly monkey tent, then has to get his jollies off looking at our porn, he thought. Disgusting!

"You want a private booth?" he snickered.

"What is private booth?"

"It's so you can buy one of these," he said, sliding a porn movie over the counter to him. "You can go in and have one of your seventy-two virgins in paradise right here on earth."

Waled stood looking confused. He didn't know whether the man was being courteous or contemptuous.

"Well, Mohammed, what's it gonna be? Choke the chicken now or later?"

As the biting remark sunk in, Waled knew he was being insulted. Pissed off, he threw a hundred-dollar bill on the counter, grabbed his merchandise, and stormed out. His bill had totaled $37.50; throwing the hundred-dollar bill was his way of showing up the merchant, who stood and smiled at his handsome profit. Waled had made his first error.

When he got into his van, he looked at his watch and determined that he was ahead of schedule, so he peeked inside one of his magazines. Feeling the heat return, he decided to find a quiet place where he could pull off for an extended look. That was his second mistake.

After he had found his relief, Waled awoke to the sound of rapping knuckles on his driver's side window. With one hand on his pistol, a state trooper motioned with his other hand for him to roll down his window.

"What is the matter, officer?" he asked.

"For starters, you're asleep in a vehicle behind an abandoned gas station that is marked 'No Trespassing.'"

"But I was only sleeping—not trespassing," complained Waled.

"Yeah, right." The trooper pulled up his flashlight and looked in the back of the van. It was empty. "Registration and license," he said with no emotion.

After the officer sat in his cruiser for several minutes, Waled's nerves became frayed. He begged Allah to forgive him this small transgression and vowed he would never again stray from his mission. He looked again and saw the trooper approaching his van. Beads of sweat began flowing down from his hairline.

As the officer reached up to hand Waled's papers back, he noticed the sweat. Pulling the papers back toward him, he frowned, gave Waled a suspicious look, and asked, "What are you so nervous about?"

"Nothing! I mean, I have never been stopped by police before. As you can see, my record is clean."

"Clean you are, young man. You're lucky. I'm not going to cite you for trespassing, but I am going to remember you. By the way—get your yuckles off at home next time."

Waled didn't understand the meaning of the word yuckles, but knew from the policeman's tone that it was an insult. His upper lip snarled and he asked, "Does this mean I can go?"

"Yes, just remember what I said. Keep your hands on the steering wheel, not in your pants."

As Waled drove off, he looked once more at his watch. He would have to hurry if he was going to make his scheduled pick-up on time. While pounding his fist on the steering wheel, he spat and cursed the police, the pornography on his seat, women in general for their disgusting sexual deviation, the Jews in Israel, and in particular, the demon he hated most—the United States. He promised Allah he would destroy the magazines he had purchased at the first opportunity. After he calmed down, he again pounded his fist on the steering wheel. He regretted making that promise to Allah.

CHAPTER 24

KYONG RAN'S FSB CONTACT HAD INVESTIGATED THE EXplosion as part of his official duties. As an unofficial duty, he had picked up a small piece of Yakov's security tape and slid it in his pocket. With a covetous frown, he looked around to make sure no one saw him. Satisfied no one had, he tapped his jacket pocket, knowing that the information he might extract from the tape could garner him a large sum of money. He had done business with the Korean before, and knowing how pathetic his financial state of affairs were, he was sure that he could ask his own price.

***

Kyong Ran was in a foul mood. He was lying on the bed in his hotel room with his shirt off, chain-smoking his harsh Russian cigarettes. His phone, which was resting on the nightstand, was set to vibrate. His eyes were closed, but he was awake, absorbed in reliving the raid on Yakov Isroel's compound. No matter how he tried to rewrite it in his mind, it had ended as an unmitigated disaster. Worse, he was the one who had directed it. It was his name that was all over it—no incompetent Russians to blame this time. The finger of blame pointed only in his direction. He threw his legs over the bed and raised himself up. He sat tense, waiting for his cell phone to ring. He was desperate to get the information he needed on the two Americans that were thwarting his every move. His connection in the Russian secret police, the FSB, had promised him information within two hours.

Kyong Ran jumped when the cell phone began spinning and vibrating on the hard surface of the nightstand. As he reached for the phone, the cigarette fell from his lips and landed on his thigh. "Shit!" he yelled out, brushing the cigarette to the carpeted floor. With one hand rubbing the burn spot on his hairless thigh, he grabbed the phone with the other.

"Hello!" he shouted.

When the FSB agent finished his report, Ran's mood improved. The confirmation that the two men were CIA agents might have given him reason to pause; however, the news that one agent had a wife living in Alaska was all he needed to buoy his deflated spirits.

Kyong Ran had been successful by always avoiding direct contact yet pouncing on the weakest points of his opponents. Julie Weston McKenzie would be the Achilles' heel of the agent code-named Trojan Horse. How appropriate—and convenient, he thought. In a matter of days, I will have my own team swarming the terrain of Alaska to blow up its oil pipeline. Kidnapping a housewife will be like…cutting out someone's heart! A horse laugh broke out at the irony as Ran got up to take a shower. Who knows, he mused, maybe all these setbacks were just part of an ordered fate, so I may have the ultimate satisfaction of making this CIA hero watch as I rape and kill his wife before putting a bullet between his saddened eyes.

The invigorating shower gave Kyong Ran a renewed sense of purpose and anticipation. He made his next call to two of his operatives driving to Seattle. He ordered them to Fairbanks and gave them the GPS coordinates of the McKenzie home. He instructed them to reconnoiter the property and return to Fairbanks and await his order to kidnap the woman. He also told them not to kill her until he arrived.

***

Devon realized that he hadn't called Julie since their stay at the house of Sergei Belova. The bloody violence of their dead images gave him pause, but also an increased sense of urgency. He was involved in something far more sinister than what he had thought in the beginning and was proving to be more treacherous in scope than he had led Julie to believe. So far he hadn't told her of the danger involved or the terrorism involving their country. He had been negligent in this same way with his first wife and he vowed he would not make that marital mistake twice. He picked up his mobile phone and made the call.

Devon felt an ache in his heart. Years of isolation in Alaska haunted his soul and this short time away made him realize how much his wife meant to him. She was never far from his thoughts and when he heard her voice, his eyes misted and the lump in his throat made it difficult to talk. "Julie, I've missed you…so much."

"Come on, Devon, tell the truth; you're having the time of your life. So how is it in old Mother Russia with Aaron?"

"Aaron is doing just fine, but that's not why I called."

"Devon, I can tell by your voice something's wrong. What's going on? Are you in over your head?"

"Look, Julie, it's not that I'm in over my head; it's just that what I thought was going to be a stroll through the park has turned out to be an issue of national security…and I can't emphasize how dangerous it is. Dangerous enough that I've asked Director Hatcher to dispatch four agents to the house—tomorrow. They're going to be there round the clock—one in the house and three guarding the perimeter."

"Is that really necessary?" moaned Julie. "And if it is, why aren't you here? Devon, you're scaring me."

"Honey, I came out here to help a friend. The truth is, I did hope that there might be a little action involved, but that was only the wishful dreaming of a bored spook. Now…things have changed. We're both CIA and there's nothing you or I can do to change that. I can't tell you all the details now, but it is national security, it is terrorism, and Aaron and I are in the thick of it. Listen, I should be able to wrap up what we need to uncover here within a couple of days. Then I promise to be on the quickest flight back home. If what I think is correct, the Alaska Pipeline is the target of this mess. We don't know if it's the drill site of Prudhoe Bay, the Valdez Marine Terminal, or any point on the eight hundred miles in between. That means I can help better in Alaska than I can in Moscow or Langley."

"Devon, I've noticed how you've been struggling with your life of inaction, but you've paid your debt to these people. You were supposed to be in retirement, damn it!" she said, holding back tears.

"I know, sweetheart, but this is who I am, and I can't change that… I'm sorry. I'm also sorry about the agents coming in, but they are necessary—and I mean it."

"Please, get here as soon as you can…and damn it, Devon, be careful! I love you."

"I love you too, Julie. Don't forget that."

As Julie slowly put the phone into its cradle, she looked out the window of their great room. All their plans for a family…all their plans for their life could be gone in a second. By God, I swear that won't happen if I have anything to say about it! Over my dead body…She began to reminisce about her former fiancé, Tim Daniels, then that horrid night her father was killed by a rogue CIA assassin flashed into stark view. Wiping her tear-filled eyes with her thumb and forefinger, she vowed she would never live in fear again.

She began laying out plans to defend her home and herself. The CIA may be covering her perimeter, but the interior was her domain, and in spite of an agent being assigned to the inside, no one knew it better than her. Over and over she pondered, What would Devon do?

CHAPTER 25

THE SKIES WERE OVERCAST AND DREARY, WHICH ONLY added to his boredom. Waled al-Ashbot had been yawning so hard and so often that his jaw began to hurt. He liked American rap music, but the last four hours of it had pushed him beyond his limit. He pushed the AM button on the van's radio and an old George Jones country song was playing. When the whining of a steel guitar bled to the forefront, Waled decided that he had had enough. He grabbed his hair with each hand and screamed. Because he had orders to make Bozeman before stopping for the night, he made an angry fist and punched the power button to the OFF position. He knew he could still make Bozeman that night, but it would take another three hours of driving and he was worn out. He rationalized that if he could just get a room, sleep, then get up earlier in the morning, he could make up the time.

The change in noise disturbed his sleeping passenger and woke him up. Waled looked over and sneered a look of disgust at him. Stinking American, he thought. They claim to be committed to jihad, but I don't trust any of them. They're all lazy and corrupt. Besides, why would any of them be willing to die a martyr's death? They have no feeling for our plight or the decades of suffering we Muslims have endured.

"Don't forget to fake getting your credit card out of your wallet," Waled said, as he pulled alongside the rusty triangular portico of the shabby motel on the outskirts of Billings. "Make it look like it is too difficult to pull out of your wallet. Then make it look like you change your mind and pay cash. And don't forget—two beds!"

Ishaq Shabazz, his identity for the trip changed to Jameel Burris, gave Waled a wide, toothy grin and decided to impress him with his inner city jargon. "Dat be coo, baby. If dey ax me where I be goin,' it be Spo'kan."

When Jameel shut the door, Waled remembered why his superiors told him he needed a homegrown to go with him. Having two Mideastern Muslims traveling alone in a van would set off alarm bells. He thought the jive talk was a bit excessive, but probably worthwhile.

After twenty minutes, Waled looked one more time at his watch. Jameel had been in the motel lobby longer than necessary to pay cash for a room. Just then, his cell phone rang. It was the North Korean.

"Hello?"

"Where are you?"

"Billings."

"You were supposed to make Bozeman."

"Traffic and weather..."

There was silence.

"You should have pushed further."

"We'll get an earlier start and make Seattle in plenty of time."

"You now have additional duties when you get to Fairbanks."

"What duties?"

"You're going to kidnap a woman from her home."

"Will there be resistance?"

"No. Quick in, take the hostage, and then quick out."

"Do we kill her?"

"No...unless there is no way you can grab her. I want her *alive*."

"What do I do with her?"

"Take her back to a different motel in Fairbanks and hold her there until I arrive."

"How do I find her?"

"I'll text you the GPS coordinates."

Waled looked up and saw Jameel saunter out of the motel office door. "What do I tell the homegrown?"

"Nothing, until you arrive at your destination. First you will reconnoiter the property, then you'll receive a notice as to when you strike."

The connection rang off.

Jameel passed in front of the van and pointed toward the end of the linear motel. He kept walking and held up the room key, indicating for Waled to follow. When he reached the second room from the end, he stopped and pointed to a parking space. As Waled got out of the van, he asked in an irritated tone, "What took you so long?"

"I guess because of my color, he didn't think I was smart enough to know that I had to stay on I90 to Spokane. I told him I did, but he pulled out a map anyway—talkative son of a bitch."

"Do you think he suspects anything?"

"No. He never even tried to look over my shoulder at the van. I don't want to piss you off or anything like that, but I thought we were supposed to change the license plates today. Did something change?"

"No, I got so tired that I forgot. We'll do it after we leave in the morning. We need to do it in a spot where no one can see us. We need to leave by six in the morning."

"Six? Why six?"

"There's been a slight change in our plans when we get to Fairbanks. We need to check something out."

"What's that?"

"Quit asking questions…I'll tell you when we get there."

CHAPTER 26

YAKOV ISROEL HAD BEEN MUCH MORE THAN JUST A SOURCE of leaks to Svetlana; they had a bond that superseded the chasm of age and sex. He was her alter ego when it came to conspiracy theories. Moreover, they shared a deep love of their country of birth—not the old Communist police state, not the corrupt Russia it had become, but the dream of a pure entity that cared for its people and treasured their God-given liberties. They both wanted a nurturing country worthy of being called Mother Russia. Yakov had grown to be a true friend and confidant as well. Truth be told, she had adopted him as the little brother that she never had.

With a face of granite, Lana said to Aaron and Devon in a slow, deliberate cadence, "I don't care what it takes or how long it takes, I want this Korean scum dead—better yet, I want him to die a slow, horrible death. I want to watch…and I want to savor the moment when I tell him that this is for my friend, Yakov Isroel." She paused as one, lonely tear escaped down her cheek. She sniffed and continued, "And I don't want anyone to tell me that pig has rights, which justice needs to serve." Then, as if the pain could no longer be contained, she exploded and let it all out. "*I want MY justice!*"

With a look of surprise, Devon glanced at Aaron and without a word looked away. Aaron gathered his thoughts while looking at the floor and with great hesitation said, "I understand, Lana. We will get this filth and we will see that he dies…and not in a court of law. This I promise."

"But," Devon said, "you have to remember that our first mission is to extract information from him. Then we can dispose of him."

With her eyes flashing a stare that could have burned a hole in him, Lana shot back, "I want your promise too, Devon McKenzie. Promise me that we will kill him, or you'll get no more help from me. That's *my* promise to you."

"I promise," he said. "Hell, Lana, I'll even let you pull the trigger if it's at all possible."

"Good, then let's get started."

Devon looked over at Aaron, who nodded, and then said, "Well, you're going to have to tell us where to start, Lana; this is *your* game— you started it, now you are going to have to run it."

"We start with Evgeny Zakorov, the Minister of Transportation. Remember, he has sources deep in North Korea. He's no fan of President Bukin or his old KGB cronies. Also, he despised Kim Jong-il and everything he stood for—and nothing has changed with the son, Kim Jong-un. A small smile appeared on her face. "Not to mention, he has always had a tender spot for me, so…who knows?"

Aaron feigned a dagger to his heart and asked, "Do you think he knows anything about the possible pipeline attack?"

"If any Russian official does, it will be him."

"Can you arrange a meeting with him?"

"Of course," Lana said. "Remember, this woman is on a mission to kill."

***

The skies were clouded over and it was beginning to drizzle when they reached a small downtown café a little after three and parked across the street. Lana told them that Zakorov was a creature of extreme habit who took his afternoon coffee break every day at three o'clock and only at this particular café. It wasn't one of Moscow's new upscale restaurants, but it was four long blocks from his office—just far enough away not to encounter any of his colleagues. He worked a twelve-hour day, six days a week, so his conscience needed no salving for taking this daily, hour-long break.

At ten after the hour, Zakorov hadn't arrived, and if he was anything, he was punctual—to a fault. Lana looked at her watched and knew something wasn't right. "I think it's best that I go in alone," she said. "If he's in there, I don't want him to see me with two bodyguards. I don't know how he'd react to that."

"Be careful," Devon said. "There may be others who are also aware of his idiosyncrasies—and his connection to you."

As Lana entered the café, she looked over the array of tables. The café was bright, with large sparkling windows, so it would have been easy to spot her friend. Evgeny Zakorov was nowhere to be seen. She sat down and feigned looking at a menu. A waitress came to the edge of the table, looked down at Svetlana's face, and remembered her from the many meetings that the girl had had with Zakorov.

"You're looking for Evgeny, aren't you?" she asked.

"Yes. I remember you also."

"I'm sorry," she said, "but Evgeny hasn't been here for two days. Each day I have had his espresso and pastry waiting, and then had to throw them out."

Lana frowned, looked around, and asked, "Has anybody out of the ordinary been in here at this particular time?"

"Do you mean FSB?"

"Could be, but also anyone else—say, Mafia or gang types?"

The waitress put her hand over her heart and blanched. "Both days that Evgeny wasn't here, there was a Korean-looking man with two Russians. They were an ugly looking bunch, black leather coats, brooding hulks…they sat right over there both days," she said pointing to a corner. "But they're not here today."

"Can you give me Evgeny's home address?"

The waitress paused, her face blushing. "Why would I know that?"

"Because I'm a woman, and your affection wasn't just because he was a paying customer, was it?"

The waitress became indignant and turned on her heels to walk away. Lana reached up and grabbed her arm. "Please, I'm worried about him also."

The waitress turned back and stared hard at Svetlana. She knew it could be a risk, but she was desperate. She eased out her pad of blank bills and wrote his address on the back of one. As she laid the paper down on the table, she gave Svetlana a pleading, desperate look. "If you find him…tell him I'm worried sick…please."

Lana covered the waitress' hand with her own and gave it a squeeze of assurance. "I promise."

CHAPTER 27

SVETLANA KNOCKED ON THE DOOR OF EVGENY ZAKOROV'S apartment. There was no answer. She knocked again, but harder. When again no sound emanated from the apartment, Devon pulled out his small roll of tools and knelt down to pick the lock. It was a bit rusty, but the lock yielded within seconds.

As Lana opened the door, she let out a gasp. Zakorov's apartment was in total shambles. Every piece of furniture had been overturned and shredded to examine its insides. Every pillow had been cut apart, spilling its contents. Books, artwork, drawers—everything had been emptied and thrown on the floor. Devon led the way with his pistol sweeping in all directions. Twice he stumbled over clutter beneath his feet. Aaron kept his weapon drawn and in firing position while Lana checked out the kitchen behind them.

As Devon came out of the master bedroom, he lowered his gun and yelled out the obligatory, "Clear!"

Aaron responded from the second bedroom, "Clear here!"

Devon turned a chair upright and sat down, indicating for the other two to do the same. He scratched his head, let out a sigh, and asked, "What now? There's no Zakorov, no sign of him being harmed—nothing except this bedlam."

Lana shook her head in disgust and then in a quiet voice said, "It's time I tell you about myself and Zakorov. We did have a relationship— but it was not sexual. I say we, but it was really more that *he* had a relationship with me. Evgeny never had any children—the military was his life." She took a deep breath to calm her emotions and continued, "I guess he took me under his wing as a daughter. I think he recognized traits in me that reminded him of himself. I mean, he told me things that he never should have told anyone. You see, he trusted me, and I trusted that he was always honest with me. When I first met him, he blew me off as just another pain-in-the-ass nuisance from the press corps. Well,

I persisted and after a while, he came to like me, or maybe he felt sorry for me. Who knows? I think he liked my brashness—like when I dug into the story on the poisoning of Victor Yushchenko.

"Evgeny knew the FSB had orchestrated that whole thing and it disgusted him—I mean right to his core. I think that's when he came to the conclusion that his whole life had been nothing but an empty shell filled with lies—from Communists to corporate gangsters. He was the one who fed me various leads on corruption, and believe me, crime was everywhere. The truth is, he ended up giving me so much and so often that I had trouble keeping up with him.

"Little by little, over time, his thinking toward the United States shifted. The more I told him of what life was really like when I went to school there, the more his old indoctrinations broke down. Then, when your country invaded Iraq and Afghanistan and was willing to sacrifice even a portion of its youth to fight the enigma of global terrorism—well, let's just say he became an admirer. You see, he lost his wife of forty years in the terrorist bombing of the Moscow subway. Do you remember reading about that tragedy? He was grief stricken and obsessed with finding those responsible. He drained me of everything I remembered and everything I discovered, all the while getting his hands on every piece of foreign news available. And he had access to communications that very few had. Everywhere he looked, he ran into dead ends. He became very bitter.

"Soon, his hatred of the FSB grew into a disgust of all Russian bureaucracies—never Mother Russia; just its bureaucrats. The dirty little secret of every revolution that ever overthrew a monarchy is that the proletariat revolutionaries simply replace the bourgeoisie as bureaucrats. They then live the high life at the people's expense. And in most cases, they live higher on the hog than the people they overthrew.

"That was when Evgeny came across information on the Gulf of Mexico oil disaster. As he began digging into who was responsible, he found that North Korean involvement was known at the highest levels in the Kremlin. He could not pin ownership on the Russian government in ordering the destruction of the rig or even providing funding, but the Kremlin knew who pulled that terrorist act off. Some people he talked to hinted that the Russian Mafia had its dirty fingers in the affair; some said the funding came from an international cabal of financiers; some even went so far as to say that the American government also knew about North Korean involvement, either before it happened or within hours of its occurrence. As in the Kremlin, it was known at the highest levels in Washington."

Lana paused for a drink of water and then continued. "Evgeny didn't want to take what he had uncovered any higher in the Kremlin maze because the information was toxic and would raise suspicions, but he was too late. Strange things began occurring around and to him. That was the moment he accelerated feeding me leads, and then one day, he dumped the whole mess into my lap. When I queried him about the Americans, all he said was, 'Even as high as their White House.'"

Lana paused and drew a deep breath. She cradled her trembling hands in her lap while her eyes looked upward to the ceiling. "That... that was just before my apartment was blown up. I haven't talked to him since."

Aaron grimaced and turned his palms on edge. "Look, Lana, the important thing is to get you out of this country while you're still alive. I mean, that *is* why we came here."

Lana fell silent as she took a moment to think. "You've got to under-stand, I've just lost my home, and more important to me, my best friend. I'm trying very hard to hold myself together. Please...my life will never be the same." After a few moments she lowered her brows, steeled herself, and said with a voice cracking with emotion, "I'm not so sure our work is done here, Aaron. First of all, I feel an obligation to find Evgeny—"

"*If* he's still alive," interrupted Devon.

She shot Devon an angry look. "*Secondly*," she said in a voice drip-ping with sarcasm, "Evgeny told me that if he should ever be killed, I was to go to his dacha where he had hidden photos of a Sang-O minisub actually being loaded into a freighter in North Korea and later landing in Cuba."

"Where's his dacha?" asked Aaron.

"I'm not sure, only that it is somewhere in the near countryside—he never told me. Maybe he wanted it that way for security reasons. Maybe he was trying to protect me. I don't really know, but I think he had enough trust in my abilities to know that I would be able to find it."

Devon looked at Aaron and said, "I agree with her. Alright, Lana, start showing us that ability, but we *are* going to put you on a short time leash."

"Not so fast, Devon," Lana said. "*Thirdly*...we haven't killed the North Korean—and I mean to do it. You do remember your promise to me?" Her glare shifted to Aaron.

"Of course. He only meant that getting you out of Russia was our top priority, not that we couldn't accomplish both."

Devon shot Aaron a quick glance that read, Good move, partner.

"Where to, Lana?"

"Back to the restaurant. We need to talk to that waitress again. Women's intuition says she's slept with him many times. And that would include his dacha in the countryside."

***

This time Svetlana felt that Aaron and Devon could be of help as she confronted the waitress, so she asked them to go inside with her. As they entered the restaurant, Devon scanned every inch, looking for the North Korean or his henchmen. While Aaron held the chair for Lana, Devon decided to check the men's room and kitchen. When he was satisfied that the inside was secure, he stepped out the front door and observed the street. All was clear. He seated himself at the table, but his eyes never stopped their vigilance. Lana saw the look in the waitress' eyes as she turned and saw them from the table she was hosting.

When they described the condition of his apartment, her face went ashen and she broke into tears. Lana reached over and squeezed her thin wrist.

"I know how this must hurt you, but you have to trust that I want to see Evgeny alive as much as you. We don't know if he is alive or dead, but we do know that we must go to his dacha if there is any hope of helping or finding him."

"I...I don't know of any dacha." Her eyes betrayed the lie.

"We both know you do. You and Evgeny are in love—you can't hide it. Please. Please let us help. The North Korean that was here—Evgeny has information that the North Korean won't allow to see the light of day. Evgeny told me that he had hidden parts of that information in his dacha. He trusted me enough to tell me that if he was ever hurt, I was to go there and find it."

Lana swept her hand toward Aaron and Devon. "These men are

from the American government. I can't promise you that they can save Evgeny, but I can promise that they can't help him if you won't help us."

The waitress hesitated, looked around to see if anyone could hear them, then pulled up a chair and sat down. With the palm of her hand shrouding her mouth, she whispered, "In the last two weeks, Evgeny had three attempts made on his life. Once when he left work to come here, I heard a car roar its engine; I looked up and saw a black Mercedes cross onto the sidewalk. It barely missed Evgeny before speeding away."

Her voice started to quiver as her eyes again misted over. "Later, when he walked up the outside steps to his apartment, he fumbled and dropped his key. As he bent over to pick it up, he felt the brick at the side of the door crack and spray onto the side of his head. A bullet had come within millimeters of killing him. He had to crawl on his belly to get in through the apartment door. Someone had taken a shot at him. He never found out from who or where it came, but that poor man lived in fear from that moment on."

She took a deep breath and covered her whole face with her hands. With a muffled voice she continued. "We were dining out one evening when this Mafia hulk walked in the door and started shooting. He first killed the maître d' and then he killed a waiter. Evgeny shoved me to the floor and dove on top of me. The killer must have mistaken the couple at the next table for us, because he walked up and shot both of them in the head."

With that, the waitress began sobbing. Lana rose and put her arms around her for comfort. Aaron followed her cue, while Devon never took his eyes off the entry door. When she was calm, Evgeny's lover told them the rest of what she knew—even disclosing the hiding place inside the dacha.

As the three got up to leave, another small detail came to her mind and she said, "I don't know what it means, but Evgeny told me twice about some financial group...families, I think is what he called them. Yes. Yes—financial families. He said they had met at the...uh, what was it—a place called Chateau d'Arbonne...It was somewhere in the French countryside. I don't know what it means, but that is all I know. Please! Tell me what you find at his dacha, even if it will break my heart."

"I promise," Lana said and squeezed her wrist one more time.

When they left the restaurant, rain was pouring down and they did their best to cover their heads as they ran to get into their car. In their haste, they missed the ominous eyes that rose up from a car across the street. A block later, two Mercedes sedans pulled out into the heavy traffic and filed in behind them.

CHAPTER 28

THE TEMPERATURE WAS DROPPING FAST, MAKING THE SKIES crisp and clear, as another front slid its way down from Canada. Waled al-Ashbot was feeling good about his overall circumstances. Since landing at Dulles International Airport in Washington, DC, he had been exposed to some of the most beautiful landscape in the world. He mused about where he would live when America was put under the sword of Allah. The big cities of the East were crowded and dirty looking and the Midwest appeared tired and worn out, but in Montana, he had fallen in love. Seeing the majesty of its mountains rising against commanding blue skies confirmed in his mind that the rest of his life would be spent there. He dreamed of how he would look in a cowboy hat and blue jeans. Without thinking, he snickered, clapped his hands together, and then pumped his fist as if the victory over these infidels had already been won.

Jameel's body jumped in the driver's seat, in a sort of spasm. His eyes had been drifting, half closed, for the previous hour. With an irritated look, he hollered at Waled, "What the hell's the matter with you, man? My driving is perfect. I mean, I may be getting tired, but you don't have to pull that clapping shit."

Waled overreacted to the criticism and flew off the handle. It wasn't just this one outburst; he had had about as much as he could handle with this inferior convert with all his jive talk and arrogance. When he finished berating Jameel, he felt better again.

"Look, the navigation system is telling us our destination is in five hundred feet—slow down you idiot!"

Jameel had an angry look as he screeched the tires of the van into the parking lot of the motel. "Do you want me to register again?" he snapped. "And if so, how many days do I book?"

"Book it for one week, but make sure they understand that we don't want any room service. Tomorrow we leave for Fairbanks."

"Hell, then why do we need it for seven days? And aren't we going to Anchorage? I mean—"

"Shut up, you stinking fool, and do what you're told. I don't question my orders; I just obey, as Allah would desire. I have vowed to die for Allah—have you?"

Jameel did what he was told and walked up to the registration desk. When he told the clerk that he wanted a double room for seven days, the clerk's response surprised Jameel.

"Ah, Mr., um...Burris, we have been expecting you," the clerk said, as he looked at his computer screen. "You will be paying cash, is that correct?"

Jameel frowned, pulled eight one-hundred-dollar bills out of his wallet, and signed for the room. Walking back to the van, he couldn't reconcile how the clerk said they were expecting him. How did he know? Was he being set up? Was he going to be sacrificed? Why did Waled just say he vowed to die for Allah? The questions bothered him. He decided not to tell Waled about this, but suspicions had jumped into his mind and could not be put back in the box.

CHAPTER 29

THE CLOUDS PLAYED THEIR PART AS THEY APPEARED TO BE the long, flowing skirt of a ballet dancer, swirling and veiling the moon in total darkness and then magically allowing it to reappear. The surface waters reflected the moon's image, adding to the artist's palette the slow, drifting waves, painting a picture of rolling fields of golden wheat. Shattering this serene image, the eye of the sub's periscope presented an ominous contrast, scanning the Alaska coastline.

Inside the sub, Captain Dong had been haranguing his men over the necessity of reaching shore quickly and silently. Over and over he hammered the difficulty in paddling fast, yet keeping stealth as their primary goal. When he paused for a breath, an alert came over the sub's intercom.

"Prepare for embarkation...ETD five minutes."

As the slowly rising sub quietly broke the water's surface, a spray of water and air hissed upward with the release of its top hatch. Two men clamored out, carefully walked the deck, and reached the mission's specially fitted storage tube. Within minutes, they had the rafts out, inflated, and tethered. Two more soldiers came out and helped them load the munitions and equipment into the bobbing rafts. They gave the signal that all was readied, and the remaining commandos poured out of the hatch, followed by Dae Dong. Five minutes later, without a sound, the sub disappeared below the waters of Norton Sound.

Dae Dong took charge, secured his bearings and steered his lead craft toward the rendezvous point. Within moments, he had his men paddling hard and in perfect rhythm. The only detectable sounds were the waves as they splashed against the rubber crafts.

Dae Dong was proud of his men and though he was a strict leader, he would do anything for them...even die. But he knew well that if it came to that, *all* of them would have to either be killed or commit mass suicide. We'll be successful, he thought. He was determined not to end up like the sub that was stranded off South Korea in 1998. We will fight with honor, and if we are to die, we will all die fighting, he thought with a certain bravado.

On board, the sub's captain looked at his exec and said, "We have accomplished the first half of our mission…the rest is up to them."

"I can't say that I will miss that son of a bitch, Dae Dong," the exec said.

The captain gave him a stern, disapproving look. "Mr. Ryu, you will do well to wish him success."

"It's just that—"

"Do not interrupt me," the captain said in a voice and look that meant business. "If he's not successful, there will be more American ships looking for us than we can handle. Even if he's successful and returns on time, the Americans will throw a massive blanket over their coastline, making it near impossible to extract his men or for this sub to escape. I don't want to have to make the decision to abandon them, thus sacrificing all of his men, or to stay and sacrifice all of us. I know he has been particularly hard on you, but remember that this mission is our honor bound duty to complete, and the enemy is the United States, not Captain Dong. Plot our course to the next rendezvous, Mr. Ryu."

***

When the last craft pulled up on shore, a few of the commandos wobbled around and slapped each other's backs for a job well done. Most were bent over at the waist with their hands gripping their knees for support. The sounds of uncontrollable wheezing told the story of their journey. What it didn't tell was the anger felt by those whose rafts had to carry the three drugged Yemenis. Each had two fewer men to paddle.

Dae Dong, who did more navigating than paddling, stood erect, put his hands on his hips, and said with all the arrogance he could muster, "Deflate and conceal the rubber rafts. It is time to move inland and whip the American dogs."

CHAPTER 30

AS SVETLANA PULLED THE CAR UP THE GRAVEL DRIVE OF Evgeny Zakorov's dacha, Devon and Aaron pulled out their pistols, checked the clips, and chambered a round. They had already agreed that Lana would wait in the car. Aaron's task was to circle the house and check the windows while Devon was to wait for his signal to enter the front door. Completing his round, Aaron met Devon, raised his weapon, and gave the signal to go in. Devon gently pushed down the latch and to his surprise, the door was unlocked, allowing him to ease his way in.

Like Zakorov's apartment, the dacha was in total disarray. This time, however, Zakorov lay on the floor with his head in a pool of dried blood. Devon and Aaron crept through with their pistols at the ready. Each room they searched yielded the same response, "Clear." As they reentered the living room, they lowered their weapons and Devon nodded for Aaron to go out and signal Svetlana to come in.

Aaron had prepped her, but as she entered and saw Evgeny, Lana went ashen and cried out a long, "Noooooo!" Her voice was so tormented that Aaron and Devon froze in silence.

Aaron tried to put his arms around her, but she broke loose and fell on her knees next to her old friend and mentor. When at last her sobbing stopped, she pulled herself together, stood up, and ran her fingers through her hair. She looked at Aaron and then fixed on Devon.

"He will die a slower, even more painful death than I first imagined. I swear I will shoot him in each knee and then I will shoot off his balls. Do you both understand me?"

There was no comment from either. They both knew better. When her pain subsided, Lana walked over to the stack-stone fireplace; she counted twelve stones up from the floor and two in from the right-hand side. She wiggled the stone, pulled it out of its place, and slid her small hand into the void. Within seconds, Lana pulled out a roll of photos bound by a rubber band.

"Got it."

Devon and Aaron moved in close and examined the photos with her.

"Shhh," Devon said, pulling his pistol out of its holster.

They all heard the sudden, crunching sound of gravel. Devon whispered for Aaron to get behind the couch with Lana and protect her. He ran toward the rear kitchen window, tore it open, and disappeared. As he crab-walked his way around to the front corner, he saw one assailant pressed against the front wall, while the other kicked in the door and entered.

Aaron was ready. From a prone position, he reached around the side of the couch and squeezed off two rounds. The first penetrated the assassin's throat below the jaw—he stood frozen, then keeled over. At the same time, Devon dropped the other killer before he was able to turn.

The engine of the Mercedes fired up and the car was thrown into reverse. Devon drew a bead on its driver and fired two shots. One embedded into the North Korean driver's arm, but he held on and slammed the vehicle into drive. Within seconds, Kyong Ran was racing down the road with Devon firing on hope alone.

When Devon reentered the dacha, Aaron was bent over, checking the pulse of the fallen assassin. He looked up and announced the results, "He's dead."

Lana crept out from behind the couch and asked Devon, "Did you get him?"

"I'm sorry, Lana. I think I only hit the driver, and I'm going to bet that our friend wasn't doing the driving."

Lana ran the palm of her hand across her forehead and then over her hair. Yakov's image flashed before her; disappointment was written all over her face. Aaron moved over to try and comfort her, but she was too distraught and didn't want to be consoled. She was torn between grief and anger. She pushed Aaron away.

Seeing her pain, Devon said, "We need to leave."

Lana turned her eyes to Evgeny and wondered, Is his death because of me? And Yakov? Did he die because of me too? Her legs weakened as she thought of her next job—Evgeny's lover, the waitress. Lana knew that she must be told, and it had to come from her.

CHAPTER 31

AS THE TRIO ENTERED THE RESTAURANT, SOME EMPLOYEES were mopping the floor and others were huddled in small groups. There was a mixture of crying and murmuring. Svetlana entered one group and questioned what was going on.

"She was shot—right here in broad daylight. She was bringing food from the kitchen when a gunman walked in and shot her in the face. Then he walked out, as if nothing had happened."

***

After they entered their hotel room, Aaron fell back on one of the beds and exhaled loudly. "I think we have enough proof on the sabotage of the oil platform to pin it on the North Koreans. We haven't been able to get the Korean bastard who masterminded it all, though…every time we're close, he eludes us. Nevertheless, I may have an idea."

"Is it based on scientific data?" Devon asked with a hint of teasing.

"No, but I think it really makes sense. Every time we make a move to get more information here in Moscow, he beats us to the punch or arrives a short time after. Moscow is his turf—he has all the people and resources he needs here."

"And that means what?" asked Lana.

"If we go to this Chateau d'Arbonne, I believe he will follow us. The difference is that we will be there first, and then it won't be his turf, like it is here in this Wild, Wild West they call Moscow. Hired Mafioso-types are coming out of the woodwork here. In the French countryside, it could take him a little longer to marshal some troops—advantage us. *We* could be waiting for *him*. Besides, we need to know for sure if this chateau is part of this or not."

Devon looked at Lana and saw her nod her head in agreement, but he wasn't convinced.

"Look, we've already got enough evidence on the North Koreans. All the U.S. has to do now is send in a team of deep sea explorers, comb through the debris under the collapsed platform, and find remnants of the sub. North Korea gets the blame and the U.S. either takes action or turns it over to the United Nations—case closed."

"The United Nations?" Lana hollered out with a look of exasperation. "Are you kidding? North Korea will be given a slap on the wrist and nothing more."

"What about UN sanctions?" Aaron asked.

Lana was quick to respond. "They won't impose sanctions because the North Koreans are already starving. All sanctions would do is starve more people for the six o'clock news. As for U.S. action, the Americans will not go to war over this. They will suppress the story, rather than be forced into another war beyond Afghanistan. That's the reality, and you know it."

An abnormal quiet held for a short period of time. Aaron wore a pensive look and then raised one finger for attention. "Alright...we're talking of going to a chateau in France to look for what? Rumor has it, there is a 'family' of international financiers that are involved in this. To find anything, we'd have to break in. We have no authority from Hatcher to do that. Are we going to risk getting caught for some wild goose chase?"

"There is no way North Korea has the money to pull something like this off," Lana responded. "There *has* to be someone else involved— someone or some group that stands to benefit from this. My instincts always tell me to follow the filthy money trail."

Aaron stood and began pacing the floor. He grabbed a large rubber band and twirled his hands in it. "We know that North Korea is involved; that seems to be an undeniable fact. Now, what's in it for *them*? The platform is owned by Hyundai Heavy Industries out of South Korea. Not only is this a crippling loss on their books, but several new platforms have already been cancelled because of this disaster. You can build all the platforms you want, but if no oil company is willing to lease them, then you go broke. A collapse of Hyundai Heavy Industries would ruin the South Korean economy. That gives the North all the reason they need. I agree with Lana that they don't have the money to pull something like this off. So, who else would—"

Lana interrupted. "A group of international financiers!"

"Oil!" Devon blurted out. "You're right, Lana, follow the money... Wait! Yakov! Remember what he said...'Follow the Korean—the pipeline is the target...then follow the money.' Those were his exact words. Cripple the oil supply in the Gulf of Mexico and then cause an ecological disaster in Alaska by blowing up the pipeline. Bingo! The price of oil explodes and someone makes trillions and trillions of dollars." He looked over at Lana for her thoughts.

The mere mention of Yakov's name brought tears to her eyes, but she knew Devon was spot on. "I'm with you on this, Devon."

"Hold on for just a minute," said Aaron, "I think it may be more. Oil has already crested to a hundred dollars per barrel and the world's commodities have followed suit. All the romantic countries of the Mediterranean are nearing collapse as we speak. The European Union might be able to bail out Greece, but they can't bail out Spain and Italy when they begin to fall like dominoes. And fall they will, taking the EU down with them."

Aaron shook his head with a look of disgust. "We have seen the Arab Spring occur and some believe this is the precursor of a global pan-Arabic caliphate. If oil approaches the hundred-and-fifty dollar range, the Saudi Royal Family will fall. In particular, with chaos everywhere, the world will be in a debt pit of quicksand, forcing the dollar to fall as the sovereign currency base for oil. As the nations of the world become desperate and reach for help from any source, anywhere, there will be demands for a *world* currency. Who will be able to provide this new currency? Well, in ride the international banking families with a new world currency to supply the world's banks. Who controls these banks? The same close-knit family of world financiers—that's who! Who sets the international value? They do! I'm not sure that the consequences could even be measured in trillions. We're talking unbelievable raw power—the power to control *everything and everyone!*"

Another moment of silence hung over the room as Aaron's theory set in. Devon grabbed a bottle of water, sat down, and took a deep breath. Nodding his head in agreement, he said, "Damn you, Cohen, I guess that's why I've always respected you...I'm trumped again by a CalSci geek."

Aaron looked over to Devon and gave him an impish grin. "It's just a theory, Devon, just a theory."

"It may be just a theory, Aaron, but I think it's a damn good one."

"Well, I'm not sure what we're going to find at this chateau," Lana said, "but as a journalist, I've struck pay dirt on a whole lot less."

"Alright, Aaron, book us a flight to Paris. Lana, let's review that wad of pictures one more time."

"I guess my lust for vengeance will have to wait," she said, "... for now."

CHAPTER 32

CHATEAU D'ARBONNE
FRENCH COUNTRYSIDE OF AQUITAINE

TRACING ITS ROOTS TO THE EARLY EIGHTEENTH CENTURY, the Chateau d'Arbonne was a historic structure whose architecture was typical of smaller baronial castles of the period, sporting high conical roofs covered in blue slate tiles, with cream-colored stucco and stone walls. Although the chateau had been modified and updated over the years, one characteristic remained the same: Its massive stone, moat-like walls that surrounded and protected it from unwanted intrusion.

The clouds were low with a mild temperature, not giving the trio as much cover as they would have liked for a midafternoon reconnoiter. The forest that surrounded the chateau was of a density that consumed daylight, leaving the ground below it free of underbrush and in a darkness that mimicked early evening. It gave them an easy terrain on which to move about, allowing only tree trunks and natural shade within which to hide. To save precious time, Devon told Aaron and Lana to scout the north side of the chateau walls while he took care of the south, meeting at the west rear.

"Lana, listen up—this is for you. There are high-tech security cameras everywhere, and we have to assume that they are being monitored as we speak. We must stay out of camera range. So keep low, say nothing, and stay back far enough so you don't get picked up. Above all, follow Aaron's lead."

Devon was apprehensive, but not with Aaron. Although he sensed there was more to Lana than he knew, he hadn't seen her perform this type of maneuver before. As he pressed forward, a smile broke out on his face. You are one tough woman, though, he thought. You remind me of my Julie.

Aaron and Lana did well, but by the time they reached the center of the west wall, they hadn't found any weakness in which to breach the perimeter. Having gone about three quarters of the way along the south wall, however, Devon found what he was looking for. The forest surrounding the chateau was cleared on a regular basis and security cameras were placed every twenty feet, but one branch from a century-old Charter Oak had grown back faster than the others. It dropped low and then swung upward to lay against the side of a camera. The rotation of that camera was impeded, but not in a way that would be apparent to anyone watching the monitors. As near as Devon could see, that limb would give them a protected sight path of almost five feet in which to scale the wall. He determined that would be just enough to gain entry.

Devon met the other two at the rendezvous point. Aaron had a look of disappointment as he told Devon that they had found no access point that could be breached without being seen. Devon smiled and said, "That's okay, CalSci, the Stanford bro found the spot…that makes us even again."

Lana grimaced as she raised her hands in a gesture of disbelief. "Am I in some kind of a time warp—caught between two college frat boys trying to outdo each other?"

Devon smiled while raising his eyebrows and replied, "Thank you, I didn't think you noticed."

Aaron turned away from Svetlana to hide his grin.

"Alright, back to business," Devon said. "We've got the access point. Now, all we need is darkness. Let's go get our night gear and return here at twenty-two hundred hours."

***

The temperature had dropped several degrees, but no one minded, as the French countryside was pitch-black from the moonless night. The chateau also had cameras that were equipped with night vision technology, allowing the security lights on the walls to be positioned at least two hundred feet apart for maximum effect.

Once in position, the three were prepared and outfitted with night vision goggles, black clothing and gloves, rucksacks, and black ski masks. Aaron carried a double-angle night periscope and confirmed that only two guards patrolled the outside of the chateau, within the walls. Their rounds were like clockwork, showing no deviation in pattern.

Devon gave the signal, and they began crawling military style toward the five-foot opening. Aaron hit the wall first and gave a bonded hand lift first to Devon and then to Lana. Lana landed with the help of Devon, who rolled her over, grabbed the nylon rope from her waist, and threw it over for Aaron. When Aaron landed on the inside, Devon took the lead, making their way to a spot on the chateau between two windows.

Inspection of the windows verified no staff was present other than the security guards.

Devon motioned for them to huddle low. "Lana, you wait here and keep an eye on these windows to make sure no activity starts up inside the chateau. If it does, come and get us, pronto. Aaron, you reconnoiter that long building over there. It looks like a garage. I'm going to go around the chateau and see if there might be another way in. We'll meet back here in ten minutes. Go!"

When the ten minutes were up, Aaron was the last to arrive. Devon reported that they wouldn't be able to gain access to the chateau itself.

"I think I uncovered something worthwhile," whispered Aaron. "That building was an old stable that's been converted to a twelve-vehicle garage. A Bentley and a couple of Mercedes are in there now, and one of the doors is unlocked. Behind it is an incinerator next to garbage containers."

"Are you suggesting we pick through the garbage?" asked Devon.

"Well, I'm just saying—"

"I might want to remind the both of you," interrupted Lana, "that some of my best material came from dumpster diving and sorting through the worst of trash."

"What about the guards?" asked Devon.

"They make their rounds every fifteen minutes—no deviation, so we should have plenty of time," said Aaron.

When Aaron gauged that the time was right with the guards' rounds, they ran bent over to the rear of the garage, hit the ground, and checked that no one had seen them. Aaron looked at his watch, raised his hand, and signaled to Devon that they had five minutes before their next chance to avoid the guards and exit back to the side of the chateau. Devon pointed to the incinerator and together they crawled to it, standing only when Lana flashed the okay sign. Devon opened the cover to find an old pile of ash. He scooped a pile onto his hand shovel and knowing its potential forensic value, took great care as he slid it off into the rucksack. They scoured the rest of the immediate area, but found nothing.

As they were about to leave, Devon spied some partially burned paper particles and ash caught in the top of the meshed spark suppressor. He started to twist the top off when a loud squeak emanated from the metal. Aaron and Devon froze. They looked at Lana, but she signaled all was clear. Devon decided to give it one quick twist to reduce the noise, but to no avail. The top came off, but the shrill screech was even louder. While Devon held the ash suppressor, Aaron pulled a small plastic container out of his rucksack pocket. He held his breath as he extracted the two shards of paper and eased them into the container.

After they crawled back to Lana, she whispered that she heard boots running fast on the gravel drive. Devon signaled for the two to take off for the wall in the opposite direction. He listened, then began running himself. Aaron and Lana made it to the wall first and Aaron booted her up and over. Devon arrived on the fly; he jumped and landed his foot into Aaron's clasped hands. He too went up and over. Aaron grabbed the rope that Devon threw over and made it to the top when the stone around him began exploding, sending shards flying everywhere. Two guards were firing their automatic weapons, spraying the whole area around Aaron. One bullet creased his cheek, one hit his arm, and as he went over the top, another hit his raised thigh. He came down on Devon and Lana with a thud.

Devon was quick to respond. He stripped the rucksack off Aaron and threw it to Lana. He picked up Aaron, threw him over his shoulder, and began running through the woods toward their car. "Go! Go! Go!" he hollered to Lana. She responded with surprising speed and led the way. As a siren wailed its screeching echo, hidden floodlights clicked on and blanketed the entire compound and its surroundings.

Lana heard trucks starting up and roaring their tires on the gravel. She turned her head and saw headlights streaming out of the compound. She kicked up her pace and reached the car well ahead of Devon and Aaron. Acting on pure instinct, she floored the car, spun the wheel, and turned back into the woods. She aimed at the area where she knew Devon would be coming. As the car skidded off a large conifer and branches whipped and lashed at the vehicle, Devon bolted into view. Lana slammed on the brakes, exited the car, and opened the rear door just in time for Devon to throw Aaron in. Jumping in over Aaron, he screamed, "Go! Go!"

The car fishtailed on the dense pine needle floor of the forest, its tires spewing dirt and debris everywhere. In a flash, the rear window exploded. Small pellets of glass came down like rain over Devon and Aaron. Lana kept her cool, eased off on the gas, and coaxed it to gain traction. Two bullets whizzed over Devon's head and shattered the passenger side of the windshield. A guard jumped onto the trunk of the car and grabbed the bottom frame where the rear window used to be. Devon had already pulled his Glock out of its holster, but decided not to put a bullet in the guard's head. Instead, he smashed the pistol onto the man's fingers, causing them to shred on the shards of glass jutting up from the frame. The man screamed in pain, let go and slid off the trunk, crashing to the ground. The truck behind them swerved to avoid him and caromed off a pine tree, rolling over on its side. The truck behind it plowed into its backside.

As their car bounded onto the pavement, Devon's head slammed upward into the roof. Tires screeched on the blacktop as the car sped forward. Devon looked behind him and saw they were safe. No one was following. He slapped Lana on her shoulder and through a voice gasping for air, said, "You're just as tough and smart as I thought you'd be. Nice job, girl. Nice job. You just passed my test."

It was a long drive back to Paris and Lana prayed that the bullet-riddled car wouldn't be seen by the police. Wanting to be the one to help Aaron with his wounds, she finally pulled the car over and changed drivers with Devon. The cut on his cheek was superficial—it had barely cut his skin. The wound in his arm was also good news, as the bullet had gone clean through the fatty underside. She saw the exit wound and knew it was only a matter of stopping the bleeding and keeping it sterile. Lana opened up Aaron's pant leg. As she felt around the backside, her fingers told her that an exit wound was not apparent. Unlike the other wounds, however, this one was gushing blood.

"The bullet in his thigh doesn't have an exit hole and I'm worried about the bleeding—it's heavy," Lana said.

"Pull off his belt and wrap it above the wound, closer to his crotch—buckle it in the smallest hole."

Devon pulled his Glock out of his holster and released the clip. He passed it back to Lana and said, "Use this clip to twist the tourniquet, but remember to loosen it every few minutes and then crank it back up tight."

Devon racked his mind to remember where the CIA had a safe doctor who could help Aaron. He remained silent for what seemed a long stretch of time and then it came to him. I just hope the guy is still there, he thought. I really don't want to have to call Hatcher on this one; we're in deep enough trouble as it is.

***

Lana was at her wit's end waiting for Devon to come out of the doctor's home. When at last the door opened, Devon came out and motioned for Lana to ready Aaron to be helped in.

The doctor had Devon lay Aaron on the gurney in his office, which was downstairs in his house. After the physician finished examining Aaron, he gave Devon and Lana the good news. "The bullet entered his thigh, but it must have been a ricochet, because it's lying just under the skin."

"How long to fix him up, doc?"

"Give me a couple of hours to remove the bullet, clean the wound, and sew everything up; then you can have him back."

"That's good! Oh, by the way, doc, do you have any Sterno? You know, the stuff you use for warming under a chafing dish?"

"What respectable Frenchman wouldn't? I keep extra here in my office, in case there's a power outage and I need to sterilize an instrument. It's behind me, first drawer on the left. Make sure you include something for it in your remittance."

"Also, I need a small pad of paper to write on—and a pen."

The doctor, trying to work on Aaron, became irritated. "Center drawer of the desk in the foyer," he growled.

"Two hours—I'll be back by then…and thanks, doc."

"Don't thank me. Just pay me the usual CIA rate when you return."

CHAPTER 33

JULIE STOOD WITH A MUG OF STEAMING COFFEE CUPPED in her cold hands as she stared out the window, looking at nothing in particular. An image of Devon flashed in front of her. It's not your fault that you left me alone, Devon; you didn't know that I might be in harm's way, she thought. You got yourself into a mess and now there is no way out. Then again, look at the mess I got you into when all you did was save my life when my plane crashed. It seems like we're fated to travel from one mess to the next. Once CIA, always—

"Excuse me, Mrs. McKenzie," interrupted Special Agent Weaver, "Langley called and told us to take security to the next level. That's where—"

"I know what the next level is, Agent Weaver…ex-CIA, remember?"

Weaver nodded and made his clumsy retreat. Julie went upstairs to the master bedroom. She had been planning her next move for some time. She pulled her Taurus Judge revolver out of the dresser and checked to see that it was fully loaded with three .410 shotshells and two .45 rounds. Verifying that it was, she opened the window nearest her bed, wrapped it in a hand towel, and laid the gun to rest on the roof shingles just left of the dormered window. A revolver that shoots a small shotgun shell is what I want in an emergency, she thought. And five shots…I'm good to go with that. I only hope to God that it doesn't come to that. She went back to the drawer and pulled out Devon's Smith and Wesson 44 magnum revolver. Also checking that it was loaded, she tucked it under her pillow.

Julie's mind was beginning to hit full defense mode. Remembering all her training, she thought about how remarkable it was still second nature. She walked over to their closet and pulled out Devon's AR15 assault rifle. Cradling it in her arms, she sat on the bed and envisioned all the rooms of her home in her head. After careful consideration, she remembered Devon's defensive hunting blind that he had set up outside of his cabin two years ago. Do I hide the AR outside or do I use it in the house to set up a total blast zone? Hmmm, she thought. Devon had his assault rifle in the cabin and my father used it to cover Devon on his way out. But in the end, it was his Glock that served him best.

Her final decision was to hide the AR 15 in the first floor great room under the rear of the couch. Now, she thought, do I keep all this firepower hidden from the special agents, and if so, how and for how long?

CHAPTER 34

DEVON GLANCED AT HIS WATCH AND SAW THAT IT WAS 10:30 p.m. Damn, he thought. I'll never find a hardware store open at this time of night. As he mulled his options, he decided what he must do. He drove the outer streets of Paris until he found a small, closed café that had no security. Within minutes, he was behind the café, knife in hand, removing the metal screen from its rear window. He then drove to an unlit, secluded parking lot.

Devon removed the screen from the frame and cut out two circles about twelve inches in diameter. He fashioned two small domes, about the size of a woman's D-cup brassiere. Next, he pulled out his rucksack and removed both the ash pile and the plastic box that contained the two scorched paper fragments. Placing an open can of Sterno on the asphalt, he looked around to make sure no one was watching. He lit the Sterno and put the butt end of his small flashlight in his mouth. He placed one of the papers on top of the first mesh dome and then gently placed the second dome over the ash.

I've only got one shot, he thought, as he turned on the flashlight.

With great care, he lowered the stacked domes over the lit Sterno. Within seconds, two words—Sang and Anad—appeared before the scorched paper disappeared into flames. Devon jotted down the words and repeated the first step on the second fragment. The result produced one word: Norto.

He gently poured the ashes out of his rucksack and with his knife, he began sifting through the mound.

After fifteen tedious minutes of careful probing and inspection, he stood up and arched his back to relieve the stiffness. Once again he searched all directions to make sure no one was watching. He debated kicking the pile to spread it and leave it behind, but Lana's words came back into his head, "Some of my best material came from dumpster diving and sorting through the worst of trash."

He knelt back down and continued to sort through the last inch of ash. Out of nowhere, he saw three unburned corners of pages; only this time, the pieces were clearly readable. With all his skill, Devon separated them with his knife and placed them in his palm. They read: Empresa Terminales and Trans-Oceanic. From a kneeling position, Devon slid onto his bottom, Indian style, never taking his eyes off the small remnants of paper. He believed he'd hit pay dirt on the previous papers, but the evidence had burned to a crisp. What he had in the palm of his hand was real and tangible. This was hard evidence. He felt like a miner striking a vein of gold after years of endless digging.

He placed the evidence into the plastic container that held the first charred remnants. As if it were divine fate, he had found them at the bottom of the pile. The wonks at Langley will have a field day with this, he thought. Minutes later, Devon was back in the rental car, heading to the doctor's office. He looked at his watch. "Right on time," he whispered.

When Devon entered the office, Aaron was leaning on a metal crutch supplied by the doctor. Devon saw the hundred-dollar bills being counted out and placed in the doctor's outstretched hand.

"That will be another hundred for the crutch," he said, "and another fifty for the Sterno and paper that your hotshot friend took."

"That's right, milk the fatted cow until you suck it dry," groused Aaron.

"You are paying for my risk," the doctor responded with a raw look of sarcasm twisted on his face. "Next time, go to the emergency room in the hospital. I'm sure they will fix up the bullet holes and never think to call the gendarmes."

"Well, this hotshot thanks you, doc, as does Uncle Sam and my friends here," Devon chimed in, giving Aaron and Lana a nod of his head to get going.

On the drive to the hotel, Devon queried Aaron and Lana about the results of the doctor's work. Lana was in the back with Aaron's head leaning on her shoulder, her hands caressing his arm in a loving fashion.

Looking in the rearview mirror, Devon snickered, "You two need a room?"

"Uh, actually we do," replied Aaron, "but get your mind out of the gutter, brother; it will only be for sleep. I'm exhausted and in pain."

They closed the door to the first of their connecting rooms and Aaron hobbled to the bed and eased his sore body down on its coverlet. Devon watched Lana help him get comfortable, then opened his rucksack and pulled out the pad of paper and plastic container.

"Sorry, CalSci, but we've got to crunch the evidence I've turned up; know full well that I wouldn't ask you right now if there was any time to wait." He pursed his lips and raised his palms in apology. "We leave early in the morning and…"

Lana was reluctant but agreed with Devon and extended her hand to raise Aaron into a sitting position. Devon began his dog and pony show by explaining to Aaron and Lana the method he used to bring up his first hidden evidence. He asked them to wait on that evidence, as it is an enigma that will test wits and take the most time.

"And now, the piece de resistance," he garbled out in a mock French accent. He slid out the two remnants that had not completely burned and said, "What we have here are two names—Empresa Terminales and Trans-Oceanic—hard evidence that we stole fair and square."

Lana moved in with a huge smile as she perused the pieces. "You're right, Devon, there is no doubt it is hard evidence. Your boss, Hatcher, will be very pleased with you two."

"Excuse me, dear lady, but there were three of us, and if any one of us had failed, we would have nothing. Got it?"

"Thank you, but—"

Aaron was quick to cut her off, saying, "He's right, Lana; we're a team. You need to remember that."

"Now remember, this other evidence is an enigma, and unless we can solve its meaning, it will neither move us forward nor guide our next move." Devon handed the notepad to Aaron for him to read. "These words are the clues that we must solve. Have at it, Sherlock."

Aaron looked the words over and passed them to Lana. "Anad, Sang, and Norto…I'm not sure where to go with that," he whispered, deep in thought.

Lana was equally baffled, but copied the words into her notebook on two different pages and passed the pad back to Devon. She kept one copy and gave the other to Aaron. Silence hung for several minutes when Aaron at last blurted out, "Watson!…Sang. It must stand for Sang-O, the minisubmarine."

"By God! You've got it, Sherlock," said Devon. "But what's the tie-in to Anad or Norto?"

Silence hung again. Then Lana spoke up, "The chatter your CIA picked up was that an oil pipeline was to be a target, right? If we assume that the pipeline is your Alaska Pipeline, then how do you get there? Only three ways get you there—by land, air, or sea. If by land, they have to cross the Canadian border. If by air, they have to parachute in. If by sea, they have to land somewhere on the coastline of Alaska."

"Norto!" Devon blurted out. "It's probably Norton Sound! Alaska I know."

Aaron was too tired from his wounds to think.

"Anad, Anad…Anadyr—that's it! It's the Gulf of Anadyr off the Russian coastline. A Sang-O sub leaves North Korea bound for Alaska, but it can't get there without refueling. So it refuels in the calmer waters of the Gulf of Anadyr. From there it takes saboteurs to Norton Sound where they disembark."

"Bingo!" Devon cried out. "Well done, Lana."

"Thank God," said Aaron, as he lay back on the bed. "Now can I get some sleep?"

"Go to sleep, brother, Lana and I will be in the adjoining room figuring out tomorrow. And don't worry; I'll be back in this room soon enough to sleep with you, sweetheart."

Devon motioned Lana to follow him to the next room. He went to the minibar and pulled out a travel-sized vodka for Lana and a scotch for himself. Lana took hers down Russian style and asked for a second. Devon obliged and sipped his scotch. He looked up at Lana, gathered his thoughts, and parsed his words. He felt like a first-time hiker trying to cross a stream without getting wet.

"You know he loves you, right?"

"Yes."

"Look, it's none of my business, Lana, but I've come to love this guy like a brother and I guess I don't want to see him get hurt. You love him?"

Lana looked away and paused. She didn't want to have this conversation, but knew Devon would not let it go. She took a deep breath before proceeding. "Years ago, I put my career ahead of my heart…I'm afraid I've already hurt him."

"That was then and this is now. Do you love him now?"

"Yes."

"When you meet my Julie, then you'll understand that there *is* such a thing as redemption…and everyone needs and deserves it. I certainly did. She saved my ass…and my heart. If you focus on that, the two of you will find the kind of happiness that Julie and I have."

Lana drank her second vodka in short order. "I'm not sure that some people are destined for the redemption you speak of, Devon."

"Hear me out. I also put my career ahead of my heart. I had it all…a woman that loved me beyond life itself and a career that could have earned us all the money necessary to live the American dream. But I put her on the back burner so I could play super spy for the CIA. I left her alone and miserable—worse, I was the cause of her death…How would you like to live with that?"

"I…I guess I wouldn't know how—"

"Of course you wouldn't," Devon interrupted. "I didn't either. Because of that, I went into seclusion in the bowels of the Alaskan wilderness for four years in a one-room cabin, with a dog as my only companion. Guess where my redemption came from? Julie…she saved my miserable-ass life."

"I didn't know, Devon."

"It's what I'm trying to tell you, Lana. That guy in the other room loves you. He can be your redemption."

Lana looked at her vodka bottle and drained the last of its contents. She then looked off in the distance and said, "Thank you, Devon."

He gave her a few minutes to let everything settle in, then said, "Now, let's get down to business. Our flight is booked for DC. When we get there, you and Aaron must get to Hatcher and show him what we've unearthed. *Now*, and this is important, show him nothing unless he agrees to fast-track you for citizenship. I mean it; there will never be another chance for you to go to the front of the line. Lana, seize this opportunity to change your life. "

"Won't this tick him off? I mean, couldn't this hurt Aaron's position at the CIA?"

"No. Hatcher will bluster that you're trying to scam him, but you hold your ground."

"Does he have the authority to grant this?"

"Believe me, Lana, he is one powerful player and he basically only answers to the president, and that man doesn't get involved in matters this small. Always remember, what may be small to someone else, could be the most important thing in your life. After that, find the time to tell Aaron you love him…he needs to know."

For the first time in what seemed like an eternity, she felt like a teenager again—and she liked how she felt. "I will," she said as a smile broke on her face.

"I won't be there—I'm going home to my wife. I have a feeling that she's going to need some serious protection."

"From what I've seen and what you and Aaron have told me, if anyone is coming after her, they're the ones that will need serious protection."

Devon laughed. "That may be closer to the truth. If Hatcher needs my help, though, I'll already be in Alaska—ready to go to Norton Sound."

"I'm sure your Hatcher is going to be angry that you're not there to be debriefed."

"Trust me, it won't be the first time. We have a history. Now, don't be jealous, but I'm going to go sleep with your boyfriend. Good night, Svetlana."

Lana laughed and said, "I'll wake you two lovers in the morning."

When the door shut, she fell backward on the bed, closed her eyes, and felt at ease for the first time in years.

CHAPTER 35

WALED SLOWED THE VAN TO A STOP SHORT OF THE BORDER crossing into Canada. He wanted, no, needed Jameel to do the talking for both of them. For the first time, he was glad he had a homegrown with him and encouraged him to lay on the jive talk—thick and heavy.

"Remember, there is a recession going on and we're looking for work in Alaska. How do you say it, there ain't shit for work in the Midwest?"

"Man, you're always so uptight. When are you going to learn to trust me? I could bullshit my way out of a hooded hanging in Mississippi."

"What is this Mississippi?"

"Never mind, just trust me. I'll get us into Canada *and* Alaska."

As they pulled up toward the guard on the American side, Jameel looked over at Waled and said, "Now be cool, brother, I can carry this load of shit all by myself, so don't screw it up." He smiled, laid on his best inner-city Philly accent, and said, "If he don' ax you nuttin,' den you don' say nuttin.' You got dat bro?"

Waled nodded and wished he had spent more time listening to Jameel's jive from the time he picked him up. Under his breath, he prayed to Allah that he had picked up just enough by osmosis.

Fortunate for Waled, the northwest weather was cooperating. The rain was pounding down, overrunning the gutters in the road and washing up to the sidewalks. Some would have said that this was at least a twenty-five year downpour. The guards on both the American and Canadian sides stood under broad metal canopies, and in spite of being dressed in all-weather gear with their hats covered in plastic, the wind was swirling, and over and over they had to wipe the blowing rain off their faces. Worse, the guards were moving through puddles that covered the soles of their boots.

Waled recognized that the weather situation was in their favor and whispered, "Thanks be to Allah."

Jameel heard the comment and was all over Waled, "I'm telling you man, no more of that Allah talk out of you—not now."

Waled sat and fumed. The guard tapped on the window and Jameel feigned surprise. "Monin,' suh," he said. "We be headin' to 'laska lookin' fo' work, but ooohweee! I sho' don' want yo' job, man. You guys be workin' hahd in dese misable conditions, and I respet dat."

"That's very kind, sir," the guard responded, showing no emotion at all. He raised his shoulders to help hide from the rain and wiped his wet face. "Now, you say you're going to Alaska?"

"Yes, suh."

"And your purpose is to find work?"

"Yes, suh; times be tough down here in da fotey-eight."

The guard raised his flashlight and shined it square on Waled's face. Waled nodded and smiled. The beam held for a moment and then moved on, searching the rest of the van. What was not detected was the false floor that had been installed, allowing a four-inch void to store their contraband. On a nice sunny day, this modification might have been detected, but not in this swirling rain.

The guard stepped back and motioned them to pass on. "Enjoy your stay in Alaska," the guard said.

As they moved toward the Canadian border, Jameel looked at Waled and said, "See, just come across as a common man that needs work, throw in a bunch of sirs for respect, and nine out of ten times, you'll be okay."

Waled gained a little more respect for the chameleon sitting next to him. As he waited in the Canadian line, scenes of the Montana landscape danced through his mind. Then he remembered his home, Yemen. I wish they had taught me more before they sent me here, he thought. There is so much more to learn other than just killing and demolition.

When Jameel pulled up to the Canadian guard, his infectious smiled covered his face. The Canadian, however, was not impressed, which was written all over his face.

"Licenses, please," the guard said with gritted teeth, trying to see through the blinding rain.

Jameel read the man right and shifted his tactic. "Yes, sir," he said, handing both to the guard.

The guard looked hard at Waled's license and said, "Your length of stay in Canada?"

"Only as long as it takes to get to Alaska," Jameel said. Recognizing the slight, he tried to recover. "Sorry, I meant no disrespect. What I meant was that we have a deadline to start our new jobs—my cousin owns a fishing business in Anchorage."

A gust of wind came up, forcing the guard to catch his hat and crush it onto his head. He frowned and looked at Waled. "What about you—going to the same place?"

Jameel popped in, "Oh yes, sir. We're both—"

"I didn't ask you. You're friend a mute?" He zeroed in on Waled with a concerned frown and asked, "Well?"

Waled straightened up in his seat, saying, "Yes, sir. I need work—you know—the American dream and all."

"That dream's not limited to the United States."

"Yes, I know, sir, but the job offer is in Fairbanks—I mean, Anchorage."

"Is his cousin in both cities?"

Waled's face went beet red. "No. It's been a long drive and I'm not familiar with Alaska, that's all."

"Is that a Mideastern accent?"

"Yes, sir."

"Are you a citizen of the United States?"

"Oh yes, my parents came over from Iraq—just before 9/11."

"Why do you still have such a heavy accent?"

Waled was approaching near panic from the questioning. "I learned your beautiful English in school, but my parents wouldn't allow it to be spoken in our home. I guess they just wanted to keep something from our home country."

The guard told them to wait a minute. He went over to another guard and conferred, never taking his eyes off the pair. Jameel felt sweat running into his eyes; he dropped his head low and wiped it with his hands. Waled asked Jameel what was going on.

"Don't say a word. Act as if nothing is wrong."

When the guard returned, he tried to trip up Waled. "Where in Fairbanks does your friend's cousin live?"

Jameel tried to cover Waled by saying, "He lives—"

"Are you hard of hearing or do I have a problem communicating with you? I didn't ask *you*," the guard interrupted. He looked over at

Waled with a scowl on his face. "Well, where in Fairbanks does your new employer live?"

"I am sorry, sir, but we are going to Anchorage. I don't know his address, but my friend here does."

The guard bit his lower lip and frowned again as he made his decision. "I'm going to have you pull off over here," he said, pointing his finger.

"As you wish," said Jameel. "Is anything the matter?"

A voice from another guard hollered out through the rain, "Let them through, the Yanks can deal with them at the Alaskan border."

The guard suddenly raised his hand and motioned them to drive forward. "Go on through," he said. "Enjoy your time in Canada."

As they drove away, Waled asked Jameel, "Why didn't you use your inner-city jive talk?"

"No two people react the same way. This guard is a western Canadian and I didn't think he would appreciate the jive talk. I use different strokes for different folks."

Waled was even more confused.

CHAPTER 36

DULLES INTERNATIONAL AIRPORT
WASHINGTON, DC

AS THEY STOPPED IN THE CONCOURSE TO SAY GOOD-BYE, Devon hugged Lana and Aaron. "Good luck with Hatcher," Devon said to Aaron.

"Are you sure you won't go with us and back me up?"

"No. I know The Agency's people are good, but I want to be at the house for Julie—you never know. I'm worried."

He turned to Lana and said, "Don't forget what we talked about last night—it's important for you. One chance and one chance only."

She smiled at Devon and squeezed Aaron's hand. "I haven't forgotten a word you said. And I couldn't agree more. Thank you for coming with Aaron, Devon. I know that you didn't have to do this."

He looked at Aaron and placed his hand over his heart. "Anything for a brother, you know that Aaron. Call me when Hatcher sends you to Norton Sound."

With a breaking voice Aaron said, "You are my brother."

***

After Aaron arranged clearance for Lana, he walked her toward Hatcher's office. Every male eye in the outer office was fixed on Svetlana Gorenkov. Most stood after they passed to get a last look.

"Holy Hannah! Did you see who Cohen came in with?" was the usual comment. Some pretended to gnaw at their fists. All were impressed. Aaron felt proud and Lana blushed. Bet you nerds never thought this geek would walk in like this—and straight into the director's office, he thought.

Hatcher's door was open and the pair went in. He pretended their presence was no big deal, but he too was impressed with the beauty of the Russian stranger.

"Sit down, Cohen," he said as he reached for Svetlana's hand. "I'm Hatcher to you, but he can call me sir. And your name is…?"

"Svetlana Gorenkov, but you can call me Gorenkov—he can call me Dear," she said with a devilish smile.

Aaron blushed as he held the chair for Lana to sit. Hatcher had met his match and knew it instantly.

"Where's that McKenzie guy?" he growled.

"On a plane to Fairbanks, I'm afraid."

Hatcher bellowed out, "That son of a—excuse me, young lady." Hatcher regained his composure. "I have a hard time dealing with an agent that flat-out disobeys my orders. And while we're at it, Cohen, I don't give a turkey's wattle what you have to show me; you disobeyed my orders too. In this league, that's strike one—strike two and you're out on your ass."

Aaron cracked a half smile and replied, "Of course, sir."

"And as for that McKenzie guy—"

"Sir, one could make a case that he doesn't work for The Agency. He, uh, just gets a paycheck."

Hatcher looked over to Svetlana and said, "See? I'll bet it isn't this way in the FSB."

"I wouldn't know, Hatcher, I'm an investigative journalist."

"I see. Well then, come on, Cohen, let's get down to business. Show me what you've got."

Remembering the words of Devon, Lana gripped the file she was carrying a little tighter. With trepidation, she said, "Excuse me, Hatcher, but the bulk of this information was unearthed by me, at a terrible cost to those who helped me attain it. So, I'd like to do a little negotiating with you before we start."

Hatcher shot Aaron a look that included both incredulity and irritation. Aaron looked at Hatcher and said, "She's telling the truth, and she deserves whatever she wants."

Hatcher's slow boil was beginning to spill over. "Are you trying to shake me down, young lady?"

"My name is Gorenkov to you, Hatcher. No, I'm not trying to shake you down at all, and I'm insulted that you think I might be."

"How much do you want, Gorenkov?"

"I don't want your money, Hatcher. When you get to know me better, you'll see that I've never been about money and never will."

"Well, then what is it you want?"

"First, when this is over, I want credit in all the news stories that are released. Second, I want a guarantee of American citizenship. That's it—painless to you and anyone else."

Hatcher let out a horse laugh that vibrated through the walls. "Gorenkov, you not only look like a fox, but you're as sly as one too. Are all you Ruskies this way?"

"Actually no, I learned everything I know when I went to school here in the States."

Hatcher looked at Aaron and asked, "So, is this the woman that you were willing to disobey me and lose your career for?"

Aaron reached over, squeezed Lana's hand, and said, "Yes, sir, this is that woman."

Hatcher stood and walked around his desk and extended his hand to Lana. "Gorenkov, you have my word on both terms. Do you need this in writing?"

"Hatcher, I've made a lifetime out of assessing people, and I believe that your word is your bond." With a firm grip, she shook his hand and said, "No, I don't require it in writing."

"Good! Now can I *please* see the intel? Good Lord, what is this world coming to?"

CHAPTER 37

ABOUT FOUR HOURS HAD PASSED SINCE THE BAND OF North Korean saboteurs had hidden their rafts and taken a break to ease their muscles and divide up their gear. Captain Dong had signaled his men to set up a perimeter patrol. The town of Alakanuk was ten miles to the south, and its population was made up of predominantly Native American Indians. He was worried about possible early morning hunters. Carrying their gear and demolition materiel on their backs was arduous enough, but trekking through virgin wilderness required enormous strength. Nevertheless, his men were committed and the distance they would have to traverse before they arrived at the Yukon River was less than five miles.

Dae Dong had confidence in the intelligence that told him where the two Combat Rubber Raiding Craft (CRRC) would be stored, awaiting his arrival. A CRRC was his choice for the rough, shallow waters of the Yukon River. They had practiced this run many times on various rivers in North Korea, but they weren't the same, and never having navigated the Yukon, its rough current left him uneasy.

One Zodiac FC 470 would carry Team One and two hostages with the bulk of the gear for the first leg. The second Zodiac carried Dae Dong and Team Two, along with the third hostage. Both crafts would follow the Yukon to where the Koyukuk River split north to pump station 5. There only Team One would continue to PS5 where the CRRCs were hidden, waiting to bring them back to Norton Sound. Dae Dong would continue up the Yukon with Team Two to where the Tanana River split south past Fairbanks. There they would cross the Big Delta Range by truck to the Copper River and pump station 11.

Dae Dong was ramrod military and willing to die for his country. He did not feel the same way about the civilian who ran the whole operation. In all his meetings with the man, Kyong Ran came across as an opportunistic killer who would always have someone else sacrificed for his country. Money drove that man—nothing else   and money was a weakness that ultimately destroyed most men. Flash enough money in front of those types of people and they will turn their backs on their loved ones and worse, their own country. Ran had assured him that enough money had been spent to secure every leg, every aspect of their mission. Ran also told him that he had paid an Alaskan drifter to buy the CRRCs and procure a bush pilot to deliver the merchandise. The drifter ended up in a fish waste grinder and the pilot crashed into the side of a mountain. Now, there were no traces back to North Korea, except for himself and his men. Will my men and I somehow die in a fiery crash or end up in a fish waste grinder? he wondered.

Kyong Ran had also given Dae Dong the GPS coordinates to other locations where camouflaged and stored Zodiacs, additional fuel, and CO_2 tanks for inflation were hidden. As he studied his handheld GPS device, Dae Dong determined that they must make the five-mile trek in less than six hours. Once there, they could rest the balance of the daylight hours, then go upriver by night. The trip on the wild Yukon would take the better part of two nights, so there would be excess time for preparation and review.

He stood and gave his men the signal to move out. Kyong Ran's sinister face and the fish waste grinder crossed Dae Dong's mind one more time.

**

When the saboteurs arrived within a mile of the banks of the Yukon, Captain Dong heard rustling in the dense woods to his left.

"Down!" he whispered loud enough for his men to hear. He halted and motioned with his arms for his men to get down and take up defensive positions.

Through the dark green fauna, he saw a large, reddish brown bear at a running clip. All of a sudden, he heard distant sounds coming from his right. He pulled up his field glasses and made out the image of a hunter stalking the Kodiak. He was coming their way.

"Captain, what should we do?" his lieutenant asked in a low whisper. "Should we take him out?"

"No! Not yet. We'll see if he stays out in front of us—he's following the bear, not looking for us. Stay low and be silent. If he's to be shot, I will do it."

"But Captain, he's sure to see us and we can't let him escape."

"Do you think I'm an idiot? He has a home and if he doesn't return to it, someone will come looking for him."

In a slow motion, the hunter turned and began moving in their direction. His eyes were focused on the bear. Within minutes, he worked his way to within twenty feet of Dae Dong. The captain's action changed in the snap of a finger. He rested his assault rifle at his side and eased out his knife. When he was a few feet away, the hunter saw the North Korean lying on the ground, poised to strike. He froze in fear.

Dae Dong made his decision. He leapt at the stationary hunter and plunged his knife into his chest and ripped downward. The stunned man fell backward with his rifle falling, without a sound, to the ground. Dae Dong hovered over the hunter like a vicious wolf till the hunter gasped his final breath.

"Should we bury him, sir?"

Dae Dong raised himself up from his hovering position. As he turned to look at the lieutenant, a strange look appeared on his stoic face. His eyes were focused, yet distant and haunting, giving them an almost crazed look. When his eyes looked at the second-in-command, they reverted to normal.

"No. Leave him where he lies. The bear will shred him overnight and be our cover. Those that come looking for him tomorrow will find nothing identifiable but shreds of his clothing. We'll be long up the river before then. Tell the men to move out."

A couple of hours later, the men reached the stashed crates that held the boats. Their GPS coordinates were spot on. By nightfall, they had their two crafts in the water, outboard motors fueled, started, and running smoothly. As the first CRRC reached its desired speed, Dae Dong stood with the cold wind whipping his jacket. His tension settled and an invigorated sense of destiny filled his spirit.

CHAPTER 38

WALED PULLED THE VAN OVER BEHIND A VACANT RESTAU-
rant. It was daylight, so he spent a good hour making sure that no local
sheriff had the road in their patrol. He was comfortable that they would
have enough time to open up the metal floor that concealed their stash
of weapons.

"Open up the tool boxes and put the weapons in them," Waled said. "Put
the suppressors and laser lights on the MK7s before you pack them. The
Glocks go in the short box and the night vision headgear goes in the paint
buckets. Make sure all the magazines are full—including the spares. When
you're done, pull on your painter overalls. I don't want some cop busting us."

"What about our attack clothes?" Jameel asked.

"Roll them up in the heavy drop cloth."

"How long before we get there?"

Waled opened his iPhone and retrieved the texted GPS points that led
to the McKenzie house. "We should have no problem reaching the house
by sunset."

***

Julie sat on her rear porch deck watching Oscar chasing an errant rabbit
through the cleared field behind their house. She was pleased because the old
dog hadn't been that frisky in months. His deafness and severe arthritis had
taken its toll, to the point where both Julie and Devon were worried. For all
intents and purposes, the day seemed as normal as any other. Evening was
approaching and the sky was filled with towering white clouds contrasting
against a vivid, dark blue background. Mount McKinley could still be seen
in all its majesty in the background and her coffee was the perfect robust
blend that she liked. "How could anything bad happen on a day like this?"
she murmured. Looking around, she noticed an agent on the porch.

"Hard to believe there's any danger out there, Bill," she sang out to her guard.

Her words startled the CIA agent, who was leaning against the house about ten feet away. He too had been looking at McKinley and was lost in deep thought. Straightening himself up, he replied, "That's for darn sure, Mrs. McKenzie, but we both know better than that. I've learned to pay attention to any reports of chatter…they're usually based on some fact."

"No, I only meant that when you look at God's glory out there, it's hard to believe that there's any evil in the world."

"That's understood, ma'am."

"But I do have to say that as I was pouring my coffee, a strange feeling came over me. I don't know how to say it other than a weird chill went up my spine—almost as if I could sense the presence of evil…as if it's close by. Do you understand what I'm saying?"

"Yes, ma'am, I think I do."

"That's why I came out here—to try and steady my nerves."

"Well, feelings are just that, Mrs. McKenzie, but I've never taken any that I get lightly. I don't want you to think that I'm some kind of nut job, but I'm a big believer in guardian angels—both the human and spiritual kind. In other words, I'm not your only protector. You trust those feelings of yours; they're mighty powerful and they will always serve you well."

"That's comforting to hear, Bill, and thank you for being so honest. Most men aren't willing to show any vulnerability. Well, I think I'll head inside to take a short nap. Come on, Oscar!"

Julie had told Bill a fib about taking a nap. She didn't want him to know how frightened she was. She pulled her cell phone out of her pocket as soon as she shut her bedroom door and brought up Devon's number on speed dial.

"Hello, sweetheart," answered Devon.

"Thank God you answered, Devon. Are you alright? Where are you?"

"I'm fine. I just got off the plane here in Fairbanks and am picking up my bag as we speak. Why? You sound scared, and that worries me."

"I don't know, Devon. I have a very bad feeling that today might be the day. I know that I shouldn't feel this way, but I do—and it seems…I don't know… somehow real. I'm sorry, but I'm frightened and—"

Devon frowned. He felt the knots in his neck tighten. "Alright," he said, cutting her off. "Listen, don't apologize for what or how you feel. You've always had good instincts and I hear what you're saying. I want you to take a deep breath and collect your thoughts. I need you to *think*, girl. Think of what I would do if something does happen before I get there. Lay out a strategy and above all, trust your instincts. You are so much more than what you may think."

There was a slight pause as Julie took a deep breath. "I…I've already been doing that. I thought through what we did at your cabin, and I've already placed the guns in hidden locations—one for each situation. I've placed my night vision goggles next to my bed and the 44 mag is under my pillow."

"Good!" he said, as tears of both fear and pride wet his eyes. His voice stumbled in response. "Julie, I love you…more than life. I…I promise that I'll be there just after dark. Keep this phone in your pocket. If something happens before I get there, press the dial button twice—it will automatically dial my number. That way I'll know that trouble has started. Don't call me otherwise. I want you in total focus mode—*total* focus."

"I love you, Devon."

"I'll be there for you, Julie, I promise," he said as he rang off.

As Devon left the airport in his Tahoe, he pulled his phone out of his pocket and set it on the seat next to him. A desperate feeling of total helplessness came over him. He slammed his open palm on the steering wheel in total anger.

"Damn me!" he screamed out. "Screw the world and all its political shit. I shouldn't have left her alone—I just shouldn't have! I don't give a rat's ass about oil or terrorists…it's just a money-power game that gets played over and over again…somebody's always screwing the world…and for what— money? All I know is that I love *her*. I screwed up once, and those I loved died. I'll be damned if that happens again!"

Devon reached up and wiped his eyes and the sweat that beaded on his forehead. He looked at his speedometer, which read over one hundred miles per hour. He looked straight ahead and saw the sun sinking below the horizon.

"Please, God, I know that I've been bitter toward you. Please forgive me, please keep my Julie safe. I know that I'm not supposed to make any bargains with you, but please, I'm begging you, my life for hers." Devon's eyes welled again with tears and his thoughts ran in a slow, rhythmic cadence…my life for hers…my life for hers.

CHAPTER 39

SPECIAL AGENT BILL WEAVER FINISHED POURING HIMSELF another cup of fresh coffee. The curtains in the kitchen were drawn, but he knew from the change to near total darkness on the curtains that a line of clouds had crossed the bright moon. The air was cool and getting colder fast. Glad I'm inside, he thought. It wasn't the darkness outside or the temperature of the night that bothered him—it was the conversation with Julie McKenzie about her gut feeling that stuck in his craw and continued to gnaw at him.

Damn! he thought. I've really come to like this woman. I sure don't want to see her get hurt. That Trojan Horse guy must be something special. Never met the guy, but I've heard all the whisperings about how he'd gone rogue—a real pariah. Man, that must have been tough; you go dark in Russia, Dagestan, Chechnya, God knows how many other 'stans' they send you to, then your bosses are corrupt and try to pin it all on you. Poor guy even lost his first wife because of it. Then, the guy proves he's a first-class hero. Gets himself secreted into a Russian submarine in the middle of the North Sea and prevents a bunch of missiles from firing at oil platforms and even London itself. Wow—the stuff legends are made of. Me? The sum of my career is pulling guard duty in the boonies of Alaska—the story of my sorry-ass life.

As he saw her face again in his mind, his sense of uneasiness came back and the acid in his stomach roiled. Guess it's time to check on the other two, he thought. Weaver lifted his wrist to his mouth and said, "Alpha, time to check in. How's the cold?"

…Nothing. "Alpha?…Come in, Alpha."

…Still nothing. "Charlie, this is Baker. Do you copy?"

…Nothing. "Damn it! Alpha, this is Baker! DO YOU COPY?"

The other end of the phone remained dead. He slammed his fist down on the countertop. He grit his teeth and knowing it was against protocol, reached up, slid the curtain back, and peered through the window in an attempt to check the compound. A muffled, cracking sound preceded the breaking of the window's glass. Bill Weaver's body staggered back, as skull and flesh from above his ear splattered the cabinet door to his right. Reeling to his left, he tried to grab something, anything, but his arm only swiped across the countertop, sending the coffee mug shattering on the tile floor. Seconds later, the cabinet door ripped off its hinges as he came crashing down in one loud thud on top of the broken mug. Blood oozed out on the floor, pooling away from his head.

***

Julie heard a crash followed by a loud thud. She froze. She had to think and think fast. She bolted from her chair and made her way to the half opened door of her bedroom. Oscar was frantic and because of his failing eyesight, was whining in circles. She locked him in her closet to quiet him down for his own protection.

She listened—no sound. The house remained eerily quiet. There is no way that Bill wouldn't call up to me if he had caused the noise. She strained to listen even harder. She heard nothing, just the sound of Oscar scratching at the closet door.

***

Waled stood with Jameel, staring at the body of Bill Weaver. Jameel pumped one more silenced round into the agent's lifeless body. "Don't waste ammunition on someone who's already dead, you fool," Waled said. "I'm going to cut the power. You go upstairs and get the woman. Put your night vision goggles on over your head, just above your eyes. Pull them down when the power goes off. Now go!"

***

Julie shut the door and grabbed her cell phone out of her pocket. She did just what Devon had told her to do—press the send button twice. As she slid the phone into her blouse pocket, the house lights flickered and went out—total darkness, total silence. Even Oscar was quiet. She heard Devon whispering in the phone.

"Don't hang up, Julie. Just *think*—think about what you need to do. I'm coming."

She put her arms straight out and moved over to her bed, clawing in desperation at her bedspread till she found her night vision goggles. Scooping them up, Julie pressed them to her chest, as if they were a lifesaver. She freed one hand and then nervously patted the bedding till she found her pillow and grabbed her 44. Pulling it to her chest also, she realized that her movements were chaotic and out of synch. Stop! she thought. Think girl—*think*!

Julie laid the gun on the bed and pulled the night vision goggles over her head. Just as she had them fitted snug, the stuttering chug of the generator's start-up broke the silence. The lights came on with a brilliance that shocked her and made her shriek in terror. She ripped the goggles off her head, and her pupils contracted as they adjusted to the normal light. Her breathing was as fast as her heart was racing.

Again the lights flickered and all went dark as the power to the generator was cut. One more time she pulled the goggles over her eyes. This time, her eyes adjusted quickly to the eerie view that the goggles provided. She picked up the 44 and took a deep breath. Julie was ready to do what she must to survive.

Do what Devon would do, she thought over and over.

Creeping on all fours, she made her way to the bedroom dormer window. Within seconds, she had crawled out the window and onto the roof. When she felt comfortable with the pitch of the roof, she turned her body and reached to close the bottom sash of the window.

Suddenly, a dark hand shot out and put a death lock on her wrist. The magnum slipped out of her other hand and slid down off the roof. Her first reaction was to pull away in terror. The man's hand wouldn't yield its vise-like grip on her. She began to panic as she saw night vision goggles appear in the window, staring back at her like some sinister fiend from hell. She lost her footing and the assassin fought to keep her from sliding off the roof. Her legs struggled to get some sort of footing and her wrist wrenched in pain as she tried to pull it away. Panic set in and began to control her every move.

Out of nowhere, she remembered the Taurus revolver that she had set outside of the window. She scratched out a small amount of footing on the rough shingles and pushed her body back upward. Her loose hand flailed to find the gun. When she found it, she gripped it tight and cocked the revolver. The mordant smile that had appeared on the assassin's face as he felt Julie's body rising upward turned to horror as she raised the pistol to within inches of his face. She squeezed the trigger and the 410 shot blasted a hole in his face. Blood splattered back at her as flesh, glass, and cartilage blew everywhere.

The assassin's grip let loose and Julie's body began a fast slide downward. In desperation, she grabbed the gutter as she went over the eave, but it let loose under her weight. Her body hit hard on the lower roof, ten feet below. The roof was of a shallower pitch, allowing her body to slow and come to a stop before going over its edge. The gritty shingles had torn through her pants and sleeves and peeled away her skin. Her left elbow felt as if it had been dislocated. Her phone connection to Devon went dead as it broke under her fall.

In spite of this, Julie kept her wits and recognized where she was and where she needed to be. She eased herself to the edge of the roof and jumped to the ground. Both revolvers were lost to her in the dark of the shrubbery that surrounded the house. The attack scene at Devon's cabin flashed through her consciousness. One thought, however, dominated all others—get to the assault rifle; but that meant going back inside. Julie's blood ran cold at the thought.

She dropped to one knee and looked over the grounds, almost as if she expected one of the agents or Devon to be coming to meet her. The stark reality glared in front of her—there was no one but her. Only she could save her life. Her hands began to shake as panic overcame her. On the verge of tears, a vision of Devon flashed in her mind. A raging anger overtook her. She knew that if more killers were waiting and killed her, then Devon would be the next target when he arrived home.

Julie's hands curled into slow, steeled fists. Rising to her feet, a new resolve transformed her. She had conquered her fear. She pulled the night vision goggles back over her head and began creeping toward the house.

"If there are more of you, I *will* kill you," she hissed under her breath. "*I will kill you.*"

Her plan was simple: She would sneak into the house and make a dash to the great room couch, where Devon's assault rifle awaited, safety off, first bullet chambered. The devil, however, lie in the details. Was there more than the one assassin, and if so, how many? she thought. Can I handle more than one in a firefight? And if there are more, where are they now…upstairs looking for me or downstairs lying in wait? Are the rear French doors locked? If so, how did they get in? The magnitude of the questions was overwhelming. Her head began to throb and with each pulse, the pain in her elbow grew exponentially.

Julie again thought of her husband. Devon! Think of what Devon would do. She shook off her doubt and moved toward the back deck. The thought of being exposed on the open deck, unarmed, made her change her mind. Shifting direction, she decided to find her fallen 44 mag. As she reached the shrubbery, she looked up and drew a line from where the gun was released to its probable landing spot. On her hands and knees, she reached in and combed the ground under the foliage for the revolver…nothing. Only seconds went by, but they seemed like an eternity. At last, her finger brushed up against the barrel. Julie pulled the revolver out and kissed its chamber.

With the gun secure in her hand, her thinking sobered. Within seconds, she had a new plan. Crawling military style, she made her way to the side of the house where the basement wall became exposed to the sloping terrain. She reached the window. As her hand slid across the glass, it was cut on the hole that had been smashed in by the assassins. The sash was slid up and left in an open position.

"So this is where you bastards got in," she whispered to herself.

Julie made her way in and reached the stairs that led up to the side of the kitchen. The door creaked as she opened it and crawled in. She nearly came undone when she saw Agent Weaver lying on the floor. The image of his murdered body caused her eyes to well with tears, but she wiped them away with the back of her hand. She steeled herself and was ready to kill, ready to take on an army of assassins if that's what it took.

All of a sudden, she heard faint footsteps on the rear deck; the wooden patio door inched open on its track. She put her ear to the floor and listened with all her might. The footsteps were of one man. She heard him take four more steps and then heard nothing more. He had reached the large, Oriental rug that was centered on the floor in the great room. Was he coming toward the kitchen? She couldn't be sure. Little by little, Julie raised herself and crawled over behind the kitchen's island. She put the chamber of the revolver under her armpit to muffle the sound of her cocking it.

She pulled the weapon out from under her arm and eased her body to face the entry to the great room. As she began raising her head, her hair came into view above the countertop. A short burst of bullets banged out of the assassin's automatic weapon. The countertop's shards ripped through her loose hair. She dropped to the floor and heard the man scramble back behind the wall that divided the two rooms.

Julie guessed that he was only a few feet back from the doorway. She crawled to the right side of the island and fired two shots into the plaster wall. Her guess was good, but the assailant was back just far enough to be missed by inches.

The killer sprang into action, dove across the open doorway, rolled once, and released another deadly burst at Julie. Wood spattered from the cabinets; the cast-iron pans inside the island rang from being hit by the bullets. One bullet creased her thigh and blood soaked her jeans, but she didn't notice and again squeezed off two shots through the wall, this time on the other side of the opening. She heard a low, muffled cry of pain. Did I hit him? She listened, but heard nothing.

The killer reached around the opening and gave two bursts of bullets. The side wall of the island was shredded; one of the cabinet doors protecting Julie blew off toward the sink. She released her last two rounds. When she squeezed the trigger again, only the blank sound of metal on metal was reported.

The assassin shoved another magazine into his weapon and snapped the slide back. He slowly rose and walked toward Julie as she frantically tried to reload her gun. He snarled and shouted, "That was the last of your bullets, you rotten, American slut. Did you think I am so stupid that I cannot count? You think you are some tough cowboy bitch, don't you?"

He arrived at the corner of the blown-out island. Julie sat defenseless. He pulled out his knife and grabbed her by the hair.

"I was ordered to bring you in alive, so you could be killed by the Korean pig in front of your husband as he watched. Too bad for you I wasn't told what condition I had to deliver you in." Spittle sprayed from his mouth as his words hissed in a maniacal outburst.

He kissed his knife and pressed it on her lower lip, forcing her to open her mouth.

"Maybe you will have no tongue. What do you think of that, you miserable whore? Or maybe I will cut one of your breasts off and use it for a coin pouch."

The knife slipped down and in one quick move, cut off the top three buttons of her blouse, while cutting her bra in half. She felt a warm trickle of blood begin to drip between her breasts. Julie looked up with a contemptuous sneer and spit in his face. The assassin squeezed the knife tighter and gave her a hard backhand across her face. Julie took the blow and gave him a defiant stare.

"You're nothing but a disgusting, little worm," she growled. "You couldn't handle a real woman."

The naked truth blinded him into a fury. In one quick thrust, he slammed her head and body downward to the floor. He bent over and jammed one knee onto her pelvis. He reached under her open bra and grabbed her breast to cut it off.

A shot rang out. A hole opened up in the killer's cheek, just under his eye. His body went rigid, weaved, and then fell backward to the floor. Devon appeared in the doorway, his two hands holding his Glock. He saw Julie, ran to her, and dropped to his knees. He scooped her up and held her so tight that she couldn't breathe, kissing her face over and over. Finally, Julie raised a hand.

"Devon! Don't hug me so tight, I can't breathe."

"I'm so sorry. I can't believe what might have happened to you."

Julie sagged; her blank eyes looked at Devon and then around at the shot up mess that was her kitchen. Her trembling hands tried to straighten her hair, to somehow make herself look more presentable. "I…I guess we came through…" She let loose with tears and covered her face with her hands, saying, "Thanks to you."

"No, honey, you saved yourself."

She took a deep breath, indicating to Devon to let her go, and then crawled over to Agent Weaver. When her fingers found the vein in his neck, she whispered, "He's dead. Check on the other agents—they're probably dead also."

Julie was in command mode. She was assessing the reality that had changed her world. Devon understood it all and liked what he saw. His heart was bursting with pride over the way she had defended herself.

He also knew there was more to do. "I'm going to turn the power back on, unless they sabotaged it. I'll holler before I flip the switch, so get ready to pull off your NVs. I have to secure the house before I check the other agents. There may have been more than one."

"There were at least two—I blew the face off one in our master bedroom."

Devon handed her his Glock. "You may need this if I flush one up. Where'd you stow the AR?"

"Behind the couch in the great room." She wanted to weep again, but found no tears could be produced. She just sat there, alone on the floor with Agent Weaver, going into shock.

CHAPTER 40

KYONG RAN SAT ON THE CORNER OF HIS BED IN THE BARD-moor Hotel. His room stunk. The time was just past midnight and he had two cigarettes lying on the bottom of an ashtray, smoldering in their own nicotine juice, while he took a drag of another in his mouth. Adding to the burning smell was his rank, sweaty body odor. Ran was in a nervous fit. He had already downed four mini bottles of vodka from the in-house bar, paced the room back and forth, and looked out the window dozens of times.

His man hadn't called; it was as simple as that. He had been sched-uled to abduct the McKenzie woman over two hours ago. Waled al-Ashbot was considered one of the best-trained terrorists al-Qaida had in Yemen. His record of success was unmatched by anyone on the Arabian Peninsula, and his ability to sneak up on an enemy and slit his throat without a sound was legendary. Ran was confident that al-Ashbot could pull this off alone, without any help from the homegrown.

Maybe that was it, he thought. The homegrown must've screwed something up…maybe he failed to get one of the agents. Why doesn't the Yemeni call? It's over! I never should have ordered them to go off mission. Did my crazed vengeance to torture McKenzie through his wife blind me? What have I done? What will happen when the families find out?

Kyong Ran sweated out another hour of self-flagellation and worked himself into a puking frenzy. I have to know! he thought. He stared at his cell phone sitting next to him on the bed. He gave in and dialed Al-Ashbot's number.

***

Devon McKenzie had returned to his house after directing the EMTs to the fallen agents. They were, of course, dead. One had his throat slit; the other two had been shot in the head. Devon was emotionally spent. The murder scenes were gruesome, especially knowing that the agents gave their lives to save his wife. He had tried to bargain with God by begging for his life to save Julie's. Never would he have wanted the agents to lose theirs. Devon had no problem sleeping over someone he killed when that person was an enemy; however, he struggled with the thought of innocent people dying so that he might live. It had almost ruined him six years ago, and the feelings were the same today. It was precisely these feelings that were exhausting him now.

As he entered the house from the rear deck, Julie was sitting with her face in her palms. She didn't move when the sliding doors rolled back. Devon noticed that she was hardly breathing. He walked over, sat down next to her, and put his arms around her. The woman that looked up into his eyes was somehow different. Devon realized that her feelings were identical to his own. The emotion she was holding back for the three agents made her seem distant and hollow—as if she was on a skiff that was cut loose and drifting away into a fog, and as hard as he stretched his hand out, he might not ever be able to reach her again. They sat like two statues facing each other, with nothing to say that would make any sense of it all.

Breaking the silence, a low ring from a phone could be heard. Devon jumped up, his mind trying to process the audible senses. He drifted into the kitchen, his head turning, trying to locate the source of the ring. Finally, he zeroed in on a pile of shattered cabinetry on the floor. The sound was coming from underneath. On the fifth ring, Devon dug the phone out of its hiding place and answered—he knew who was calling.

"You miserable piece of shit—your hired guns have drawn their last paycheck. Now, you're going to deal with me. I know where you are and I'm coming to kill you—that I promise. But first, I'm going to shoot each of your kneecaps off, then your elbows, and then I'm going to shoot you in the balls while you writhe in pain on the floor. You will beg for mercy, but there will be none. You will just bleed to a slow, painful death… while I watch."

With his rant in full stride and the phone to his ear, Devon failed to notice that Kyong Ran had broken the connection after he told him his hired guns had drawn their last paycheck. When he finally noticed the dead zone, he looked at the phone and screamed out, "Son of a bitch!"

The two dangerous men made a stark contrast. One knew that he should never have made the call; the other knew that he should never have answered it. One was now in fear of his life; the other was in fear of not being able to terminate the other's life. Both knew they had someone to answer to. One had to answer to his superiors, who would not accept this fiasco; the other knew that he would have no time to pull the GPS location he needed to find the filthy psychopath. Worse, he looked around and saw that his wife had heard every word of his rant to kill. Her eyes told him everything he didn't want to know. Devon felt the heat rise from his neck into his face. Julie was shocked to hear Devon's rage, not remembering her own just a few minutes earlier.

"Tell me that you didn't mean every word you just said. Tell me that the man I love and trust has not turned into some killing machine—a machine without a sense of what is right and wrong. Tell me that the man that I too would die to protect has not become a savage animal, with only vengeance to guide him."

Devon walked over to put his arm around her. "Julie, please—"

"Don't touch me, Devon McKenzie, unless you honestly answer my questions!"

Devon was taken aback. He knew that he would never operate outside of the law to that extent, but in his heart, he did want the man dead. "Listen, you don't know the death that I have witnessed from this man's hand. I shouldn't have said the things that I did, but I do want him to die for what he has done and what he tried to do to you. I can't leave him out there and go back to being hunted like an animal by a man who wants to kill you in front of me. I can't sleep for the rest of my life with a gun under my pillow."

Devon paused and turned his head, but not in shame. Julie stood up, wrapped him in her arms and hugged him with all the agony of knowing he was right and he must kill that man. "I know," she whispered. "I know."

"No, you don't know, but I swear that you are all that matters to me in life. And I swear that I will bring him to justice—legally...if I can."

***

Within minutes, Kyong Ran packed his bag and left the hotel. He pulled his car into a dark, vacant lot. After he got out of the car, he pulled out his cell phone and ground it under his heel on the pavement. He bent over, picked the SIM card out of the rubble, and with his cigarette lighter, melted it down to a smoldering mass. Opening his trunk, he unzipped his bag and pulled out another phone.

As he drove away, he assembled new plans in his head; plans that negated the need to have his terrorists caught in a Seattle motel by the FBI. The homegrown and the Yemini had been essential for cover, but were no longer a part of the equation. As long as the remains of some terrorists were found at the explosion sites of the pipeline, al-Qaida would still be blamed. This is what he would justify to the family members, but only after he came up with a plausible excuse for his latest screw-up. His fate depended on the success of Dae Dong and his saboteurs. Then it hit him—if all depended on those men, what need was he now to the family? A cold chill ran up Kyong Ran's neck and he shuddered at the only answer he could come up with. *He* was expendable.

CHAPTER 41

DIRECTOR HATCHER STOOD LOOKING OUT HIS WINDOW; his mind was thousands of miles away at a house outside of Fairbanks, Alaska. He had received the report of the bloody death of three of his agents. That kind of news always upset him—right to his core. To Hatcher, these men were family. It came with the job, but he had always described himself as a "hard-ass Christian man." To him, that meant that God forgave him for all the terrible decisions he had to make. Nevertheless, he still had a conscience, and along with that conscience was a heart that felt pain.

He remembered Julie Weston well and liked her. Thank God she's safe, he thought. As for that son-of-a-bitch husband of hers, he's nothing but a bore hog running around like a chicken that knows it's his turn to be supper. Damn loose cannon! Why for two cents I'd—

Hatcher was interrupted by his secretary announcing the presence of Aaron Cohen and Lana Gorenkov.

"Come in, Cohen, and you too, Gorenkov."

"Good morning, sir."

"Good morning, Hatcher."

Hatcher chuckled, "You know, Gorenkov, the more I see you, the more you remind me of me."

"Is that a complaint or do I take that as a compliment?"

"Well, I guess...oh hell, it's a compliment. Now, let's get down to business. Cohen, I'm sure that twin of yours in Alaska called you about last night."

"Yes, sir, he did. It was a close call for Julie, and I am so sorry about our three agents."

"A terrible day for The Agency. Damn fine performance by Julie, though."

"Yes, sir."

"Now, tell me your best guess as to where, if it's true, al-Qaida is supposed to hit the pipeline in Alaska."

"Sir, as I have said before, I don't believe that it is going to be al-Qaida. Devon, Ms. Gorenkov, and I all believe in the information we showed you from the Chateau d'Arbonne. I know that it's not concrete and a stretch to tie it to the North Koreans, but in my estimation, it's hard evidence. The root of this is money, not terrorism. It's got the dirty fingerprints of international banking all over it."

"Well, that's not what the president's national security advisor thinks, nor do Homeland Security, DOD, and the flippin' FBI. They all just about snickered at me in the security meeting yesterday. I felt like a hen that was picked up by the neck with no eggs underneath her."

"But—"

"What do you mean, but? The two dead terrorists that attacked the McKenzie house are both al-Qaida. One's a Yemini and the other is a homegrown, for God's sake!"

Lana spoke up, hoping to break a potential deadlock. "What he's saying, Hatcher, is that while it may be true that *they* are al-Qaida, it doesn't negate all the other intelligence that I gathered and our group of three expanded upon. There is a direct tie-in to North Korea. We think the al-Qaida boys are merely a ruse to shift the blame elsewhere. Aaron has a credible theory that has to do with the value and control of international money. Your own Federal Reserve may be complicit in this."

"Tell me, then, why in the hell al-Qaida operatives tried to kill Julie McKenzie?"

"That we can't figure out."

"Well, in any case, the whole mess has been turned over to Homeland and the FBI. Cohen, you know damn well we aren't allowed to do domestic spying."

"Are these the same agencies that 'shared' all their information on the terrorists prior to 9/11?" Lana said, her response dripping with sarcasm.

Hatcher looked at the floor and said, "No, that would be the FBI and…well…*us*."

It was Aaron's turn. "And now we're all one big, happy family under Homeland Security."

"Look, Cohen, I did my best at the meeting, but I couldn't get anyone to listen as long as the smell of that pig, al-Qaida, was stinking up the room. However, they threw me a bone to cover their asses anyway. They're going to divert two drones from border security in Arizona to Alaska."

"So, are they doing this today? And what else are they doing? Two drones can't cover the pipeline well enough in that unpredictable weather! My God, what arrogant idiots they are."

"I don't have the answers, Cohen," Hatcher said, shaking his head. "What they mean is anybody's guess. They're also going to mobilize the National Guard, and how well they cover the pipeline is questionable."

Aaron's voice mirrored his dejection when he asked, "How many?"

Hatcher grimaced and raised his eyebrows. "Look! It doesn't matter how many; it's out of my hands. This is no longer CIA business—federal law, remember? We have no jurisdiction in the states—period!"

"So that's it?" Aaron asked.

"No. I'm sending you and your little Ruskie up to Alaska—but only to visit the McKenzie folks. You know...to console them. Whatever else you do while you're there, well, that's your business. Maybe you four go sightseeing or whatever. Now, get out of here."

Swinging her ponytail, Lana looked back over her shoulder and winked at Hatcher. "Thank you, *sir*."

Hatcher smiled as he looked up at her from his desk. "You know, *Miss* Gorenkov, I'm reminded of the farmer that just harvested a bumper crop—enough to save his farm. Everyone slapped his back and cheered his effort, but down deep, he knew that the Lord had blessed him with incredibly good weather. I hope that *you* are our good weather."

"Perhaps I am...by the way, my friends call me Lana, sir."

"Aw, get out of here and take that jackass Cohen with you!"

CHAPTER 42

A SPECIAL MEETING HAD BEEN CALLED IN RESPONSE TO THE attempted break-in at the chateau. The fact that no one had gained entry to the chateau itself delayed the group from the necessity of gathering at once, so when all the participants arrived late in the day and tired, they were grateful to go to their assigned rooms. No one slept well because an unrelenting thunderstorm accompanied by ferocious lightning had kept them awake most of the night. However, the new day opened in bright sunshine, and most members had a cheerful breakfast before getting down to business.

The first family leader clanked his glass of Perrier when the long table had been cleared and all attendants had left the room. The members quieted and sat upright and stiff, as if on cue.

"This special meeting has been called to update the membership on the status of our mission. There is no agenda in front of you because we have only two items to discuss. The first is the breach of security that occurred within our overall compound. The second item is an update on the progress of our missions in both Russia and Alaska."

"As I understand," said the second family leader, "the outer walls were breached, but the intruders were chased off by our security guards before any attempt was made to enter the chateau itself. Is that correct?"

"Yes."

"Do we know who was responsible for this breach, that is to say, was it intentional or random?"

"Unfortunately, the security cameras were dodged, which leads us to believe that those involved were professionals. Our security guards are certain from their unsuccessful chase that it was two men and a woman."

"Have we any leads as to who these professionals are?" asked the third family member.

"Yes. The woman is believed to be Svetlana Gorenkov."

Murmuring filled the room as members began whispering to each other. The first family member again banged his knife on his glass for silence. All obeyed.

"Svetlana Gorenkov is the Russian journalist that Kyong Ran has been unsuccessful in eliminating. Not only has he failed to eliminate her, but he has failed on numerous occasions to find Minister Zakorov's cache of photographs."

This time the room broke out in loud discussions between members who were now fearful of exposure. The fourth family member wiped his forehead and raised his hand to be heard.

"Go ahead, monsieur. Quiet! Please!"

"When we talk of a failed elimination, does that mean that there are some that have been successful?"

"Yes. Zakorov has been eliminated, as has Sergei Diemchuk of the Ministry of Justice and Viktor Chortina of the Ministry of Emergency Situations. Arkady Banketik of the Ministry of Trade and Economy has not."

The fourth family member blanched in a combination of disbelief and outright fear. "All of these ministers have been killed? Are we just meting out death sentences, as if they were common criminals or terrorists? It was my understanding that only Zakorov was to die, and that was only if we could not secure the photographs that connected the Koreans to the Gulf of Mexico platform destruction. My God! What have we become?"

This time the first member rose to his feet and demanded silence. He assumed a power position in his body language and stared directly into the fourth family member's eyes, freezing the man in his seat.

"In the first place, we are not even sure that any photographs still exist. We terminated one Yakov Isroel, whom we believe had all of Gorenkov's information on his computer system, which *was* completely destroyed. Secondly, do not lecture me or anyone else in this room on 'what we have become.' For centuries, our families have had to make the hard decisions to move the world forward in a manner that we deem is in its best interest. Millions of people die every day and their deaths mean nothing to the march of time. Nothing! They are merely chaff blowing in the wind. If you, or any other member, have a problem with our methods, I suggest that you remind yourselves that this membership is not revocable. You are here to stay—for generations to come. No one leaves our organization voluntarily…or alive."

The room became still, the dead air could have been cut with a knife. No member dared look at the person seated beside him or across the table. Their eyes merely fixed on the intricate inlay of the table below. The first member's words were as sobering as a bucket of ice water thrown in their faces.

As if on cue, the phone in the center of the table rang in, breaking the tension. The first member answered it and listened. Minutes went by and still he said nothing, and then, "Keep me apprised. It is essential that Dae Dong be successful. Do I make myself clear?"

He rang off without waiting for a response. Turning again to the members, he said, "That was Kyong Ran. I never finished with the information on the chateau grounds break-in. The two other men that were with Gorenkov are believed to be agents from the American CIA. Ran not only botched killing them in Russia, but he made a foolish and misguided attempt to kill one of the agents' wives in Alaska. He diverted two of his terrorists to the agent's home; however, they were unsuccessful and both were killed. We now have lost part of our al-Qaida cover that was essential to our cover-up."

"What reason could he have had for doing this?"

"He gave me one, but I don't believe it. The man has shown himself to be not only incompetent, but a liar as well. I have tracked his every failure with our connections in the Russian FSB. I am now convinced that he is no longer of any use to us. He must be eliminated. Are there any dissentions?"

Not one hand was raised. For a second time, they all stared down at the conference tabletop. The first member was now sure that the threat of violence was a good stick for whipped dogs. He took his time looking left, then right, viewing the entirety of the table. When he was confident that they were like putty in his hands, he snapped, "The motion is carried unanimously. Now, the last item on our agenda is the transfer of funds to the Greek government. Have they been transferred?"

The last family member to speak shuffled his papers, aligning all four corners. He was a timid man of slight build. His mouth was dry, so he quickly took a drink of water from his cut-crystal glass and in an effeminate way, dabbed his lips with his napkin before spreading it in a dainty fashion across his lap.

"Yes," he said, making sure his posture was prim and correct. "All thirteen deposits from the New York bank have been conveyed and all transfer data wiped clean, showing it to be in total conformance with international standards. These funds, shall we say, are one hundred percent untraceable and the Greeks are only too happy to launder it for us."

"All parties are on the same wavelength—they know what they have to do?"

"Yes. The New York bank will have its money back as soon as the EU buys into the Greeks', uh, stability, and makes the necessary bailout loan. The Federal Bank will then pocket one hundred twenty-five million in commissions and will be happy. The Greeks get their money, so they don't have to make any unpleasant social cuts for the time being, and the EU is happy because they think the problem is resolved. When they discover that they have sunk further money into a beggar nation with an inability to repay, it will be too late. Therefore, we have our debt and we are happy."

"Excellent!" said the first member, as he closed his folder. "Now, if there is nothing—"

"Wait!" said the skittish fourth member. "You haven't said anything about what we're going to do with the two CIA agents or the Russian journalist."

The room fell still. All eyes moved to the first family member. "Nothing at this time. We wait until Dae Dong and his men have destroyed the pipeline and left their al-Qaida hostages at the scene. We have a contact within the American Federal Reserve, who in turn has a contact in a high-level position in the White House, specifically their NSA. It is obvious that we need to eliminate the agents and the woman, and that we need to hire people who are more adept at killing them. We *will* handle them—of that you can rest assured. Finally, we will reconvene here in fourteen calendar days unless summoned sooner... Au revoir."

CHAPTER 43

YUKON RIVER, ALASKA

CAPTAIN DONG WAS PLEASED WITH THE WEATHER HE AND his men had encountered the last two nights. The skies were mostly overcast, but not with the heavy clouds that carried rain. On the Yukon, the wind whipped hard, especially when they tried to gain speed, which was seldom. He had studied every piece of information on the river that he could get his hands on and believed he was as aware of its natural hazards as anyone. His only concern was the floating debris for which the river was famous. As long as the moon was not a factor, their chances of being detected were reduced to near zero. What he hadn't prepared for was how pitch-black everything was. This total darkness left him and his men on edge, in spite of their night vision goggles.

He sensed the moon was about to break out of its cloud cover, so Dae Dong motioned for the boats to pull off and tie up at the shoreline. It was time for a break anyway. Even without excess speed, the ride on the rough river was exacting on his men, and a short stretch would be good for morale.

Dae Dong checked his GPS and was satisfied that their mission was on schedule. With another four hours of running the river, they would come upon the town of Nulato. The town was big enough to have its own small airport, even though it only had a population of 336 people. The townsfolk were primarily employed in the local hotels, restaurants, and outfitting stores that catered to sports enthusiasts. Best of all, there was an island in the river that ran almost the length of the town proper—a perfect cover.

Dae Dong's plan was to lie up well short of the town before daybreak, pull the boats up on shore, and stay camouflaged while they slept the daylight hours. His only worry was the possibility of a stray fisherman or hunter coming upon them, but he was confident that he would handle that in the same manner as with the first hunter.

When the sun disappeared, he would order his men to paddle upstream, staying between the island and the north shoreline of the town. Their next exposure would occur on the long, open stretch of water that ran along the airport, whose runway paralleled the river. After they cleared that, they should again have decent coverage, allowing them to use their motors.

Ten minutes later, they were back on the river, bucking its current.

CHAPTER 44

DIRECTOR HATCHER WAS STILL STEAMING OVER THE dissing he had received at the last security conference. Damn it! he thought. Now Cohen has me questioning the Federal Reserve, for God's sake. And the NSA! Why were the majority of people at the table so willing to disregard my report about the pipeline chatter, though? The president sat back in his chair like he was either disinterested or bored—neither of which was true. The information that my two agents and Gorenkov had supplied should have raised red flags all over the room. Maybe that's it! Maybe I misread his actions—maybe he was hiding his real feelings. There's something going on with the president and the NSA and it stinks. I can smell it! I need to find out what it is before it's too late, but I've got to be careful. Hell, you don't go picking up a skunk's tail to find out what the smell is. Hatcher wondered if going forward with this wouldn't cost him his job.

Then it hit him. Our national security is supposed to be more important than my job. What the hell is going on with me? Am I turning soft...tired? Worse yet, am I losing my integrity? He picked up his phone and got the NSA director on the line.

"Say, Jim, there was something that I forgot to brief the president on at yesterday's meeting. Would you set up a meeting with him in the Oval Office? It's important."

"I'll check his calendar with his COS and get back to you. Do we need to make it a full security meeting with NSA and the other usual suspects?"

"No, I don't think so, Jim. Don't worry, I'll keep it brief."

LaSpesa sensed the old country boy was up to something—he'd never been this nice. "Do you want to tell me what it's about?"

"There's been some foreign chatter about the Federal Reserve and the NSA. I'd rather not go into that over the phone—you know...security."

Hatcher picked up on LaSpesa's pause before he responded.

"Well, uh, sure…sure, I understand. Uh, okay, I'll get right back with you."

Hatcher rang off and pounded his fist on the top of his desk. He frowned and whispered to himself, "Damn you, Cohen, you'd better be right. Now what line am I going to feed the president to flush the weasels out of their hole?"

Within minutes, LaSpesa called Hatcher back. "You're on for this afternoon at one o'clock. Make sure you remember your promise."

"I know, keep it brief."

***

After he hung up, LaSpesa looked over at the President and took a deep breath. "I don't like this, Mr. President. He's onto something, but I can't figure out what…and that worries me."

"Do you think he's still fishing about the North Korean connection to the oil rig explosion?"

"Personally, I think he's gone beyond that. He took that as a given, and now he's like a bloodhound. He wants to know where it leads. He may be bluffing, but he's practicing the age-old adage, 'Follow the money'…Should we inform Sarris? He was the biggest bundler of questionable donors."

"No, Van Leuwen at the Fed is Sarris' friend, not *ours*. He can decide to tell him or not."

"How will he get the message?" LaSpesa asked.

"My guess is Sarris already has a mole in the NSA. Truth be told, he probably has them in the CIA and FBI as well."

"God help us."

"Money has an ugly trail, Jim. The potholes are filled with mud and leave footprints."

"And they always lead upward to the top."

CHAPTER 45

HATCHER SAT ACROSS FROM THE PRESIDENT'S DESK. THE president normally liked to sit on the couches for a more relaxed atmosphere, but this time he wanted his CIA director to feel the power of the office. He guessed wrong. Hatcher read through the ruse and became more convinced that the rats were scurrying.

"So, Ernie, what's this about some chatter going on with the Fed and NSA?" As his eyes darted around the CIA director, he feigned seeking some sort of folder. "May I see what you have?"

"You can, Mr. President, but because this meeting was called on such short notice, I didn't have time to prepare a report. You see, the intel has been streaming in sporadically—in fact, I'm expecting some new data when I get back to my office. Rest assured that I've got the bulk of what we already have committed to memory."

The president glanced at LaSpesa and said, "I see. Well, what is it you have committed to your memory?"

"Sir, the chatter has been garbled at best, but over and again, we hear what appears to be a name followed by what we can clearly make out as Federal Reserve. Then, after we hear that, another name is garbled, followed by what sounds like NSA. We have run the names through the analysis computers, but have been unsuccessful thus far. Is there any reason you can think of that might explain the connection between the two?"

The president held his head with his forefinger and thumb as if he was in heavy contemplation. He leaned back in his chair and appeared to be wracking his mind for some connection, but all the time, he was looking at Jim LaSpesa, hoping that he might come up with a credible explanation.

Hatcher's hawkish eyes darted back and forth between the two men, catching every nuance.

LaSpesa finally grimaced and said, "I don't know about you, Mr. President, but I have collated every major person in the NSA and the Federal Reserve, but I can't come up with anyone who may know someone else in the Reserve. There could be people at lower levels, Ernie, but I sure as hell don't know—how about you, Mr. President?"

He nodded in agreement, snapped his chair upright, and stood with his hand extended to Hatcher. "Ernie, I wish I could help, but I'm not sure where any of this goes, and I don't see how it's relevant to us. So, keep us informed and do send us your report. Thank you."

With that, Director Hatcher was dismissed from the Oval Office. As he exited, a sly smile broke out on his face. He felt like a kid at elementary school that had just thrown a harmless rat snake into a gaggle of girls. "Hoooeee!" he whispered. "There *is* something rotten in Denmark, after all. I knew there was a reason I liked you, Cohen."

As he reached the outside, he took in a deep breath through his nose and thought, Best set the bobber high, ol' boy, we got some real bottom-feeders here.

CHAPTER 46

THE BRIGHT SUN HAD MADE IT AN ALMOST PERFECT DAY in Alaska. Aaron and Lana spent a half hour at the luggage carousel and then made their way to their rental SUV. Looking for the vehicle, Aaron shielded his eyes with his hand. He made a mental note to get a pair of sunglasses before they left Fairbanks for the drive to Devon and Julie's house.

As Aaron leaned into the rear cargo area, he froze. It took a second, but he was positive he had just seen an Asian man staring at him over a car, two aisles over. Aaron quickly backed his body out and looked over in that direction. There was nothing—just the car as he remembered it. He frowned and tried to shake it off, but he couldn't get rid of the nagging feeling that it was more than the sun playing tricks on his eyes. What he and the Asian man didn't notice was the glint from a pair of field glasses at the opposite edge of the parking lot.

Their drive was relatively quiet. Both Lana and Aaron were tired from their flight—too tired to notice the car that had followed them through Fairbanks as they purchased Aaron's sunglasses and a bottle of expensive wine to give Devon and Julie. That same car was still behind them.

It wasn't until they were about an hour out of Fairbanks that Aaron finally noticed the tail. He woke Lana, who had been catnapping on and off, and said in a matter-of-fact tone, "I think we're being followed."

Lana brushed her hair off her face and looked behind her. "Are you sure?"

"It's hard to say. I didn't notice the car until an hour ago and we haven't passed any roads for the car to turn off on. This is a fairly desolate stretch."

"How far are we from the McKenzie place?"

Aaron looked at his in-dash navigation guide and said, "It shows about another half hour."

"Fairly isolated out here, aren't they?"

"He lived far worse than this for four years, and as far as I know, she grew up here and loves it."

"How would something like this suit you?"

Aaron was taken aback. Was she projecting some sort of life for the two of them? He wasn't sure, but if she was, he liked where she was headed. "That depends on who I was with."

Aaron looked again at the rearview mirror just in time to see the car turn off onto a small road he had just passed. "I guess I was a little paranoid about that car—it just turned off. I didn't tell you, but when I was loading the luggage, I could have sworn that I saw Kyong Ran staring at me from a car a couple of aisles away. When I stood up to get a better look, there was no one—just the car."

"Was that the same car that was behind us?"

"It looked like it. Yes, I think it could have been."

Maybe we're both overly tired. Three days ago, we were in France—now we're in Alaska. It could be jet lag. However, after all we've been through, I can't disregard your concern. Let's stay vigilant."

"Okay, I guess."

Aaron kept driving and their tempting conversation seemed to have drawn to an end. Lana noticed and with her face staring out the window, she murmured, "There's something that I need to tell you, Aaron. It's been so long since…well, since I've let myself feel…I mean, I have always, you know…"

"Are you trying to say that you love me?"

"Yes!" she blurted out as she turned around to look at him square in the eye. "Yes, Aaron, I love you. There! I've said it."

Aaron smiled, reached over, and pulled Lana in for a kiss. "I can't tell you how long I've waited to hear you say those words. I love you too, Lana."

As they drove along, they both contemplated what this new commitment meant. After a while, Aaron broke the silence. "Looks like their house should be off this next dirt road."

Lana strained her tired eyes and said, "There it is—on the left. Wow, looks like a nice place. You Americans can certainly live well."

Aaron reached down and squeezed her hand. "I hope the term 'you

Americans' will soon apply to you as well."

Devon and Julie hurried out the front door as soon as the SUV crunched to a stop on the gravel drive. They hadn't counted on their visitors stopping in Fairbanks and had been anxiously awaiting them.

When the introductions, hugs, and kisses had run their course, Julie waved her arm and motioned for Lana to come in. Lana glanced back toward their luggage.

"Listen girl, let the men get it. It's a great way to keep men as gentlemen. And allow them to open our doors—it's a nice civilized gesture."

"But—"

"No buts," she said with a twinkle in her eye, "just give them a little smile of appreciation and a thank-you. That's how we keep them well trained."

CHAPTER 47

WHEN DINNER WAS FINISHED, THE FOUR RETIRED TO THE great room and opened the bottle of wine that Aaron and Lana had brought. Halfway into the bottle, Devon sat pensive for a moment. Finally, he looked up and said, "I've had some time the last couple of days to do some thinking, and Julie and I have come up with a thought or two. I...*we* think the four of us could make a great team." There! It's out in the open, he thought.

Lana looked at Aaron, who seemed as confused as she was. She turned her palms to an open position and asked, "What are you talking about?"

"I'm talking about us—us as a foursome. You know...in business together. We could form a company that works with, but outside of, the government. Doing...you know...what we do. I mean, what we've just done—in Russia and France. And if you wonder what Julie might bring to the table, well, she's as good on a computer as anyone I've ever met. As far as action goes, she just survived an attack by two al-Qaida terrorists and is here to talk about it."

"Slow down, cowboy!" Julie said. "Let's not forget that some very brave agents died to protect me, and in the end, *you* still saved me."

Aaron was the first to break the silence that ensued. "Are you suggesting that we form a company that would provide intelligence services to the government?"

"Yes."

"But you, Julie, and I already work for the CIA. What's to be gained?"

"Well, the fact is, the government pays out far more in professional fees for security and whatever than it costs them to use their own people. We would be able to follow our own hunches and leads without all the bureaucratic red tape that only stifles what we do best. And to have someone like Lana to sniff out corruption, well...I like the idea."

Aaron had a distant look on his face and then looked at Lana. She raised her eyebrows and pursed her lips as if to say, why not? Aaron returned the look and with a serious face, looked at Devon and said, "Well, I've got two serious questions. First: Where will we be based? You know, as in headquarters?"

Julie looked at Devon and motioned for him to handle this one.

"We had a long talk on this one, ourselves. Julie's primary duties would be on the computer and doing field support and coordination. She's comfortable enough to be here by herself and is reasonably sure that she can defend herself, if I add better security equipment. If there is a crisis, we'll add some private security contractors. But she also wants to do a certain amount of field ops. If Lana is not with us in the field, then she can stay here with Julie, if she chooses. We'd like to have our headquarters right here. We've got the acreage to grow as the business expands, and you and Lana could move in with us until you decide where you want to live. That could be here on the compound...in DC... in California...wherever. That's the beauty of what we do—we can do it anywhere. May I remind you, Fairbanks is as close to Russia as you're going to get, Lana."

Aaron looked over to Lana and read her sign of approval. "Okay, my second question is: How about the name Phantom Four?"

Devon glanced at Lana and Julie, and with a smile, raised his glass. "Sounds like something out of a comic book...but I like it! To the Phantom Four?"

"To the Phantom Four!" was the resounding toast.

***

The clock chimed midnight; Julie and Svetlana had gone to bed, and Devon and Aaron were nursing a Lagavulin scotch, neat. Their legs rested nicely on ottomans and their bodies were slouched down into the sofas with the scotch snifters resting on their stomachs. All seemed well, but their work on the current situation wasn't finished—Phantom Four would have to wait.

Devon spoke about it first. "So, what does Hatcher recommend, or are we to improvise?"

"Let me put it this way: Lana and I are here on a well-earned vacation, and where you take us sightseeing is up to you. We're free to enjoy ourselves at Uncle Sam's expense. Now if we happen to stumble on someone trying to blow up the pipeline…well, we *do* have an obligation to react—in the interest of national security, of course."

"I like your thinking—that is, Hatcher's. If I were a betting man, I'd bet that you have already done several algorithms that show the likely targets. "

"Right on, brother. Pull up a map, paper or electronic, and I'll show you my conclusions—not my equations, mind you."

Devon got up to retrieve a map and mumbled, "I don't know what Lana sees in a geek like you."

"Guess it's my curly hair."

Devon returned and noticed that Aaron hadn't moved. "Where are your notes? Aren't you going to get them?" he asked.

Amazingly, Aaron had committed every coordinate to memory, stored in his head in descending order of probability. Devon cleared the coffee table and spread a large map out.

"Here," Aaron said, placing his finger on the map. "This is numero uno." His finger rested on an area just north of the Arctic Circle latitude. He slid down to an area southeast of Fairbanks and declared, "And this is the big number two."

Devon stood with his mouth hanging open; a puzzled look written all over his face. "What about where the pipeline crosses the Yukon River? I mean, it doesn't take an algorithm to figure out that a massive oil spill into a river that cuts Alaska in half would do the most damage."

"Ah," Aaron said, sitting up and preening like a peacock. "That's the difference between a SoCal man and a CalSci genius. We CalSci dudes never assume the obvious." His smile disappeared into a look that begged attention. "And neither do the Asians."

Deflated, Devon sat down and poured himself another Lagavulin, knowing full well that he was about to be taken to school and get "the rest of the story"…and that might take a while.

"You see, the Yukon River Bridge was designed to span a half of a mile using an orthotropic box girder design. What is most peculiar is that its design, meant to handle seismic earthquakes, was twenty years ahead of its time. It not only carries the oil pipeline, but also carries the Dalton Highway as well as a natural gas pipeline. The ability to blow up this bridge would require engineering analysis to the nth degree. The bridge was designed in only three months, but its engineering is so complex that, although anything made can be blown up, the study to blow this one up and leave a gaping rupture spewing oil, natural gas, and debris would require a degree of sophistication that is probably not available in North Korea—especially considering the time available."

"Then what's with the two points?"

"The two points are pump stations 5 and 11. PS5 is a relief and re-injection site. It has an RGV, which is, to the great unwashed like you, a remote gate valve. This valve is actually intended to open and divert a large volume of oil into a holding tank, thus protecting segments of the line in the event of a catastrophic pipeline break."

"And that means…?"

"You can't just shut down the pipeline with the snap of a finger. The backup pressure from a sudden stoppage would be so great that it would cause ruptures in a half dozen locations behind it before the pipeline is fully shut down, thus isolating sections of it. Think of trying to stop a roaring freight train on a dime—all of the cars it was pulling would crash into the one in front, each with its own momentum, crumbling into a massive ball of destruction. Now remember, the pipeline is forty-eight inches wide, no matter where it is. So the environmental damage, as long as it spills into any tributary that connects to the Yukon River, would be exactly the same as being right over it!"

Devon nodded his head in agreement and cracked a smile. He knew Aaron had done his homework and Devon was proud of him. "What about the second point, southeast of Fairbanks?"

"That's where the pipeline crosses the Gulkana River with a conventional suspension design—easy to take down and right in the heart of the Copper River Delta."

"Yeah, that delta is the largest wetlands complex on the Pacific Coast of North America," added Devon. "You devastate that river and you demolish the salmon industry for years."

"Exactly. In my calculations, I've taken into account the flow rate and the time sequence of oil flowing in the Tazlina River and then dumping into the Copper River. Even under perfect weather conditions and allowing for a quick response, an infusion of oil will pass all the containment sites on the Tazlina that were built to stop the flow and will absolutely dump into the Copper River. The estimated response time for containment is a little over six hours. Now here's the kicker: The pipeline service company has no—no as in zip, zero, nada—containment sites on the Copper River to address such a disaster. My calculations show that if a breach in the pipeline released oil into the Tazlina River, that oil would be eighteen miles down the Copper River, past the confluence of the Tazlina and the Copper Rivers, all *within* those six hours."

Devon whistled and shook his head. "Looks like our government's at its bureaucratic best again."

"Should oil actually enter any of the rivers crossed by the pipeline, it's unlikely that a high percentage of oil would be recovered by any one containment site on these fast-moving, multiple-channel rivers. I'm telling you, *none* of their design or containment models really address terrorism breaches. This pipeline was designed prior to 1975. What was our geopolitical thinking in 1975?"

Devon scrunched his face and answered, "The Cold War. Who could possibly have foreseen the events of 9/11?"

"Bingo! We didn't even begin to see terrorism like we know today for another twenty-five years. Those engineers were concerned with seismic disruptions and mechanical failures, not terrorist attacks. It's all ivory tower conjecture—you know, like your car being rated for nineteen miles per gallon on the highway, and no matter what you do, you can't get but fifteen…and that's downhill."

"Are there more of these RGV valves?"

"Yeah, up to seventy of them."

"What's to prevent the control center from operating all of the other RGVs? Certainly that should minimize the disaster."

"Everything is controlled by the OCC—that's the Operations Control Center in Valdez. SCADA, or Supervisory Control and Data Acquisition, monitors and controls these remote facilities. Everything operates through a data general minicomputer at the OCC, but…are you ready for this? Either the OCC or *any* local pump station can override and control *all* of the line's RGVs!"

Devon ran his fingers through his hair and squeezed the back of his neck in exasperation. "Holy shit! So, if a terrorist knows what he's doing…"

"You got it, brother."

"Let me guess: This computer system can also be hacked?"

"North Korea has already had incidents of hacking into the Pentagon. And may I remind you, this is *not* the Pentagon?"

"Why, then, did you put the Copper River Delta as the second choice?" asked Devon.

"Distance, SoCal, just distance. Remember, they're supposed to land somewhere in the Norton Sound area. That presumes the Yukon River as their delivery vehicle."

"Why wouldn't they split up, with one half traveling southeast, and get them both?" Devon asked.

"That would be too big an operation. That would require doubling the size of the mission; men, boats, and materiel, which increases the possibility of them being seen by someone—too many risks. They would have to split their group to hit the pipeline simultaneously, and then wait for the other half to return to the Yukon River and use it to escape back to Norton Sound. Or they'd have to wait for the first half to travel south, rejoin them, and then use the Copper River to exit to the Gulf of Alaska…all of this with too many saboteurs—my algorithm says it's not feasible."

"So, you think they will hit PS5 in the center, travel south and hit PS11, and then what? Take the long way out by going back north to the Yukon and down to Norton Sound where their sub picks them up? Or redirect the sub to the Gulf of Alaska and take the short way out—in the most crowded waterway of Alaska?"

"What does your analytical, Western mind think?" asked Aaron.

"If PS5 blows first, followed by PS11, I would look south for their exit. That's where I would concentrate the surveillance of the drones and troops."

"Exactly! But the Asian mind might do the unexpected and go back up north. My algorithm deals with the most likely scenario—until I plug in the Asian mind. That's when it changes. "

"I know—you're blinding me with science. Listen, I've lived in this wilderness for over five years of my life and you just took me back to school. Well done, CalSci. But…my gut isn't sold on the escape route."

CHAPTER 48

THE FULL MOON AND CLEAR SKIES WERE GIVING DAE Dong's crew fits. Tensions were high and the men were bone tired. They were having a hard enough time battling the swift current, but now their leader seemed edgy and irritable. The men were growing disgruntled by his constant demands. He doesn't touch a paddle himself, yet he constantly harps for more speed yet less noise, a crewmember thought. The two don't go together.

Dig and pull, dig and pull—their lungs burned as if on fire. The night seemed as if it would never end, that they would never pass the island that hid them from the small town on the river.

Ul al-Sarary, one of the Yemeni hostages that was intended to be sacrificed at one of the pump stations, had been busy sliding his snap-tie arm restraints across the blade of a collapsed military shovel, hoping to free himself. He had seen the lights of the town as they approached Nulato. When the island obscured them, he knew this might be his only chance. He pressed down harder on the shovel blade in spite of the snap tie cutting into his flesh.

Feeling it finally break, al-Sarary felt warm blood flow again in his arms. The Koreans had secured him to one of the raft rings with a nylon rope, which was rendered useless when his arms separated. Fortunately for him, they had made a larger mistake in not securing his feet with restraints.

Dae Dong was the first to hear the splash as al-Sarary rolled overboard into the river. Dae Dong lunged for his assault rifle, but thought better about the noise it would create. He motioned to his best commando to go in pursuit. The man stripped his shirt off and had his knife in his teeth within seconds.

"He must be brought back alive. *Alive*! Do you hear me?"

The commando nodded, jumped overboard, and began swimming hard, the cold water a shock to his system. The Yemeni never looked back. His concentration was on reaching the island's shore and nothing else. He could swim, but not well; al-Qaida had never emphasized swimming in any of their training.

As his feet touched the gravel of the shoreline, al-Sarary could hear the commando gaining on him. He could even hear the man's lungs pull the air in with every third stroke.

There! The Yemeni saw the smoldering embers of a camper's fire as he ran stooped over toward the campsite. He wasn't the brightest bulb in the chandelier, but al-Sarary knew exactly what the North Koreans had planned for him and this campsite represented his only chance to stay alive.

Just as he raised his arms and opened his mouth to scream, a heavy weight encompassed his shoulders and a hand placed an iron grip over his mouth. His body collapsed under the weight and the commando's other fist delivered a knockout blow. The Korean lay on top of the hostage as his eyes honed in on the two tents. A man came out of one of the tents and seconds later, another emerged.

"Did you hear that noise? It sounded like a large thud."

"You don't think it could be a bear, do ya?"

"Don't know—better get your rifle. I'll stay here and see if anything moves."

The commando tightened his grip on al-Sarary's mouth, just in case, and with his other hand, he pulled his knife from between his teeth. Every muscle in his body went into attack mode. He knew he could handle the campers. It was the collateral damage that he worried about. His captain would be furious if they had to make this look like another bear attack.

The second camper came out of his tent with his hunting rifle and a bewildered female in tow, cowering behind him. As he approached the first camper, his arm rose upward and presented him with a revolver. "Where's Jenny?" he asked.

"Still sleeping, I guess."

The first man spun the cylinder of his revolver, making sure it was fully loaded. He moved over to the fire pit and threw two logs onto the smoldering fire. A huge plume of sparks shot upward.

"Damn it!" the second said. "Why don't you just start singing 'Kumbaya' and ask whatever is out there to join us for cookies and milk?"

He followed with his girl, sat down on a log, and put his rifle across his lap. "Crap, I don't know what it could be if it isn't a bear."

"Well, it sure as hell isn't Sasquatch and this isn't a beef jerky commercial. The thought of a Kodiak coming into camp makes my ass pucker."

The commando's tension grew exponentially as he debated whether to go in and kill them all. He knew the Yemeni wouldn't stay unconscious much longer, and now there was a rifle and a revolver that he had to contend with. He also knew that Dae Dong wouldn't tolerate any more lost time. He wasn't sure if there was enough time left to sneak by the airport, and even if there was, that window of opportunity was fast running out.

Then, as if some god had smiled on him, he heard underbrush moving on the other side of the campsite. A short, low snort was delivered. The campers jumped to their feet and raised their weapons in a defensive position aimed away from the commando. The woman screeched and dove into her tent. The men dropped to their knees and trained their flashlights and weapons in the direction of the snort.

The Korean moved on instinct. He cut the sleeves off the hostage's shirt. He cut the cuffs off and stuffed them into al-Sarary's mouth, and with a hard tug, he wrapped and cinched the rest of the sleeve around the gaping mouth. Slowly, he raised himself up and hoisted the Yemeni over his shoulder. Within minutes he had slipped away. As he fought the strong current back to the boat, his lungs burned in pain. He was grateful the hostage had not stirred or given him additional resistance.

When his hand finally reached up and grabbed the rope of the boat, Dae Dong was in front of him and irritated. "What took you so long? This time, tie him up like a wild pig." He snapped his wrist up and looked at his watch. As he turned and looked eastward, the horizon was showing the first signs of sunrise.

"Move out!" he growled.

***

With the island behind them, they had lost their cover as they attempted to pass the airport. Dae Dong ordered his crew to shut off the motors, forcing the crew to again struggle with the heavy current of the Yukon River.

"Dig! Dig!" he said, sounding like a broken record. The men were lean and muscular, but pushed beyond their endurance. The current proved to be too strong. Dae Dong knew the sun would be up momentarily and the dawn's light would highlight them against the eastern shoreline.

They still had a half mile to travel and the captain realized his only chance was to risk the noise of the motors, even at low throttle, over having their boats silhouetted in the water by spotlights.

"Turn on the motors and set the throttles for ten knots," he said.

The hum of the outboard motors as they broke the morning silence startled even him. Dae Dong gnashed his teeth and prayed they wouldn't be seen or heard, but they had no choice but to risk everything. Finally, they passed the last spotlight of the runway. He breathed easier. When upstream a good distance, he became confident no one had seen them and gave his order, "Prepare to turn off the main river on my command." When they found the intersection of the Koyukuk River, Dae Dong swung his boat northward into its mouth, where Team One would proceed alone under the leadership of Lieutenant Kim. He again breathed easier, as the Koyukuk was a smaller river with a less turbulent current; plus Team One would have only two small towns to pass before arriving at PS5. He found his confidence in this part of the mission returning. Perhaps it can be accomplished, he thought.

CHAPTER 49

TO ANYONE WHO WAS BLESSED ENOUGH TO RECEIVE AN invitation to enter, Jonathon Van Leuwen's office carried the trendy moniker of uber-plush. Not only did it have generous square footage, soaring ceilings, and a spectacular glass wall that presented a commanding view of the city's skyline, it also possessed all the accoutrements that were expected of the power and privilege it bespoke. The finest works of New York's past and current rising artists adorned its walls. Its bar held the crème de la crème in spirits, from cognacs to vodkas. Contrasting with the ultra-modern decor was a massive, antique desk that had once served a Pope that had held court in Avignon, France. Even his impressive collection of first-edition books was not the result of a labor of love, but had been selected, book by book, by a grand dame of decorating who rode the social circuit with widely exposed cleavage, an unlimited budget, and a keen nose for large commissions.

Jonathon Van Leuwen was young, good looking, and carried himself with an arrogance that was born of the confidence he had in himself and his inherited position. That confidence was not fleeting, but real. After all, he was one of the chosen ones. His Dutch family had long ties to New York's financial world—ties that could be traced to the immigrants who founded New Amsterdam in 1613 and later renamed it New York City.

After receiving his master's degree from Harvard, young Van Leuwen was put on a fast track that wound its way through the labyrinth of global hedge funds. He now worked for one of New York's largest banks and held the vice chairman seat on the Federal Reserve's Board of Governors. He was part of a world that had no time for mundane tasks, let alone the paying of taxes or reporting one's real income. He didn't even know his own income. What did it matter? He was born into such a vast empire that it had never crossed his mind.

On his desk was his smartphone, which his colleagues and friends used to contact him, but in his left pocket was a special phone—a phone to which no more than a half dozen people had access. Even his wife was not one of those privileged few. When it vibrated against his leg, Van Leuwen motioned to his well-endowed secretary to leave the room. When the heavy, ten-foot-tall, bronze door closed, he looked once more at the caller ID and answered the call.

"Is this call necessary?" he asked.

"Of course it's necessary. Or maybe you'd prefer to meet at some public restaurant?"

"No. What's this call about?"

"The last NSA meeting."

"What happened?"

"CIA's Hatcher—I told you in my last call that he knows about the North Korean connection to the Trans-Oceanic oil rig."

"So? What has changed? It's my understanding that the president was able to put a damper on that."

"What has changed is that Hatcher is like a starved bloodhound. He had another meeting with the president and told him he has discovered chatter about a connection between the NSA and the Federal Reserve."

"Maybe he's just on a fishing trip. How do we know if he really has anything?"

"And what if he's not bluffing? If he accessed our bundled campaign funds, you know damn well where that could lead."

"He's not allowed to do domestic surveillance. You're making too much out of this."

"Half of those funds come from overseas, and did you not agree to have AmeriCorps Bank make thirteen odious transfers to prop up the Greek government—as in overseas? Yes, he can follow the money trail. And do I need to remind you of just how powerful the CIA is? I think you'd better brief Sarris, so he can inform the families. They will want to be out in front of this."

CHAPTER 50

HATCHER SAT ALONE IN HIS OFFICE. MIDNIGHT WAS AP-proaching, and he rubbed his tired eyes. For once, the CIA Director didn't have an early meeting the next day, and on these kinds of nights, he appreciated the fact that he had no one to go home to. His cigar was only half consumed, so he poured another glass of Blanton's single barrel bourbon. In one motion, he kicked his feet up on his desk and stretched to reach the photograph of the Chateau d'Arbonne that barely caught the desk's edge.

Everything springs from this fortress, he thought. Beautiful place, but why is it that getting any information on this place is like walking through a dark forest at night? I run the most powerful spy agency in the world, but every which way I turn ends up in a shroud of secrecy—one rabbit hole after another.

He turned the photo in his fingers and mulled over his dilemma. If I can't get anywhere, I may have to lay this photo on the president's plate and see how he reacts while I feed him a few lines of bullshit.

The bourbon slowly trickled down his throat, giving him a warm feeling inside that grabbed his thoughts and pulled him momentarily away from the conundrum at hand. When the president's face reap-peared in his mind, guilt descended upon Hatcher.

I should have more loyalty to the guy, he thought. He *did* appoint me to the directorship, after all. But damn it, it's still my country that I'm sworn to protect. I guess it's hard to believe that he's involved in some misdeed that's contrary to the country's interest, yet I can't ignore my gut, and it's been roiling ever since his and LaSpesa's reaction to my discussion of the North Korean connection.

He took another glance at the chateau and another sip of his Blan-ton's. He cracked a smile and murmured to himself, "You are indeed beautiful to look at and truly appear to be a lady of high stature, but even the finest of ladies can hold secrets. And sooner, rather than later, I will get a peek under your lovely skirt."

CHAPTER 51

JULIE HEARD THE LOW RINGING OF AN ALARM CLOCK IN the guest room. Rolling over, she felt the empty side of the bed and noticed that Devon was already up. The master bath shower reported that water had just been turned off. She was bone tired and wanted to sleep longer, but figured the men must be up to something, and her instincts told her that it couldn't be good. As she entered the bathroom, Devon looked up from under the towel that was drying his head and gave her a smile.

"Sorry, honey, I didn't want to wake you just yet."

That was all that was needed to confirm her suspicions. She pulled the towel from his head and said, "Just when were you going to tell me that you and Aaron are up to something—a trip to where?"

"I was going to make coffee and then wake you up. Aaron and I decided last night to take a trip to Fairbanks. We want to check out the bridge that carries the Dalton Highway and the pipeline over the Yukon. While we're there, we'll stop at the pipeline field office and check out some details. You know, just to rule out—"

"I know the bridge well, Devon; don't insult me. Look, if we're going to do this Phantom Four thing together, it's going to have to be based on mutual trust, respect, and work. There won't be any of this 'I can't tell the little woman anything to protect her' malarkey."

"You're right. I'm sorry...Aaron believes that terrorists are going to attack the pipeline at pump station 5, which is just north of the Arctic Circle. He ran an algorithm on where the attack would most likely occur. After he went to bed, I stayed up and tried to blow holes in his theory, but I couldn't—it's a brilliant piece of work. However, there are possible flaws in how Aaron projects them exiting the country. I need to see some things in person to make sure everything squares in my head too. We need to leave the day after tomorrow for PS5. We're going into Fairbanks today to pick up some additional gear to outfit Aaron—you know, California dude and all."

"What about me—and Lana? Are you telling me that you're going to leave us out in the cold?"

"I was going to tell you over coffee."

"Uh-huh. I have a better idea. Lana and I will go into Fairbanks with you today, and I'll show her the city while you two do whatever it is that you have to do."

"Sounds good." Devon's face turned sober. "I'm sorry, Julie. You're right about everything. No more secrets. Maybe this morning we can show our guests that pair of AR-14s that we bought. You know, squeeze off a few rounds to get Lana comfortable. Then we can go to Fairbanks."

"Sounds like a plan—wish I had thought of it. Kind of a Phantom Four plan, wouldn't you say?"

"I don't want to leave you alone again. By the way, more agents arrive tomorrow afternoon. Besides, with the way you handled yourself the other day, do we really need them?"

"That's funny—real funny. All the talented comedians out of work and with my luck, I get you," Julie said. "Get dressed…I'll make the coffee."

CHAPTER 52

THE MORPHING OF KYONG RAN FROM CRIMINAL MASTER-mind to cheap assassin with an obsession was now complete. No longer could he contain his rage toward the four people who had thwarted his every move across the globe. In his mind, his plan had been perfect, and this denial of personal failure fed the cancer of his twisted compulsion. Day after day, his only thoughts were the immediate deaths of Goren-kov and McKenzie's wife. He still planned torturous deaths for Agents McKenzie and Cohen, but first he wanted their loved ones killed. Only in this way could he physically feel their pain. Only in this way could he tell them it was he, Kyong Ran, who tore their hearts out before he put a bullet between each of their eyes.

***

While Devon and Aaron procured gear at an outfitter in Fairbanks, they also picked up more ammo to use on their trip. Their gear included four Kevlar bulletproof vests—one for each of the Phantom Four members.

With Devon's vehicle loaded, the pair reconnoitered the bridge and Aaron pointed out in detail why he gave it low priority on the pipeline target list. Devon concurred and they returned to Fairbanks to find the women.

***

Kyong Ran had maintained surveillance on the four and had followed them into Fairbanks at a safe distance. When Devon and Aaron dropped the women off in the downtown area, Ran parked his car and followed them on the sidewalks. As they hailed a cab, he was close enough to hear them give orders to drive to the Pump House restaurant. Ran felt the heat of a twisted adrenalin rush. It was the killing hour. He knew the restaurant would be packed and he could take them out there. He ran back, got into his rental car, and caught up to the taxi by the second traffic light. Ran pulled his Sig Sauer pistol out and screwed a silencer onto its barrel. He pulled the slide back and loaded the first bullet into its chamber before returning the pistol to his jacket. He took a deep breath through his nose and filled his lungs. He smelled blood and it was intoxicating.

As he entered the historic restaurant, he saw the two women being seated on a verandah overlooking the river. When the hostess approached him, he requested a seat outdoors as well, but was told his wait would be a few moments. After a short wait, Ran began to fidget. He had clicked into killing mode and the wait was beginning to rattle him.

When the hostess tapped him on the arm, asking him to follow her to his seat, he nearly jumped.

Kyong Ran sat down and feigned reading the menu, but his eyes never stopped scanning the environment. He not only needed an opportunity to kill, he also needed to create maximum chaos for a clean and swift exit. When a waiter came to take his order, Ran asked for an unsweetened tea while he formulated his plan. Over and over, he raised the menu to keep his distinctively Korean face from being recognized by Lana.

***

Julie kept their conversation light, as she didn't feel comfortable asking Lana about her Russian past. She mainly concentrated on selling Lana the benefits of living in Fairbanks. As far as cities went, Fairbanks was a far cry from the urban sprawl of Moscow, and Julie was worried about the cultural shock.

Reacting to her days as an investigative journalist, Lana's eyes continually scanned her environment, all the while maintaining her focus on their conversation. Julie was in her spiel about small-town America when Lana froze. All life came to an abrupt stop. It was him! She knew it. Kyong Ran had reentered her life. Lana immediately shifted her eyes away from Ran and carefully reached over and slid her hand over Julie's wrist.

"Keep looking at me and don't turn your head," she whispered.

"My God, Lana, what is it? You look like you've seen a ghost."

"I have," she whispered, tightening her grip on Julie's wrist. "There's a man sitting alone a few tables over on your right. I'm a hundred percent sure he's Kyong Ran—the North Korean who masterminded all the attempts on my life in Moscow. I caught a glimpse of him at a dacha as he backed away in a car. It's him, alright. I know it is."

Julie's CIA training kicked in. She knew her 38 Special was in her unzipped purse. She looked over the surroundings away from Ran and took into account the potential collateral damage if there was a shootout. She casually took a drink of water, looking past and around the Korean, formulating their best and safest exit strategy. Her eyes locked back on Lana.

"He's sitting with his right hand in his coat pocket—as if he's holding something. My guess is that it's a silenced pistol."

"What do we do?" asked Lana.

"We've got to quickly separate—that negates his ability to use his gun without pulling it out of his coat. I'm going to feign a trip to the restroom. I'll see if I can't get behind him without him seeing me. If he makes a sudden move when I stand, make a dive for the floor—it'll be your only chance."

"What if I'm wrong and it's not him?"

"No time—just shift in your chair so only your side is facing him. Do it now!"

As Lana shifted, Julie wiped her lips with her napkin, placed it on the table, and stood up. Ran followed suit. He pulled his pistol from his jacket and aimed it at Lana. From behind her, Julie heard a short, telltale spitting sound and dove to cover Lana. It was a shot, but it was one that had pierced the forehead of Kyong Ran. His body froze in place, his eyes wide open. He remained motionless, slightly tilting as blood began to spill over his eyebrow. His body fell over his table, sending everything sprawling. Patrons began screaming in horror.

Julie pushed hard on Lana's shoulder, forcing them both to crash to the floor. A second shot from the same direction grazed Lana's upper arm between Julie's fingers. As mayhem ensued, Ran's killer disappeared as quickly as he had come.

Julie's training never left her. She remained covering Lana when her cell phone rang in. She stretched to reach her purse and pull it out. The ID showed that it was Devon.

"Devon! Where are you?" she screamed, while fumbling the phone. "I thought it was *you* who killed the Korean."

"Killed the Korean? What are you talking about? Julie! Are you okay—what's going on?"

"Lana and I are alright—we're at the Pump House. Get here! Fast!"

***

Devon threw his screeching SUV into park as they reached the restaurant, slamming Aaron's forehead onto the dashboard with a thud. They had beaten the police. Both men jumped from the vehicle and raced through the mass hysteria of people. Devon had his Glock chambered and held low against his side. When he saw Julie helping Lana to her feet, his heart leapt and his pistol returned to its concealed holster. He slammed his way through the last of the crowd and grabbed her in his arms. Aaron followed in the path cleared by Devon, grabbed Lana, and held her to him. Kyong Ran lay below them in an ever-spreading pool of blood.

As Aaron tried to guide Lana away from Ran's fallen mass, she pulled away and knelt down next to his lifeless body. It took all the courage she could muster to place her fingers on his carotid artery and verify that he was dead. After grabbing Aaron's arm and pulling herself back up, she leaned over again and spit on Ran's corpse. "Burn in hell, you bastard!" She spit again. "Burn for Yakov—burn for Evgeny—burn for all eternity!"

CHAPTER 53

OVAL OFFICE
WASHINGTON, DC

THE PRESIDENT APPEARED EXHAUSTED. IT WASN'T ANY ONE of the myriad of world crises in the making causing his weariness; it was the daily rigors of Washington's political life. His tie was pulled down, his collar was open, and his sleeves were rolled up. More than that, he had a hang-dog look that signaled he was reaching the end of his rope with politics. His NSA director sat across from him on the sofa, knowing full well his words would have to be carefully selected. He glanced at his watch and sighed.

"Mr. President—"

"Hang on a second, Jim. I'm tired…It's this job. It has turned me into nothing more than some sort of political hack. I fly off to Hawaii and pretend I'm there for whatever half-baked reason, yet all I do is grovel for more money. This reelection is going to cost upward of a billion dollars, and—"

"Mr. President, much of that will come from PACS," LaSpesa interrupted.

"People are already complaining that I vacation too much."

"Well, you can't keep telling the American people that you won't take money from lobbyists if you have to fundraise right here in the White House. Besides, you know as well as I do that it's illegal to do it here."

"You're not hearing me, Jim. These vacations are nothing more than a few of rounds of golf and spending the rest of the time shaking down sycophant fat cats for money. I'm damn sick of it."

"Well, at least the media's still on our side and reporting them as working vacations."

"That's all well and fine, but they only report it that way because their bosses tell them to…and why? Because they gain their power from the position of influence we give in return. It's called being in the tank for us, Jim."

"Is that so bad? I mean, they *do* share our political agenda."

"They rail against lobbyists, but what in the hell do they think *they* are? They're lobbyists too—just with a different name. My God, I feel like I can't even wipe my ass without first checking to see whom I might offend. Money, position, and power, that's all that matters in this town."

"Wait a minute—are you not seeing the reality of it all? Everyone is a lobbyist. You, in fact, lobbied the American people for this position by promising jobs, a better economy, lower taxes—you *bought* their votes the same as any lobbyist. And you're doing it all over again. Washington is a pack of savage hounds, each chasing the tail in front of them. It's just the way it is, and it isn't about to change anytime soon. Besides, you knew all this going in."

"Yeah, you're right, I did know it—I even loved it. But now I've grown weary of it. So how and when do I get out of the vicious cycle?"

"If and when you're defeated, I guess, Mr. President."

Coleridge looked at his glass, tilted and whirled the whiskey inside, and stared at the long legs his action produced. "I'm just like this whiskey, Jim. The New York money people swirl me around in a glass until they get the results they want."

LaSpesa cleared his throat and carefully couched his words. "Speaking of the New York people, we need to move on and talk about the matter of…why we are willing to bury, or let's say, keep secret, what the North Koreans may have done in the Gulf of Mexico."

Coleridge blew his stack. "Damn it! Let's stop all this '*we*' shit. *I* didn't know about it until *after* the deed was done! You and those money grubbers are the ones who talked me into turning a blind eye."

"We did what we thought was in the best interest of the country—period!" said LaSpesa.

"That doesn't cut it anymore. I'm sick and tired of dealing with the heat from that crummy decision."

"Mr. President, I understand…but we *were* made aware of the contents of the Russian naval report before it was written. And we *did* keep the information from the American people."

"I wasn't even sure that it was true! And you advised me not to confront the North Koreans at that time."

"Remember, we were continuing to clean things up in Iraq, and the situation in Afghanistan was rotten to the core. The American people wouldn't have tolerated another military action. Besides, BP was somehow convinced that they were in the wrong. We had our scapegoat and someone to pay for the cleanup," LaSpesa said.

"I should have insisted that it go through the whole security group instead of kowtowing to the Fed's people."

"Again, I understand; however, it was still *you* that made the final decision to stand down and bury the story."

Coleridge took another long hit and drained his glass. Silence held as both men passed the bottle and refilled their own glasses. Neither was keen on looking the other in the eye. Their collective fall from grace had a price that couldn't be ignored, couldn't be denied.

LaSpesa took a gulp of his drink and mustered the courage to continue. "In the final analysis, I guess it comes down to how much longer we are willing to continue the dance."

"Dance? You're spinning it to be a dance? Go ahead and say it, Jim—you mean the *cover-up!*"

"Alright! The cover-up," LaSpesa blurted out. "The money trail will remain buried—the families will make sure of that. We just need to keep up the illusion of national security as our only motivation."

"No matter how you dress up the pig, Van Leuwen dictated to us the directive of the families. Quid pro quo! And if that ever gets out, Jim, no one in this country will believe that it was in their best interests."

LaSpesa allowed the president's words to hang. After a deep breath he said, "We do have one small problem...the two CIA agents and that Russian journalist...they have some sort of evidence that they uncovered at a place in Aquitaine, France called the Chateau d'Arbonne. Hatcher's playing coy and hasn't shared everything he has with me, but apparently the families have conducted ultra-secret meetings there."

CHAPTER 54

CAPTAIN DONG CHECKED HIS GPS. HIS DEMOLITION TEAM One should have been in the right place at PS5 and ready for the third phase of his operation. They had to get off the river, secure their boat, and turn east on foot to reach the Alaska Pipeline's PS5 valve. His Team Two had gone as far as they could go by the Tanana River, and now prepared to cross the Big Delta range by truck where they would again inflate their Zodiac boat and continue south to PS11. He had to admit, everything that Kyong Ran said that he would have in place was exactly that; from the Zodiacs and the additional buried fuel to the truck needed to cross the Big Delta—all in pinpoint locations. So far, everything was on schedule.

With the GPS signal acknowledged, his mouth twisted in a sardonic grin as he felt the satisfaction of knowing that he was about to deal a major blow to the nemesis country he had been raised to hate from birth. His jaw muscles tightened as his face twisted in anger.

Our people have starved because of you, he thought. You and your invincible army—ha! I will put your neck under my boot! You will choke on the black slime that will dump into your rivers, forcing an ecological disaster that will be felt for generations to come. Your salmon and tourist industry will die off for decades, your gasoline will be rationed out to an angry people, and you will be seen on the world stage as the hapless clowns you are. Worse, you won't even know who did it to you. You didn't defeat us before and you never will!

At PS5, the job of concealing the boat was arduous. The Koreans deflated and carried it inland, away from where anyone would look along the river. They dug two enormous holes, covering everything with tarps, and then meticulously buried their gear. When Dae Dong was satisfied that the site was as natural as when they arrived, he marked the GPS coordinates, raised his arm, and moved his men out toward PS5, kicking and shoving the al-Qaida hostages with them.

Dae Dong's plan was simple: His saboteurs would set their charges on the PS5 valve as well as critical sections of the pipeline well above the relief station. If the valve and the relief it provided were destroyed, multiple fissures would occur upstream of the break, as the backup pressure would exceed its design capabilities. The damage to PS11 at the Copper River would occur shortly *after* PS5, causing Homeland Security to assume the saboteurs would move east to escape into Canada. Dae Dong and his men, however, would move south to the Copper River in a daring dash to the Gulf of Alaska. Only this time, speed would be on their side as they wouldn't have the burden of taking the hostages with them.

CHAPTER 55

IN THE LARGE CONFERENCE ROOM, ANOTHER DAILY GATH-ering of the usual suspects was taking place. Representatives from CIA's Counterterrorism Unit (CTU), FBI's Counterterrorism Division (CTD), and their counterparts in the Department of Defense, among others, did their due diligence by attending. Unless there was an imminent crisis, the president rarely attended these meetings, but he did receive a daily report. The meeting started promptly when the last of Alaska's National Guard staff had taken their seats at the long conference table.

Secretary Jenna Martinez was only five foot two inches tall, so she assumed her usual tougher-than-you stance. She opened the meeting by grabbing a wooden pointer off the table and swinging the rubber tip to a monitor on the wall, where a diagram of the Alaska Pipeline was on display. Several attendees had to wait until their eyes rolled back down.

"People, our focus today is the ongoing chatter regarding a potential attack on the pipeline. The intel in your folders is murky, at best, but we are continuing to take this threat as serious and viable."

"Madam Secretary, is there any concrete evidence that an attack is imminent?" asked General Collins of Alaska's National Guard. "I mean, should we raise the threat level?"

"In spite of an enormous amount of chatter, there remain just two Mideastern—excuse me—one Mideastern and one American terrorist of whom we are aware. Both were killed in a shoot-out at an ex-CIA agent's house outside of Fairbanks. The van that transported these two terrorists has been thoroughly searched and forensics found nothing to change our assessment that they were acting alone. Their phones are being examined as we speak, but so far only prepaid phones were used—untraceable. Nonetheless, DHS released funds to increase pipeline surveillance by means of drone units."

"As I'm sure you are aware, Madam Secretary, Alaskans are an independent sort and would be uneasy about the appearance of these drones…well, let's say, spying on them."

"We fully understand, General, but those concerns are best handled by the politicians, are they not?"

"Where are these drones going to come from and when can we expect their deployment to be up and running?" asked the FBI's terrorism director.

"We will divert two from the Arizona border patrol. We have authorized a C-130 Hercules to go to Arizona where the drones are being disassembled and packed into their coffins as we speak. We will notify the Arizona governor today."

Waves of grumbling and jokes made their way around the table in quick order. All were centered on the current governor and a controversial sheriff.

"Did I say something funny?" asked Secretary Martinez. Her eyes circled the table, sending the room into dead silence.

Whacking the pointer into her open palm, she continued, her irritation out of control. "So, General Collins, look for that program to start right up, which means zero six hundred day after tomorrow."

The Secretary looked around the table for closure and then summarily dismissed the Alaska contingency before starting the next discussion.

Walking down the hall, General Collins commented to his aide, "More bullshit as usual. Nothing will come of this other than more red tape from the Pentagon. Mark my words, Major, for every drone that is put in place over any state, there will ultimately be a 5% cut in the funding of its National Guard troops."

"Should we raise our alert status?"

"Of course, but the decision on where to deploy our troops will have to wait until the wonks monitoring the results of those creepy fliers actually find something to be concerned about. Where do we start? The pipeline is eight hundred miles long."

"Understood, sir, and let's not forget that the pipeline is considered by the experts as virtually fail-safe, anyway. Major environmental damage from an attack just isn't going to happen."

"That is what they say, Major."

CHAPTER 56

FAIRBANKS, ALASKA

JULIE AND LANA LEFT THE RESTAURANT IN DEVON'S
vehicle and headed for the hospital. Lana's wound appeared to be superficial, but Aaron insisted they have it attended to by a doctor. Devon knew the dilemma they faced: Wait for the local police, contact Hatcher, or just get out of the way. As always, Aaron weighed in with the best advice.

"You and I need to stay close to the restaurant. This is still a civilian killing and we can't risk any damage to The Agency. And yes, I do have to call Hatcher."

"Things are about to get sticky, Aaron" replied Devon.

"The question looming in my mind is this: Was Kyong Ran acting on pure revenge or was he in Fairbanks as part of an attack on the pipeline? You and I know that the answer is yes, to both," said Aaron.

"If you're correct, then the attack on the pipeline is imminent, and us staying to cooperate with the locals is going to negate our ability to help; any news of CIA involvement will tip off the saboteurs."

Aaron paused, looked at his partner, and said, "We still gotta do what's right, brother. Let me start with Hatcher. If he tells us to hightail it out of here, then our backs are covered."

Devon heard the sound of sirens roaring closer. His gut told him to run, but his loyalty to Aaron said to stay.

He bit his lower lip and growled, "If you're going to do it, get on with it, but call him from across the street. At least that way, no one can say we left the scene and you get to make your call in privacy."

Aaron started to go, then paused and turned to Devon. "There are a couple more questions that need to be addressed too. I understand Ran tried to shoot Lana…but who the hell shot Ran? And why?"

***

"You two just did what?" Hatcher's voice bellowed through Aaron's cell phone, loud enough for Devon to hear it. He was beside himself. His first instinct was to order them back to Langley, but in his heart, something told Hatcher the country may be better off with them near the pipeline.

"What's your gut telling you, Cohen? You two girls must have worked out some 'rithm on when and where."

"That's the other reason I called, sir. We both agree that PS5 is the priority target, and the fact that Kyong Ran was here in Fairbanks tells me it has to be soon."

"You figured that out how?"

"It was a North Korean sub that took out the oil platform. Ran is—or was, a North Korean. For me, that's all the evidence I need to say it's going to be a PRK operation."

"What about the fact that it was al-Qaida that made the hit on the McKenzie house? Let's not forget that the one flew in from Yemen, picked up a homeboy, and drove across the entire continent to what—to take out McKenzie's wife? Doesn't make any sense."

"I understand—that is, I don't understand and I can't explain it beyond the fact that they are working for whoever is the big employer. Yes, they were al-Qaida, and yes, Ran was North Korean, but there's something else going on. Who's funding all this stuff? To us, it will be a North Korean sabotage unit, but we don't think they are doing the funding."

"Well, then who? Are you still looking at that international money angle? What does that buddy of yours, that McKenzie guy, think?"

"We're both certain that its roots can be traced back to that chateau in France. It has to be the source."

"Alright, Cohen, listen…I want the four of you to cooperate with the locals…tell them the women were not a target and you're as baffled as they are. The cover story is that you and Gorenkov just got engaged and you took her to Fairbanks to introduce her to McKenzie's wife. You and McKenzie were elsewhere in town and they went to lunch. If anything comes up regarding your employment at The Agency, don't deny it. You're within your rights as normal citizens to go where you want. End of story—you know nothing."

"You didn't say whether you've made any progress on the chateau. Anything we need to know?"

Hatcher shifted in his chair. The last meeting with the president and his NSA director flashed before him.

"I've got a team on it, but there's no satellite recon and nothing happening there at the present that we might be able to hack in on. For whatever reason, Interpol won't lift a finger to cooperate—strange, but true. I'm personally working on the Federal Reserve angle, but I don't have anything yet."

"Mind if we take a boat ride or do some sightseeing in the woods tomorrow?"

"You girls enjoy yourselves and warm the cockles of your hearts with good friendship. By the way, those extra agents are coming to visit the residence late this afternoon. They're mutual friends of yours and the McKenzies, aren't they?"

"Best of, sir."

CHAPTER 57

IN SPITE OF THE FACT THAT DEVON AND JULIE NEVER DIS-
cussed any aspect of their professional lives with anyone, tales of Devon
McKenzie had become iconic, urban legends all around Fairbanks.
Everyone had heard of the recluse hermit who had been a hunted man
for over four years. Some said it was the mob, some said it was foreign
governments, some even whispered that it was our own government that
had hunted him. His rescue of Julie Weston from a plane crash was well
documented, and the shoot-out in the woods that killed two would-be
assassins was also a given. However, fact and fiction blurred after that.
Most bailed out on the alien abduction angle, but somewhere in the back
of their minds, who knew?

As for Julie, those in the know claimed she ran the Iditarod when she
was only twelve. She would've won except some woman-hater recluse
shot her two lead dogs a half day out from the finish line. She buried
the dogs and hitched herself up as lead, pulling the weary dogs over the
finish line. Even the latest shoot-out at the McKenzie home had morphed
into Julie saving Alaska from the ravages of al-Qaida. They were sure
that the Muslims had picked their residence as a forward compound
to train fanatics where they couldn't be seen. Well, thanks to Julie, a
modern-day Annie Oakley, the last frontier had been saved and was in
good hands—at least for now.

Needless to say, the local police were willing to give them all the
leeway they needed. Lana returned with Julie within the hour, and the
police asked them, nearly begging, if they needed any help getting back
home. Because of the aura that surrounded Devon and Julie, the police
believed that they had a fortress of munitions and security, and any
opportunity for the local camels to get their noses under the McKenzie
tent would be a real score.

***

With blankets draped over their legs, Lana and Julie relaxed in Adirondack chairs on the back porch, sipping cabernet to relax after their horrendous day. Lana's wound had been superficial, requiring only a small dressing. Devon and Aaron stood around the grill while the steaks seared to medium. The sun was beginning to set over the mountains in the distance, and for the moment at least, the four were enjoying a moment of rest. Devon poured Aaron another drink and eased into what he knew was going to be a debate by saying, "I've been doing a lot of thinking about your theory on the saboteurs' escape route."

"With the intel we picked up, we pieced together the Norton Sound drop-off point; what's the matter with that?" Aaron asked. "You yourself told me that Frederick Schwatska ascended the Copper River in 1885, crossed into the Tanana River, and then descended down the Yukon River to its mouth. Where's the problem?"

"It's not that it can't be done—it's what you said to me two nights ago. You said, 'We CalSci dudes never assume the obvious—and neither does the Asian mind.' It's the Asian mind part that's got me hung up. We believe that this group is willing to commit suicide to insure the success and secrecy of this mission—correct?"

"Okay, but I still don't see—"

"Just give me a second," Devon interrupted. He stood up, walked around for a moment, and gathered his thoughts. He began, "If their leader is willing to die to carry this out, why not go all the way? Why not set his explosives at PS5, head south to the Copper River, and blow up PS11—just as you predict? But why not then take out the heart of the pipeline—its computer station at the Operation Control Center in Valdez? That way, it is total destruction—total mayhem. You said it yourself. Without being able to use those particular pressure valves, the whole system becomes a house of cards. Once everything comes crashing down, there's plenty of time to commit suicide."

Aaron stared at Devon, lost in thought. Finally, he responded, "You're right. Once the pipeline is ruptured, if you mess up the sequencing of the valve shut-down system, the spine would fracture everywhere."

"Actually, taking out the OCC doesn't negate them heading back North to the Yukon River and out," conceded Devon.

"It only makes it more difficult," Aaron added. "Nevertheless, you're right, Devon, the Operation Control Center has to be put into the mix—at high priority."

"You and I can only be in one place, bro. Do you need to do another algorithm or has your genius mind already figured out where you and I are best needed?"

"Nope, I'm going with *your* gut feeling on this one, Devon. Look, I told Hatcher that everything is imminent and he said he would send an urgent memo to DHS stating that, with extra emphasis on PS5 and PS11. He also said that drones would be in the air starting tomorrow. I have to assume that Secretary Martinez will have ordered the Guard to mobilize around the valves."

Devon grunted at Aaron's last sentence. "I wish I had your confidence in that group of political clowns."

"Well, no hits since 9/11—that has to say something."

"Way too many near misses, though," Devon replied. "Let's just say a lot of luck, and leave it there."

"Okay, back to your original question. Your gut says that the Operation Control Center is the place to be. No more formulas, Devon; I'm going to trust you on this one. When do we leave and how do we get there?"

"We're going to need a lot of logistical help from Julie, and Lana needs to see what other information she can gather on the chateau. Maybe she can shake down that Arkady Banketik."

"Well, let's get them up to speed over dinner—steaks ready?"

"Yes. Get the ladies."

"Drink up," Aaron said. "We've got a train wreck to stop."

CHAPTER 58

AFTER DINNER JULIE CONTINUED TO CHECK ON LANA LIKE a mother hen. Lana's upper arm was sore, but it could have been far worse. Devon heated up some leftover pie and the group moved into the great room. All were quiet, with their heads downward, avoiding the five-hundred-pound gorilla in the room. The only sounds were small clinks as forks poked through the servings and hit the plates. Devon was the first to put his utensils down and speak.

"Ladies, Aaron and I need to go to Valdez tomorrow. Our thinking has changed to a degree. We believe that the pipeline's Operational Control Center may be the linchpin in this operation."

"Is there a reason that you two need to be there?" responded Julie. "I mean, wouldn't a phone call do just as well?"

Devon looked over at Aaron for help.

"If the computer system is disabled or rigged, all of the oil in the pipeline could end up in Alaska's rivers. We're talking a catastrophe," Aaron said.

"Why not just call Hatcher?" Lana asked. "Surely he could alert your Homeland Security people."

"Well, that's just it. They're part of the whole bureaucratic mess that incestuously relies on each other's sound-bite conclusions. The pipeline authority says its shutdown system is fail-safe. DHS accepts that premise and is obsessed with the idea that their drones can save the day."

"And...?" queried Julie.

"Well, the algorithms I've created say they're dead wrong." Aaron paused, then said, "It's been a long day and I don't want to come across as arrogant, but these conclusions are real and they're based on *today's* knowledge, not thirty-year-old conjectures."

Devon jumped in, adding, "We can't help the fact that our government is bloated with ivory tower idiots. I've spent a lot of time reviewing Aaron's conclusions, and in the pit of my stomach, I know he's right.

Look, I was forced to live in Alaska, Julie, but I've come to love it as much as you do. I can't stand by and watch it be destroyed—not now, not ever."

Julie looked over at Lana and with a sigh of resignation, said, "It was a very short time ago that Devon came to me and said, 'I have to go to Russia. I need to help a friend.' Well, that brought me a new friend." Julie squeezed Lana's hand and continued. "So I guess my response is the same now as it was then. When do you leave and what's our role?"

"Book us the earliest private flight into Valdez Pioneer Field and have a rental vehicle waiting. Have it on standby for a return to Fairbanks. That's as far as I can plan right now."

"What about me?" Lana asked. "I'm also part of this Phantom Four business and I've got the wound to prove it."

"You're right," said Aaron. "We'd like you to stay here and contact some more of your friends in the Russian government—see if you can dig deeper into the ownership of the Chateau d'Arbonne. We may be able to avert this crisis here, but until we can expose the people funding this terror, we'll be doing it all over again—just somewhere else and in some other fashion."

"Julie, please secure the compound like you did before. No suggestions on my part, just do what you know will work. By the way, I think I forgot to tell you, those Langley agents are scheduled to arrive here..." Devon looked at his watch and continued with a grimace, "well, right about now."

"Devon, I'm going to shoot you!" Julie said, as she sent her napkin flying through the air at Devon.

CHAPTER 59

IN FLIGHT TO VALDEZ PIONEER FIELD AIRPORT

"SO, MISTER CHARGE-AHEAD-WITH-YOUR-GUT-FEELING, what's the plan of attack after we land?" asked Aaron. "We can't just go into the OCC and tell them they're about to have their computers blown away by a bunch of terrorists."

"I know, I know. We're the bloody CIA and we're not allowed to interfere domestically."

"Well...?"

"After we land, grab our gear and get our vehicle; it'll be time to get breakfast."

"Aaron rolled his eyes and said, "You're a beaut, Clark."

***

In what seemed to be one continuous motion, a waitress slid two plates off her arm to the table, poured a second round of coffee, and laid down the bill—all without saying a word.

Devon snickered as he caught an astonished look on Aaron's face. "We like 'em quiet, but efficient in Alaska."

"Then what am I going to do with Lana?"

"Like me, just make sure you always get the last words in."

"And those words would be...?"

"Yes, dear!"

Aaron laughed, but then got down to business. "Seriously, do you have a plan or are we winging it?"

Still chewing on his crisp bacon, Devon scratched the stubble around his scar, winked, and replied, "Winging it."

Devon let the words hang for effect, but only briefly. "I actually do have a plan, but as always, your input is welcome. I thought we would reconnoiter the area today—you know, make sure no one suspicious is doing the same. Remember, from a distance, the North Koreans are

— 183 —

not going to look a whole lot different than some of our indigenous population. Us—a displaced Scotsman and a Hebrew—we're the ones who'll stand out.

"Having said that, if there's nothing going on outside, we could walk into the facility and fake something so we can get a peek. If all appears cool, we could consider going to the National Guard HQ and give them some blarney about being sent by the CIA with some, you know, blah, blah, blah. That way, we can see what they're up to."

"That's your plan?" Aaron asked, sarcasm dripping all over his words.

"Not all of it," Devon said in mock defense. "If we think that the National Guard isn't up to speed yet, we can try to coerce them into mobilizing to PS5 and PS11. Also, you can call your buddy Hatcher and have him kick up the heat at DHS. If all is really quiet in and around the OCC, we could consider going up to the Copper River and checking out PS11 ourselves."

"Now you're talking. Normally I deal with the abstract—you know, sitting in an office conjecturing on what the next big crisis might be. This is the kind of life I want—a little action mixed in with having to think quickly on your feet."

"Glad you like it, bro."

"I haven't had—no, that's not true. I haven't *taken* the time to thank you for going to Russia. It hit me last night when Julie remembered you saying, 'I have to go to Russia. I need to help a friend.' You barely knew me and yet you came and put your life at risk. That says a lot about you, Devon."

Aaron ate some more eggs and caught Devon's attention. "We were able to save Lana's life and uncover a huge plot. In the process, you've also taught me a lot. Thank you."

"You're welcome. Now, stop the babble and pick up the tab. Let's get our gear and get over to the OCC."

As Devon rose, he added, "And make sure you turn it in at the Pickle Factory. We haven't set up Phantom Four just yet."

CHAPTER 60

LANA LEANED BACK IN HER CHAIR, TUCKING HER LOOSE hair into a ponytail. Looking around the room, she felt a strange comfort in the rugged, western décor that defined the McKenzie house. She understood why it was called a log home, as opposed to a log cabin. It was not only large, but its handsome ruggedness spoke of native strength, the same kind of mettle that was required to live in this wilderness. She heard Julie in the kitchen and pictured Devon in there with her. It may have seemed almost idyllic, but she knew that this family had the spirited determination that she wanted in a life with Aaron Cohen. In her heart, leaving Russia would be hard, but this strange land seemed to tweak the strings of her own inner being—as if it was drawing her into its bosom.

A shadowy figure passed outside the French doors that opened to the patio; it was one of the agents who had come in early the night before. His image brought her back to reality and the task at hand: What to do with the information that lay before her on the desk.

Alaska time was 10 a.m., but it was 11 p.m. in Moscow. She had been trolling nearly the whole morning, plumbing the lowest depths that most of her Russian governmental contacts preferred as their milieu. They were all high-ranking officials, but when they dared to step outside of their bureaucratic maze, they favored the murkier depths of bottom feeding. Sitting upright in her chair, she looked at her computer screen. She was positive she had scored. How big, she wasn't quite sure.

Arkady Banketik of the Ministry of Trade and Economy had responded to her encrypted icon. Like her friend, Evgeny Zakorov, he had had taken her under his wing and confided secrets that should have never seen the light of day. Unlike Zakorov, he lusted for her body and tried to grope her every time they met. Normally, she was aggressive at parrying his moves. Her inaccessibility while in his presence drove him crazy. Today, however, she was extra careful, so as not to let on that she was out of the country. It was a delicate dance, but if she was able to hold him at bay in the physical world, she had no problem dancing around him in cyberspace.

His information was scattered and wrapped in conjecture, but she knew it was a good start nonetheless. Banketik stated that he was aware of the Chateau d'Arbonne, having discussed it with Zakorov at his dacha. For sure, this place was cloaked in the heaviest security, the type he wished his motherland produced. The Russian FSB had interest in the comings and goings of the chateau due to an unusually large dump of the ruble on the world market. The ruble tanked, to the point where the government began to lose its control and faced massive inflation.

Their espionage had traced several phone transactions that wound up in a maze of dead ends, yet somehow always led back to the U.S. Federal Reserve in New York. He remembered a name that was never quite clear, but Banketik thought it was of Dutch descent.

He gave her one more interesting tidbit: A North Korean, named Kyong Ran, had entered and left the chateau on at least one occasion, possibly two. He told her Ran was a cutthroat mercenary who had been tied to many crimes in Russia and elsewhere in the world. Ran had close ties to the highest levels of the North Korean government, but left no paper trace—he was an enigma. The FSB has not seen or heard of him in several days. Out of courtesy, Lana returned a message that said she heard of his demise in Alaska only yesterday.

She wasn't sure how long she had been in a daze, reliving the death of Kyong Ran, but when Julie came by with an assault rifle strapped over her shoulder and a Glock 45-cal in her hand, Lana caught her presence and paid attention.

This is a good time to prep for trouble. I'd like you to come with me so you'll know where everything is—just in case."

"Sure," Lana replied. She rose and followed Julie.

"Did you come up with anything from your connections in Russia?"

"Actually, yes. Most of it is hearsay, but I did get a good lead that might help point to what Aaron's been saying about international financiers. Unfortunately, it points to involvement with your Federal Reserve."

"Listen, girlfriend, don't ever worry about offending me over those ruthless people. I don't live in a bubble—well actually I...*we* all do. We live under the financial bubbles these people create so they can profit as they expand and then sell off and get out just prior to their preordained collapses, saddling the middle class with losses from which they can never recover. One day people have modest nest eggs, and then suddenly they don't. Their wealth just disappears. Then somehow, our benevolent government rides in to rescue us with more entitlements that only further entrap us with more taxes."

"You sound cynical," said Lana.

"You've lived under a different yoke in Russia, but the end results are the same; our corruption just has a different name and style of oppression."

"In Russia today, that corruption is a hybrid of Western capitalism at its worst and old-style Communism with lipstick."

"Pig's still the same, though, isn't it?"

"This is why I do what I do, Julie. I have to fight them—to stop them."

"I understand, but remember this: *They* will always be there—in one shape or another. You can wound them, but they heal and morph into another beast. If you want real happiness, you have to make your own. Find the love that fulfills you and makes you the best person you can be. Then, fight like hell to keep that love alive. I have a hunch you've already found that love in Aaron."

Julie stared at Lana long and hard, hoping her words would sink in. "Now, let's lay these weapons out where you and I can get to them—in an emergency."

CHAPTER 61

DEVON LOOKED AT AARON AND SHRUGGED HIS SHOULDERS. For three hours, they had been watching from across the street of the OCC. Aaron nodded agreement—it was time to go inside and rattle some cages.

Once inside, Devon did most of the talking while Aaron visually inspected the overall operation, focusing on its computer system. His immediate conclusion was that it would be adequate if it were serving some nonessential private corporation in the farmlands of Iowa. The computers were older models with updated software. State-of-the-art security of the building didn't appear to be present, so Aaron knew its computer system hardware could be hacked into by any twenty-year-old kid working a computer call center. Moreover, most could backdoor this system within minutes.

They gave their identification to the receptionist, along with a line about being sent by DHS, which got them escorted into the manager's office. He was a typical middle-aged manager who was comfortable in a job that required very little; most of the time, it could be done on auto-pilot. He was irritated at being disturbed from his do-nothing routine, but the fact that he had already received a visit from a colonel in the National Guard quieted him down and allowed him to fake a toothy smile of cooperation.

Following a well-rehearsed line of scripted company talking points, the manager said, "Yes, we do know that we're on high alert, but I can assure you both that the shutting down of the system is fail-safe and is designed to eliminate any risk to the environment."

Aaron proceeded to explain his theories about what would happen to the Copper River should PS11 be taken out. The manager stifled a yawn and made every effort to politely shut the conversation down and get the two interlopers to leave.

"I understand your concerns, but as I have stated, we have the capability to shut this pipeline down in a heartbeat. Now, if you'll excuse me…"

Aaron wouldn't let go, saying in frustration, "I want to reiterate that my calculations show that if a breach in the pipeline released oil into the Tazlina River, that oil would be eighteen miles down the Copper River, past the confluence of the Tazlina and the Copper Rivers, all *within* your six-hour containment period!"

"Thank you, gentlemen, your warning is duly noted and appreciated, but I really do have to get back to work. So, unless you have anything further to add…"

Aaron gave a last-ditch plea as the door to the manager's office was shut in his face. "The pipeline service company has no containment sites on the Copper River to—"

Devon put his hand on Aaron's shoulder, spun him around, and guided him to the front lobby. Once outside, Devon squared their bodies to face each other. "Just accept it. His reaction is no different than you expected. C'mon, let's head over to the Guard's headquarters."

"This is asinine!" Aaron thundered.

"No, it's a bureaucratic snafu—no more, no less. C'mon, time to move."

"Are we going to get the same reaction at the Guard?"

"Probably—but let's hope they're not quite as pigheaded. Let's go, time is spare."

***

"You're damn right General Collins is taking this serious," replied Major Pratt, "about as serious as his own heart attack. Come over here and I'll show you how well the drones are doing their job."

Devon stood looking over Aaron's shoulder as he leaned in to observe the monitor.

"There! See? There's that PS5 you keep harping about. The drone's able to react to anything that generates heat. Humans, wolves, bears—the drone doesn't care—but we do. If we've got any a-Qs out there, the birds will see 'em and we'll rack 'em up—and el-pronto, if you know what I mean."

Devon straightened his back and had a puzzled look. The major caught it and asked, "What's the matter? You unconvinced?"

"What happens when the drone passes by the target? You know, the time between your bird's next flyover? I mean, I didn't see any thermal images of your men actually guarding the station."

"Hell's fire, we've deployed almost all our assets on this pipeline. That's why we'll be able to get to a spotted a-Q in a flash. Remember, we've got eight hundred miles of pipeline to protect."

Aaron stood erect and said, "Are you not listening to me? It's not eight hundred miles! Did you not see the memo from DHS making PS5, PS11, and the OCC your highest priorities?"

"Seems to me that we did…yes," answered the major. He looked at both visitors with a confused look.

"And…?" Devon asked.

"What I mean is that I, rather General Collins, fully understood the implications of the memo and we increased the actual coverage time of the drones over those valve stations. You know, it's kind of a rotational thing—that leaves our coverage lapse time to a minimum. And don't worry about the OCC…hell, it's damn near next door. Valdez isn't New York City."

"Major," Aaron said, "either of those valve stations could be blown out of commission within minutes. Are you telling me that your coverage lapse time doesn't exceed a few minutes? Are you telling me that your men are actually guarding these stations—hands on—during this lapse period?"

"Well, as I said, we have all our assets deployed and we can't be everywhere all the time. Sure, we could put all our troops around the valve stations, and they could blow the pipeline a quarter of a mile upstream or downstream. Look, we may be the National Guard, but we are still professional soldiers. Right now we're responsible for this pipeline, and we have to trust our instincts, not just what some bowtie-boy in Washington happens to think might be the best protection."

"Major, with all due respect, do you fully understand the operational function of these particular valve stations?" Aaron asked.

The major shifted awkwardly from leg to leg. He was insulted, but he didn't want to appear as ignorant or uncooperative.

"A valve by any other name is still a valve. You turn it one way and it opens. You turn it the other way and it closes. This isn't rocket science, guys. Besides, the OCC has assured us that they will have these or any other backup valves closed down within seconds. It's all fail-safe, gentlemen—fail-safe. Capiche?"

"So was the Titanic, major. Have you ever seen the pictures of it lying on the bottom of the North Atlantic?"

Devon reached for Aaron's arm, as he was leaning into the major's face. "It's time to go, Aaron." He looked at the major and extended his hand for a handshake. The officer refused.

As they walked away, Devon stopped and turned back to the major. "One more question, if you don't mind: When the drones fly over the valve stations, why aren't they magnifying on any of the valve buildings—you know, like looking for access tampering?"

"That's simple—the weather—the fog is too thick and there's too much rain this time of year. Besides, each station has a maintenance staff."

"I thought the Predators were equipped with synthetic aperture radar to look through clouds, smoke, and haze?" Aaron asked.

"Remember, these sweethearts were diverted from Arizona. Down there, in the southwest, clouds, smoke and haze aren't problems, so it was removed to reduce weight and conserve fuel. These aren't the MQ-1B Predators that you boys at the CIA get. Let's not forget that there is a pecking order in the services. You spooks guard all the skeletons in the closet, and 'whatever Lola wants—Lola gets.' And in case you haven't noticed, there ain't anybody in the National Guard named Lola."

CHAPTER 62

CIA HEADQUARTERS
LANGLEY, VIRGINIA

DIRECTOR HATCHER WAS IN A SURLY MOOD. HE HAD STAYED late the night before, wrangling every which way to "peek under the skirts" of the Chateau d'Arbonne. He had come in that morning with the conclusion that he was digging a pipeline to a dry well. It was now four in the afternoon and he had just pulled his round, frameless glasses off and was massaging the bridge of his nose. He jumped as his buzzer went off.

"Damn it!" he shouted as the noise startled his frayed nerves. "What is it, Helen? I told you no calls unless it was an emergency."

"I know, sir, but I assumed you'd make an exception for Svetlana Gorenkov."

Hatcher's demeanor changed on a dime. He snagged the phone from his desk and smooth was all over his tongue. "Ms. Gorenkov—I mean Lana—how are you this beautiful afternoon? Are you recovering from your injury?"

"I'm well, sir—"

"No, no, no. Until I can figure out a way to hire you, you've earned the right to call me Ernie, or as I prefer, just plain Hatch."

"Alright…Hatch, I'm well. I thought it important that I share with you the information I just picked up from one of my Russian colleagues."

"High up?"

"You know I wouldn't waste your time otherwise—Arkady Banketik of the Ministry of Trade and Economy."

Hatcher whistled and conceded, "No surprise, I guess; you did say you moved in mysterious ways."

"Not mysterious, Hatch, just the result of years of tending my garden. Anyway, he confirmed everything we already knew about Kyong Ran, but he said that Ran never worked with the North Korean government— not even in a quasi-fashion."

"I see." Hatcher paused a moment, closing his eyes as he connected the dots. "What else did he say?"

"Apparently the Russian FSB has also been trying to look into the chateau. Six months ago, there was a heavy sell-off of rubles—damned near destroyed its value."

"I remember…but what's the tie-in?"

"They picked up heavy communication between the chateau and your Federal Reserve around the same time. Most of it was garbled and they had a tough time trying to enhance it, but they did come up with a name, if you want to call it that. They think it was a Van-something—of Dutch descent was how Banketik phrased it. Aaron told me that you were working on a connection with the chateau, so I wanted to get this to you as soon as possible. I'm sorry if I've disturbed you."

"Disturbed me—are you kidding? Listen, Lana, you can rustle up this old country boy anytime, even if it's only on a hunch."

"Banketik told me he was going to be in New York in a few days for a trade mission. If I hear anything else, Hatch, I'll be in touch," she said and then rang off.

Hatcher was pleased with her information. She was top tier as an investigator and her sources were impeccable. He decided it was time to ramp up the pressure on the president and his NSA toady. When you're huntin' a boar hog, there are times when you've got to get out of the tree stand, he thought.

He buzzed his secretary. "Helen, connect me with Jonathon Van Leuwen at the Fed."

CHAPTER 63

FEDERAL RESERVE
NEW YORK CITY

JONATHON VAN LEUWEN SAT READING HIS NEWSPAPER IN the rear of his black, stretch limousine. As always, in downtown Manhattan, traffic was snarled, bringing its flow to a standstill. He looked out his window and sighed at the teeming mass of humanity that swelled over the sidewalks in every possible direction. How this city is able to function as well as it does is quite a tribute to the raw power of its commerce, he thought. It's not the politicians; they come and go and are bought and paid for. No, it's greed that runs this city, and not just this city, but the entire world. In reality, all these people may be on their own treadmills, but it is still the greed of commerce that regulates their moves and motives. And it is the very few elite like me that control all the world's commerce. A small grin crept over his face. The sheer arrogance of his self-aggrandizement caused him to raise his nose and take a deep breath, feigning moral superiority.

Turning the page, his mind drifted to the contrasting pastoral beauty of a drive through the rolling French hills to the Chateau d'Arbonne. He yearned for the tranquility of that sparsely populated countryside and knew in his heart he would soon have a chateau of his own. And why not? he thought. A person of my stature *should* be entitled to it.

As his eyes caught the article he had been looking for, he failed to notice an old wino cross the street and stumble onto the hood of the limo. His chauffer laid on his horn, then rolled his window down and began cursing at the bum, yelling for him to get off the hood. A sharp rap on the window on his side diverted Van Leuwen's attention. Looking over, he saw a stunningly beautiful woman in her twenties appearing to beg for help. He rolled down the window and opened his mouth to speak. Before his first word escaped, she shoved a small pistol into his mouth.

"Unlock the door—NOW!" she hissed. "Now! Open it up."

Fear gripped Van Leuwen and he obeyed without protest. In the flash of a second, the woman pulled the gun from his mouth and shoved it into his rib cage. "Slide over—now!"

It happened so fast, his chauffer never noticed. When the woman saw the chauffer look into his mirror, she pressed the gun into Van Leuwen's ribs even harder, covered his mouth with hers, and held it there. The driver was stunned, but assumed his boss must have expected the visitor. The drunk had wandered off, Van Leuwen seemed to be enjoying the woman, and traffic began to open up, the cars behind them still honking their horns. The chauffer drove the limo forward.

"Say one word and you're a dead man," she whispered. "Notify the driver that you've changed your mind. Give him this new destination." She slipped him an address on a small piece of paper. Van Leuwen obeyed.

The new address took them to an abandoned warehouse in a seamy section of Harlem. Upon arrival, two rusted, rolling metal doors slid open, begging their entrance. The driver put the car in park, lowered the window screen behind him, and turned to question Van Leuwen. Before his eyes could focus, the woman put a bullet between them. His head and body bolted back, blood splattering on the driver's window. A man opened the driver's door, shoved the body over to the passenger side, and slid in behind the wheel. Within mere seconds, he parked the limo inside the abandoned building. Van Leuwen sat speechless in a state of total emotional shock.

Without hesitancy, the woman pulled the gun from his ribs, raised it to the side of his head, and fired two shots. She nodded to the man in the driver's seat as she slid out the passenger door. He pulled the limo forward up a ramp into an enclosed auto carrier in front of them. The man got out, threw a set of keys to the woman, and then jumped up into the auto carrier's cab.

Within hours, four steel jaws hoisted the limo into the air, swung it around, and dropped it into a gargantuan car crusher. Its next destination was a large vat of industrial acid.

***

Director Hatcher tried to multitask while waiting for his secretary to contact Jonathon Van Leuwen. Hatcher was not a patient man. His finger slammed the intercom button.

"Damn it, Helen. When are you going to get that Van Leuwen guy on the phone?"

"I'm sorry, sir, but I just hung up with his secretary for the third time. He left his office about two o'clock and hasn't returned. He missed a Board of Governors meeting scheduled at four. He hasn't called in, his cell phone's gone dark, and no one has seen hide nor hair of him. This is totally out of character for him, and everyone I've talked to is in a panic."

CHAPTER 64

THE DAY BEGAN CRISP AND COOL, ALMOST ENERGIZING, but now the sun was setting and the temperature was dropping—and dropping fast. Ahead of a massive front that had come down from the north, a bone-chilling, foggy drizzle had crept its way in. Dae Dong's leader of Team One, Lieutenant Kim, sat shivering as he waited to break into the building that housed the main valve. What he and Dae Dong hadn't taken into consideration was the sudden influx of a small cadre of National Guard troops that had rolled in earlier that morning. Kim and Corporal Pak watched their moves for the entire day and concluded that the soldiers had no set pattern to their guard duty, so Kim would have no difficulty gaining access to the pump valve.

During the day, Kim had moved the hostage further up the pipeline and had returned to set the Semtex-10 charges on the valve itself. When he had finished, Kim set the timers and eased himself out of the building, secure in the knowledge that his job was properly done and the Semtex would not be seen before it was too late.

When Kim finished, he made his way back up the pipeline to meet Pak, where they would set more explosives. After they drugged the hostage, they would leave him secured with his own smaller charge. The difficulty lay in disguising the body of the hostage so as not to be detected by the drones. When finished, they were to make their way back down the Koyukuk to the Yukon and out to Norton Sound where the sub would be waiting—but the sub would only wait for four days before it would leave for the Gulf of Alaska...with or without them. Those were the orders given to Corporal Pak.

Like his commander, Lieutenant Kim was a hardened, sadistic man who placed no value on human life—his or others. He too was fully prepared to commit suicide and would have no problem helping any of the men under his command do the same should they waiver.

The chances of him hearing any drones were next to nil. Still, he kept looking from his watch to the sky. No one could be sure, however, whether the drones had even been ordered to monitor the pipeline. Dae Dong had assured him that with eight hundred miles of pipeline to guard, he was not to worry about the possibility of drones. Kim was to evade whatever maintenance staff should be on site and any soldiers of the National Guard, who were not expected at this location. A part of him hoped that at least a few soldiers might appear so he could personally slit their throats.

The Semtex-10 explosive felt cold in his hands, as he carefully pressed and molded the clay-like mass to appear as part of the pipe joint itself. Pak was off setting more charges a hundred yards upstream to assure maximum damage. Kim had already placed a small amount of Semtex on the hostage's body along with native brush as camouflage. Timing would be critical before he administered the knock-out drug and placed the detonators.

Suddenly, a beam of light flashed above his head. He ducked, but he was left in an awkward position—half squatting, half standing. Two American soldiers were walking, rolling their flashlights back and forth in front of him. They were within an arm's reach. Grousing about a temperature in free fall, they were wishing they could get back to nice cup of hot coffee and warm shelter.

Without making a sound, Kim reached down, slipped his fingers around the shaft of his knife, and squeezed it tight. The muscles in his legs tensed; he readied for an attack, his blood racing through his veins, his heart pounding. I can kill them both, he thought. No! Wait—follow orders—hold off. It was all he could do not to kill. Why have they stopped? Something's not right...

His eyes strained to catch a glimpse of his watch. Time seemed to stand still. His legs started cramping beyond belief. The soldiers flashed their lights at the joint and then at the area surrounding it. Minutes went by. Pain dominated his every thought. The soldiers continued to talk, but didn't move on. More time passed. They began telling jokes and laughing. Kim closed his eyes and tried to think of his family back home, anything to take his mind off the pain in his muscles. His legs shook out of control. Nothing worked. The pain! I can't stand it!

He lost control. He slid the knife from its sheath, raised it high, leapt up, and plunged it into one of the guardsman's back shoulder blades. A loud, piercing scream broke the silent air. The second guardsman pulled his assault rifle off his shoulder and began spraying aimlessly into the dark bush. A bullet hit the Semtex taped to the hostage's chest. An immediate orange and yellow blast blew the shooting guardsman onto his backside. He scrambled to his knees and emptied his rifle's magazine into the darkness. Everything was pitch-black.

I need light! the guardsman thought as panic overcame him. He bent over, his fingers clawing at the earth, desperate to find his flashlight. Where is it? Where is it?

There! His fingers felt the round shaft and slid the switch upward, its beam finding his fallen comrade, face down. He ripped off a glove and felt the man's carotid artery.—A pulse!

***

At the Alaska National Guard Headquarters, a short memo began printing out the identifying logo of DHS followed by a notice:

NOTICE:

SEND ARMED GUARDS IMMEDIATELY TO PS5 AND PS11 TO BE POSTED 24/7.

SIGNED:

JENNA MARTINEZ, DEPARTMENT OF HOMELAND SECURITY

The on-duty corporal was in the next room wooing a brunette private. He was half sitting on her desk, with his back to his office, when the distress call screamed in. Coffee spilled everywhere as the corporal jumped off the desk.

"I need a medic! PS5! I need a chopper at PS5! Guardsman down! One terrorist shot. Repeat—terrorist has been shot. Need medivac and support! No damage to the valve. Repeat: No damage to valve."

***

Lieutenant Kim vanished as soon as the shooting started. Within a short time, he met Pak and told him of the shootout. The two disappeared into the Alaskan wilderness. Their "official" orders were clear: Should anything go wrong, they were to make their way back to their boat and retrace their journey to Norton Sound within two days. There, they would rendezvous with the submarine. If that was not possible, they were to take their lives. No exceptions. But Kim knew the "real" orders and was prepared to carry them out. He ran his hand over the small pocket of his military trousers. The thin lump telegraphed that the vial that contained the cyanide pill was still secure. He and Pak would go down the Koyukuk, as far away from the pump station as they could travel, but then they would stop and he would kill Pak, burying him and the Zodiac away from the river. Kim would strip his own body of all items that might trace him to North Korea, then hike deep into the woods, take the cyanide pill, and let the bears do the rest with his carcass. End of mission. End of story.

"Did you get the charges set on the pipeline?" Kim asked.

"No. Should we go back and set them off?"

"Not without orders. I set the timers on the main valve. That will have to do."

"But surely they will find the Semtex and disarm it."

"So be it. I repeat: We have orders. You know this."

"I will not leave this country without inflicting some form of horrific damage. I can't," said Pak.

"I share your hatred, but we must obey our orders. Move out."

***

Lieutenant Patrick Raleigh had his men fully deployed around the perimeter of PS5. He stood watching the bomb squad remove the Semtex that wrapped the pump's valve. A shiver ran up his back as he thought about how the soldier dismantling the explosive had a family of his own, no different than he. What a sick, twisted world we live in, he thought. Even here in Alaska, we can't get away from the bastards.

"Sir!" The sergeant broke his train of thought. "The valve is clean, the area's been swept, and there's no sign of any other a-Qs anywhere."

"Are you trying to tell me this was a lone suicide bomber, sergeant?"

"Must have been, sir, because there aren't any tracks to be seen anywhere."

"Sergeant, it is pitch-black out here, and either the cold has frozen your thinking process or you must have shit for brains, because there is no way this operation would have been carried out by one, lone terrorist. Do I make myself clear?"

"But—"

"No buts, sergeant. You will continue to deploy your men all night long if that's what it takes, and then have at it in the morning again with a fresh crew until you find something. I don't care if that something leads you to a skunk's ass—find something!"

CHAPTER 65

WHEN DAE DONG LEFT TO GO TO VALDEZ, HE WAS CONFI-
dent everything at PS5 was under control and he knew firsthand the
explosives had already been secured to the PS11 valve. Unlike what had
been done at valve five, Dae Dong let his arrogance take charge and
decided to alter the mission. He would leave no hostage behind, thus
freeing the two commandos for other duties. One would go to the Zodiac
and run it downstream to where the highway crossed the Copper River
at Chitina. There, he would wait until Dae Dong and the rest of the
saboteurs returned from his newly planned attack on the OCC in Valdez.
The other commando would go with the two hostages to Valdez.

***

Major Pratt was en route to PS11 when the call from General Collins
came through. "Major, make no mistake about it, we are under a full-
scale terrorist attack. The intel points to destruction of the pipeline,
with the primary targets being PS5 and PS11. Operation Intercept is
underway. Deploy your men immediately."

"Yes, sir. General, has the deployment been expanded to include the
OCC in Valdez?"

"No it has not, major. The protocol is to guard the pipeline with the
primary focus on PS5 and PS11. If DHS gives us further instructions,
we will react accordingly. For now, we follow the protocol."

"Yes, General, it's just that these two guys from CIA—"

"That's enough, major," Collins said. "*We're* running the show here,
not two spooks from Washington. Have I made myself clear?"

"Yes, sir!"

With the station in full view, Pratt raised his hand for the driver to
stop the vehicle. Something was wrong. He could feel it. The drone had

given PS11 the all-clear sign, but something was amiss. He motioned for his men to form a tight circle and do a wide sweep of the area. He raised his binoculars to his eyes and saw Semtex charges shaped to a joint in a pipe upstream. They were barely visible, but they *were* there. He gave word for his men to fan out while the bomb squad deployed.

CHAPTER 66

AARON AND DEVON SAT HUDDLED IN THE BUSHES ACROSS the street from the Operations Control Center. Aaron looked at Devon; the hours of waiting were wearing on them. Their confidence that the terrorist's ultimate target was the OCC was beginning to crack. Hatcher had called and briefed them on the PS5 attack, then the PS11 attempt, but hours had passed and nothing had happened. They were cold and hungry.

Aaron was the first to speak the unthinkable. "What do you think, brother? Have we made our first mistake? I mean, maybe the OCC isn't a target after all."

"Hard to say…what I do know is that these fanatics have not traveled this far and gone through this much misery to walk away with so few results. No, they'll come, Aaron. I don't know when, but they will come. We both have that same gut feeling."

Aaron looked down at the ground and then back up at Devon. With an apologetic look, he said, "Sorry, my head says you're right, it's just—"

"Shhh. What was that?"

In the failing light, a murky figure was moving, then four more, one after another. Two were wobbling, as if they were bound. They converged at the entrance to the OCC.

Devon's iron grip pulled Aaron down low, pressing his face hard against the ground. Leaning over, Devon whispered in Aaron's ear, "It's them. I knew those filthy scumbags would come here. This is their Holy Grail. There's no way they could have resisted it, buddy."

"What should we do?"

"Get on the phone to the Guard, tell 'em who's here and that we're going in."

Aaron hesitated, unsure as he gathered a plan in his head. "Shouldn't we wait? The Guard's not far away."

Devon again pulled Aaron in close. This time his voice was raspy with a mixture of anger and authority; his cadence was slow, his message deliberate. "We don't have time—understand? We have to move as soon as you call—*now!*"

Aaron was on the phone within seconds to the Alaska National Guard. "Major Pratt, this is Aaron Cohen from CIA; I talked with you earlier. Terrorists have entered the pipeline control center in Valdez. I repeat; they have entered the building. CIA operative McKenzie and I are going in to intercept."

Pratt stood dumfounded; his cell phone line went dead. "That son of a bitch hung up! Get General Collins on the line. Move! Move!"

Dae Dong and his men formed a position as if every motion had long been planned. In fact, it hadn't. By instinct, they knew that killing every person in sight was the first order of business. There was no need for stealth, for there would be no prisoners. No sounds were heard outside the building as their silenced weapons systematically cut down the staff. With the agility of a cat, Dae Dong leapt atop a desk in the central room and viewed the carnage. He raised his arm and his men came to immediate attention. The silence was deafening.

He pointed to one man, signaling him to the front. He responded post haste. Next he pointed to his second in command, Lieutenant Kwon, who understood the message that the rear was his to cover. Kwon then grabbed satchels and, like a programmed machine, began placing Semtex on the computer mainframe panels.

Dae Dong jumped down, walked behind the two bound al-Qaeda hostages, and slammed each one on the back of the head with his pistol. They slumped to the floor. Wasting no time, he dragged them over near the computer banks and propped them up onto chairs so he could begin taping charges to their chests.

***

Devon knew the small explosive he had placed was enough to do the job without taking the whole entrance wall down. All he wanted was access. He looked over at Aaron, held up three fingers, and slowly laid them down, one at a time.

The explosion not only blew the door off, but rocked Dae Dong's men back on their heels. Devon and Aaron flew through the door with their assault rifles blazing. Dae Dong was stunned. His men retuned fire from every direction. Devon and Aaron hit the floor, rolled, and took cover behind desks. Dae Dong turned the two hostages in their chairs and positioned them as shields in front of him. His assault rifle delivered fire in between them. Devon answered, pumping short bursts into the chest of the first and the head of the second.

Dae Dong knew it was over; it would be only a matter of minutes before the National Guard would arrive and the charges hadn't been set. Time was his enemy and it had just run out. His only hope was that the explosives he had set at PS5 and PS11 had succeeded in doing their job. But even of this he couldn't be sure, because he had let his arrogance get in his way. Kwon was right. He realized that coming to the OCC was wrong. They needed to retreat. He motioned to his lieutenant, who nodded agreement in return.

Dae Dong and Kwon alternated laying down a fierce barrage of fire, while one by one, his men slipped out the rear door. Devon and Aaron returned fire as best they could, but were running out of ammo.

"What have you got left, Devon?"

"I'm down to one magazine. What about you?"

"Only what I've got in, maybe half. Guard better get here quick," Aaron said.

"Don't worry. Haven't you noticed? They've been ducking out the back door."

"What? How do you know?"

"It's the count, bro, the count. Only two of them are firing—it's heavy, it's alternating, and they're firing from the rear."

"Now what do we do?" whispered Aaron.

"We need to stay alive, let them escape, and then go track the rotten bastards down."

The room went quiet. Devon listened, assessed the situation, and stood up. He looked around; a cloud of smoke hung below the fluorescent lights that alternately flickered on and off. Paper and human bodies were strewn helter-skelter; pools of blood were everywhere, dripping down walls and shot up furniture. He offered a hand and pulled up Aaron. "C'mon, CalSci, we've done what we were supposed to do; we saved the computer station. Call that buddy of yours, Hatcher, and tell him he can keep his superhero medals for another day. Right now, we've got some vermin to track and bag."

As they turned to go out the door, soldiers from the Alaska National Guard poured through the entrance with assault rifles aimed at their chests and heads. "Down! Down! Drop your weapons! On your knees! Now! Now!"

Devon stopped, looked over at Aaron, and motioned him to follow suit. He lowered his assault rifle and dropped to his knees. When his hands were raised and clasped behind his head, he looked at Aaron and said, "I rest my case, bro. Our government says we're winning the war on terror. We sure are, aren't we?"

CHAPTER 67

HATCHER'S FACE TURNED BEET RED. "WHAT THE HELL DO you mean, Cohen, that they held you up for two hours?"

"I'm telling you, sir, the terrorists got out the back door, and when we went to pursue them, the stupid Guard bastards drew us down at gunpoint and held us there until Major Pratt stormed in; then he held us in a 'bureaucratic paper' lockdown until General Collins finally cleared us."

"And all that took two stinking hours?" bellowed Hatcher.

"Damn near."

"Alright! Enough is enough. Is the control center secured?"

"Affirmative. The Guard has a full squad around it as we speak, and it's fully operational. None of the computer mainframes were damaged. They've already replaced the personnel that were killed."

"The pump stations were never damaged, Cohen. You and McKenzie were spot on in calling those. PS5 was close—we ended up with one dead al-Qaeda plastered with Semtex. Talk about lucky that it never exploded. The Guard got to PS11 and disarmed the Semtex there just minutes before the timers were set to go off."

"That's good news, sir."

"The nation owes a debt to you and McKenzie."

"Thank you, but the job's not done. We still have to find the ones that got away."

"How many a-Qs did you two kill in the OCC?"

"Two."

"And how many got away?"

"Why are we still having this dance about al-Qaida? These terrorists are North Korean."

"Damn it, Cohen, just answer the lousy question…Homeland wants to know—alright?"

"Can't say how many escaped, sir. As you know, the Guard gave us the bum's rush. You'll have to get your intel from Homeland on that question."

"I already have—they're clueless. I was hoping you two knew. The Guard thinks nobody got away. Homeland has no idea how many got away, but at least they acknowledge that some did. Their theory is that the al-Qaida terrorists are making their way north to take another shot somewhere along the pipeline, after which they will try to get into Canada."

Aaron paused; he knew he was headed for an argument with his director. "Sir, Devon, that is, we…believe the three terrorists that got away are North Korean—plain and simple. I don't know how many other ways to say the same thing."

"Did you just say three?"

"I did." He paused again, waiting for Hatcher's reaction. The phone was silent.

Finally Hatcher's voice came through, lower and raspier, almost as if he were looking over his shoulder to see if anyone was listening. Only this time, Hatcher *was* looking. An uncomfortable feeling crawled over him, reminiscent of the chill he felt after Treasury Secretary Jonathon Van Leuwen's sudden disappearance. Hatcher realized that his secretary, Helen, had been working abnormally long hours and seemed to be silently present in the background, always nearby. Why hadn't he noticed it before? he wondered.

"Damn it, Cohen!" he hissed into the phone. "Don't you get it? Homeland does not want to see North Korean involvement here—period, end of story. Now, move on and let me see what I can do behind the scenes."

"Is that Homeland as in security or White House as in politics as usual?" asked Aaron, not able to stifle his disgust any longer.

He could hear squeaking as Hatcher grew ever more agitated and shifted in his chair. "Think about it. Does it matter a rat's ass?"

Aaron let out a heavy sigh of resignation. "Well, it damn well should. I just wanted to know where we stand, that's all."

"Look, Washington's roads are littered with bullshit politics, Cohen; we all step in it every day. I go home and clean my shoes the best I can, but at day's end, they still smell like I tromped through a pig sty. It's just the way it is and the way it's always been."

Aaron paused, rubbed his forehead with his fingers, and took a breath. His mind understood what Hatcher was saying, but it still sickened him. He went silent.

"You there, Cohen?" Still silence on the other end. "Now don't you go playing Johnny Boy Scout with me, you hear? It's an ugly-ass world, and sometimes we don't get to choose our bedfellows."

"Understood, *sir*," Aaron said.

"Did that Trojan Horse cowboy put you up to this?"

"No, and I'm going to say this only once, sir. With all due respect to your position, if you ever show disrespect to Agent McKenzie again in my presence, you'll have my resignation on your desk immediately. Let me be perfectly clear; as we indicated before, we believe that North Korean saboteurs are behind all of this; they took al-Qaeda hostages in an attempt to leave them dead at the scene, hoping to throw everyone off the trail. The North Koreans then escaped from the OCC and are heading *south*, not north."

Aaron waited for a response; as he again started to speak, Hatcher broke in, "What smidgeon of proof can you give me that they're North Korean?"

"Kyong Ran tried to kill Lana on numerous occasions and we have his corpse for God's sake!"

"That still doesn't tie him to the pipeline—sorry."

"Alright, then nothing concrete; Devon caught a glimpse of one of them in the firefight. He's comfortable the face was Korean."

"Excuse me, but don't the Native Alaskan people have a look that could pass for a North Korean in a smoke-filled room in the middle of a shoot-out, for God's sake? Is that not possible, Cohen? I mean we're talking about a stinking firefight!"

"I suppose," Aaron responded without any hesitation.

"Then tell me again why I shouldn't be on board with Homeland on this."

"Because you know damn well that Devon and I have a sixth sense about things, and we're usually right. Now, if you'd like, we could whip up a quick algorithm on this, showing you the mathematical *unlikelihood* of them wanting to take another shot at PS5 on their way to the Yukon River, where they will make a mad dash down to Norton Sound to escape on an awaiting submarine. Shouldn't take too long—or...or you could just trust us—sir."

Hatcher closed his eyes and shook his head. He ran his fingers through his hair, pausing to give the knot in his neck a deep massage. "God, you two girls are a proverbial pain in the ass. Go ahead and find them. I already feel like a whack-a-mole at day's end."

CHAPTER 68

DIRECTOR HATCHER WAS AGAIN THE FIRST TO ARRIVE TO the 7:30 a.m. security briefing. The conference table had completed reports laid out in front of empty chairs. Ernie opened his report and reviewed the pages in rapid order. Blah, blah, blah, he thought, another easy al-Qaida whitewash. As he closed the report, others began filing in, most in early morning jocular moods, now that the country had averted another crisis, thanks to the diligence, of course, of Homeland Security.

NSA Director LaSpesa opened by congratulating Jenna Martinez on the fine job Homeland had done on the pipeline situation.

All five foot one inches of the Homeland Security director stood and turned from side to side, as if the entire meeting had been called solely in her honor. "Thank you. But as you can see in the report, we do owe a great debt to our Alaska National Guard for their takedown of the terrorists at not only the pump valves, which if breeched I might add, could have been an ecological disaster of the worst possible magnitude, but also of their protection of the Operations Control Center in Valdez as well."

As Martinez continued to slap her own back, Hatcher reopened Homeland's report and looked deeper, but couldn't find the names of Cohen and McKenzie anywhere. I guess I'll be cleaning the dung from my shoes again tonight, he thought.

"Speaking of the Control Center," said President Coleridge, "have any of the terrorists from Valdez been rounded up yet?"

FBI Director Kearns replied, "No, sir. We know that they headed north toward Canada. We are currently working with the RCMP to make sure the border is secure on both sides."

"Is there any chance of them heading south? I mean that would seem to be the shortest route—you know, to get to the Gulf of Alaska?"

asked Coleridge.

"No, sir," replied Martinez. "Al-Qaida has no assets available to pick them up even if they tried to make that run. In any case, we do have a Coast Guard cutter patrolling Prince William Sound. Our primary focus is to concentrate our drones in keeping the pipeline secure for the present. We cannot be certain that they may not try another attack, but we will be vigilant."

Hatcher had his fill of the endless crap. "Excuse me," he said, "I see no mention of any North Korean connection whatsoever in this latest report. Is that intentional?"

A sudden pall came over the room. Coleridge shifted in his seat and turned his eyes to LaSpesa, telegraphing the need to close the topic. LaSpesa answered in dry sarcasm. "Are we going with that DPRK crap again, Ernie? And if so, why?"

"Why? You're asking me why? Because this report is filled with nothing but bullshit, that's why. I have two agents who were on holiday in Valdez the day all this went down at the OCC. And guess what? They are the ones who broke up the terrorists taking over that building—not the Guard. You want to know something else? They saw North Koreans get away from that building—not al-Qaida."

"Are you telling us you had CIA agents working on U.S. soil?" Martinez asked.

"I said they were on holiday—hunting. You got a problem with that, Jenna?"

"Hunting with assault rifles, Ernie?"

"Glad to see that you are *finally* acknowledging them. And yes, hunters today do use assault rifles when they hunt."

Director LaSpesa stood to signal the meeting was over. "Let's all understand, we simply can't have CIA personnel involved in domestic affairs—no matter how well intentioned. There is physical evidence of al-Qaida involvement and absolutely none of it points to the DPRK. Therefore, this report stands and this meeting is closed."

CHAPTER 69

CIA HEADQUARTERS
LANGLEY, VIRGINIA

DIRECTOR HATCHER'S MIND WAS DEEP INTO THE POSSIBIL-
ity of the ramifications of a North Korean connection to the pipeline
when a light rap on his door startled him, forcing a gruff response. "Yes,
Helen, what is it?"

"Ms. Gorenkov, line one."

As always, the name Gorenkov was a game changer that brought an
instant smile to his face. "Thank you; I'll take that call."

He thought for a moment, and then decided to wait for the door
to shut before picking up the phone. It didn't take long for the smile
to vanish as he watched the softness at which Helen closed the door. It
was the telltale behavior of someone who was lingering, listening on the
other side. Hatcher didn't like it. He'd been in the spy business far too
long. Helen was a good secretary and she had been properly vetted, but
she had only worked for him for a couple of years. In any case, he didn't
trust her, or maybe it was that he just didn't like her. His gaze lingered
after the door closed.

"Lana, is there anything this old polecat can help you with today, or
have you got a special treat for me?"

"I'm not sure, Hatch. Do you remember the other day when I told
you that Arkady Banketik had contacted me about the Federal Reserve?"

"Yes...yes, I sure do."

"Well, he contacted me by email again today. He has come upon
more information."

"Information? About what?"

"I don't know any of the details, but he indicated that what he had
could 'blow a hole in a fortress called the Chateau d'Arbonne'—his
exact words."

Hatcher paused, deciding to play his cards close to his vest. "I see.

— 214 —

How do we get our hands on this information?"

"*We* don't. His email said he would only give it to *me*, in person—no one else."

"So where does Banketik want this meeting to take place?"

"He said he's going to be in New York City the day after tomorrow to attend an international commerce conference. He wants me to meet him there—alone. Can you arrange a flight for me?"

"I don't know. I don't like it, Lana; something smells fishy. Why does Banketik want to give you intel on the Chateau d'Arbonne?"

"I don't know, Hatch. What are you worried about?"

"What am I worried about? How about you! I'm not putting you in danger—period."

"Please remember, I don't work for you or your CIA, Hatch. I've been digging through this cesspool for years without you, the United Nations, or any other kind of protection. So with or without your help or blessing, I'm going and I will meet Arkady Banketik."

"What about Aaron? Have you discussed this with him?"

Lana paused; she was embarrassed that she hadn't. "We haven't talked," she whispered.

"Don't you think it wise to talk this over with the man that just saved your life and pulled you out of that snake pit you were in?"

"That's not fair. You and I both know he's facing life or death with Devon, and I didn't want to put any more stress on him."

"I'm not your confessor, Lana. Life is about making choices, and I'm not sure this will prove to be one of your finest. God knows I've made a slew of my own bad ones, but if you're hell-bent on going, have Julie book your flight and I'll make sure two agents meet you at LaGuardia day after tomorrow. Call me back with your schedule. But Lana, I still don't like it."

"I'll be fine…don't worry. How will I recognize the agents?"

"They will find you, my dear, they will find you."

"You are a sweetheart, Hatch."

When he rang off, Hatcher pressed the button for Helen's desk, looked down at his watch, and noted the time it took for her to answer the pager.

"Yes, Director?"

"Helen, could you bring me the latest intelligence on the Pakistan drone strike, please?"

He reckoned that the seconds it took for her to answer was about the time it would take to hurry back to her desk from his door where she had been listening to his conversation. While pounding his fist into his open palm, he winced and ground his teeth. Hatcher knew full well he had a problem and the mere thought of a mole in his midst sickened him. This was one more problem he would have to deal with. If Helen really was a mole, who did she report to…and why?

CHAPTER 70

THE CAR RIDE BACK TO PIONEER FIELD AIRPORT WAS LONG and tense. Looking down, Aaron became aware of the pain in his hands and realized that he had white-knuckled the steering wheel for what seemed the entire drive. Covered with debris from a storm that had blown in the night before, the asphalt road appeared to dance in and out of a hazardous patchwork quilt. He found it almost impossible to concentrate on driving as his mind kept drifting to Svetlana and what danger she might have encountered.

"Damn!" he blurted out, as he released his grip and pounded his fist on the steering wheel. "The least she could do is to call me back!"

He looked over at Devon, whose body jolted out of his delirium. Aaron's eyes telegraphed fear—fear for Lana's life, fear that he might lose her again. Exhaustion was taking its toll on the pair. Svetlana hadn't returned any of his calls, and all Julie could tell him was that she had suddenly left to go to New York City…something about meeting the Russian head of commerce.

As always, Devon was quick on the uptake. The bond between them couldn't be measured in time, because it ran deep, more than just respect or friendship. They were brothers to the core. "Don't let your mind get ahead of you, Aaron. There's more to her than you're willing to give her credit for."

"Well, I'm pissed off at Hatcher for letting her go."

"Hold on, now. Julie said that he sent two experienced agents to meet her there."

"Then why doesn't she answer my calls?"

"Don't have an answer for that, bro, but you have to stay focused on what we've got to do here. Remember, Julie's got a boat waiting for us on the Copper River. I don't know how the hell she did it on such short notice, but that woman is a whiz. She has a plane waiting so she can fly us over there as we speak—also unbelievable. Look, we're not far from the airport. When we get there, I'll load the gear in the plane. That way, you can call Hatcher and see what kind of update you can get on Lana—fair enough?"

"Yeah, I suppose. Look Devon, I still think we should have Julie fly us up to PS11. I have this lingering hunch the Koreans will try to take one last shot at it. I mean, right now, they have nothing—zip, zero, nada. That valve could very well be their last hope of wreaking havoc on America. They may consider mass suicide without at least having accomplished *something*."

"Any other time, I'd like to help them in that decision, but we want to capture them alive. Don't lose sight of that."

"And your point is what?" asked Aaron.

"Homeland put the National Guard in a virtual lockdown on that valve and the pipeline for a mile each way. My gut says Dae Dong's had it and he's going to fake going north to throw us off, as if he's going back to PS11, but he's going to turn east to the Copper River and follow it south to the Gulf of Alaska."

"Then what? The Sang-O sub dropped them off in the Norton Sound. Isn't it still there?"

"Is it? My gut says they planned all along to move the sub south to the Gulf of Alaska. It's the shortest way out—with the least margin of error."

Aaron grimaced, "Biggest exposure, Devon, greatest chance of getting caught."

"That's just it. On the one hand, he can't risk getting caught—he's out of hostages and there absolutely can't be a North Korean fingerprint. On the other hand, time is his worst enemy."

"Are you sure about your theory? Before we left your house, I ran two different algorithms, each pointing to them descending the Yukon back to Norton Sound."

"Aaron, you want one o' *my* al-go-rithms?"

"Cute…real cute."

"Seriously, it's what I would do—it's my gut feeling, bro."

"Don't get me wrong, Devon, I'm still on board. Sometimes, that which is staring you in the face is the hardest to see. Remember, we work best together when we keep testing each other's ideas."

Devon shrugged his shoulders and added, "Science or years of experience...?"

"Experience wins—I'll call Hatcher."

CHAPTER 71

"COHEN, WOULD YOU CUT ME SOME SLACK? FOR PETE'S sake, there was no way I could stop her. Hell's fire, man, you know her better than I do, and I don't think you could have stopped her either. Listen, I've sent two of our best to protect her. Believe me, she's going to be okay. I promise."

Hatcher sensed that Aaron was holding back. Something didn't seem to sit right. "Sir," Aaron asked with apprehension, "I'd appreciate it if you'd double that guard."

"I think four agents are unnecessary, but I'll do that for you, Cohen. Now, tell me what's going on with you and McKenzie."

"We're about to fly to the Copper River—Julie's flying in with some special gear and will pick us up at the airport at Valdez. We're certain the North Koreans are going to make a run for the Gulf of Alaska."

"Impossible!"

"No, it's not. And anything you can do to help us throw a ring around the Gulf of Alaska would be appreciated."

"Hell's fire, Cohen, I can't…Homeland's rules; you know that. Besides, they're concentrating all their efforts on PS5 and PS11 in the north. It's out of my hands."

Hatcher knew Aaron's patience had hit a brick wall. He heard Aaron take a deep breath before speaking, "Sir, I have to go; thanks for nothing."

"Damn it, Cohen…Cohen…?" The line was dead.

Hatcher was pissed. His hands were tied. He was tired of Washington politics; the never-ending, politically correct games that never allowed the right actions to be taken. Hell, he cared for his agents, every damn one of them, including Svetlana Gorenkov, agent or not. Why had his job become so personal? The faces of Cohen then McKenzie, with that scar from eye to ear, flashed through his mind. He knew his two mavericks were right—they *were* tracking North Koreans; however, nobody in the White House or State Department wanted to deal with the international ramifications if they were actually caught. Better that terrorists get away so we can sweep it under the rug and pretend it never happened.

Hatcher growled under his breath as the North Korean leader came into mind, standing at his podium watching his missiles roll by. "Well, you're not going to get away with it, you fat little crud. You may be the head of a communist, backwater, third-rate country, but the best part of you was left on the sheets," he whispered to no one.

He picked up his phone and ran through the stored numbers. His thumb stopped sliding when he got to the name Stoker, Harry. He reminisced of his early days in the Navy. Harry Stoker was Hatcher's XO on a light cruiser in the Persian Gulf. He was tough and ran a tight ship, and when he had the helm, he never shied away from making hard, even controversial decisions.

"Harry? It's Ernie Hatcher."

"Hatch, you old weasel, how the hell are you?"

"I'm doing great, Harry. Listen, I've got a proposal that's going to make you a national hero."

"I've never been interested in being a cock-o-the walk. You know that, Hatch. You always told me, 'A hen that struts like a rooster is often invited to dinner.'"

"I said that?" They both laughed out loud. "Well, seriously Harry, this might even get that whole motley crew of yours a presidential citation. What would you say to that?"

"These citations…they get passed out in the light of day…somewhere other than the basement of the White House?"

"Probably not, Harry."

"What would I say, Hatch? I'd say run away as fast and as far as you can."

CHAPTER 72

LANA WAS STARTLED WHEN A MAN STANDING AT THE crowded carousel reached in ahead of her and pulled her luggage off the ramp. "Excuse me!" she blurted out in indignation.

"Easy, Ms. Gorenkov...I'm here to help—Special Agent Curtis. If you would please, take the handle, go about your business, and know there are three other agents posted in the airport. We will be following you to your destination...Director Hatcher's orders, ma'am—you must be high priority to rate the four of us."

"Please! I didn't request any protection, nor do I need any. I can't be seen with any body guards. Okay?"

"Understood, ma'am. Now if you don't mind, I'll excuse myself, as if there has been some mistake. Have a nice day."

With that, Agent Curtis waited for the next matching piece of luggage to come around before he pulled it off and proceeded in the opposite direction. Lana walked outside to the curb and hailed a taxi. As the cab pulled away, she didn't notice the unmarked car behind her.

When she was dropped off at the Marriott, a half mile from the Jacob Javits Convention Center, Agent Curtis relaxed, as other operatives had already swept Lana's room minutes earlier. Lana wasted no time cleaning up and was back out the door, walking the short distance to the Russian Pavilion at the JJCC.

Upon arriving at West 34th Street, the enormity of the all-glass structure overwhelmed Lana. She was already suffering from jet lag, when, as she looked up, she momentarily staggered backward, and then felt a firm hand grab the underside of her upper arm, righting herself. "Excuse me, ma'am," was all that was said by a man in a dark suit as he passed by.

Once inside, Lana made her way to the second floor where the

Russian Pavilion stood in stark contrast to other world exhibits. The Russians, free of the communist yoke, were now spending money as if it was in endless supply—nouveau, crass and vulgar. Young, blonde, scantily clad girls acted as hostesses, attempting to lure Western businessmen into capital ventures.

She had a prearranged meeting spot, just outside the pavilion at a café with tables and chairs viewing the main concourse. Lana sat down and waited with an espresso in hand. A full hour passed, but Banketik did not show. She pulled out her smart phone and checked one more time—perhaps with all the noise, she had missed his call—nothing. She looked around, worried whether the agents may have scared Banketik off. Odd, she thought, I don't see Agent Curtis anywhere; but then again, if he's doing his job, I'm not supposed to.

Thirty more minutes passed, still no Banketik. Anxiety, coupled with jet lag, began overwhelming her; her eyelids grew heavy and her head started to bob. Lana stood up and decided to walk over to a nearby market area to stretch and move. The area was close enough to keep an eye on the table where she was to meet Banketik.

As she wandered through the small marketplace, she found a small, cuddly Russian bear. A perfect gift for Aaron, she thought. She bought it and the clerk placed it into a paper tote bag. As she headed back to the table, a man in a trench coat and hat bumped into her, while dropping an envelope into her bag. She looked up, but only caught a glimpse as he rushed past. Her heart wanted him to be Arkady Banketik, but she couldn't be sure. He had caught her by surprise and she was unsure of what to do next. She wanted to blurt out his name, but realized this was no accident. Discretion cleared her mind. As if he had come in and out of a mysterious vapor, the man vanished as quickly as he had appeared.

Svetlana Gorenkov, always the investigator, was back. She gathered her thoughts and with a cool demeanor, as if nothing had transpired, purchased another coffee and the day's newspaper, returned to her table, and waited another half hour.

When that half hour passed, Lana feigned irritation, grabbed her bag, and with her chin held high, walked back to the first floor and out to 34th Street, where she hailed a cab for the short distance back to the Marriott.

Before the cabbie started up, she asked him to pause for a moment.

She looked left, right, and fully behind her; there were no signs of Special Agents Curtis, Johnson, or any other member of the security team.

Lana frowned, looked at the cab driver, and said, "Cancel going to the Marriott. Just drive around."

"Where should I go, madam? And for how long?"

"I don't care. Just drive till I decide where to go, and then I'll tell you my destination."

Lana was nervous. As the cab pulled away from the curb, she looked from side to side, hoping to see any sign of the CIA detail that was sent to cover her. She knew that she needed to check in with Hatcher, but decided to make the call after she perused the contents of the envelope. She looked down at her tote bag and put her phone into her purse.

CHAPTER 73

JULIE WAS STANDING ON THE TARMAC, USING THE AIR-plane's wing to shield her from the lightly falling mist. With one arm akimbo, she brushed her hair back with her other hand as a dirt-covered SUV ground to a halt in front of her. For Devon, her tall silhouette contrasting against the cloudy, billowing, gray sky, commanded an image in which all things warm, loving and sexy lay. He was dog tired; more tired than he could remember in years, but thought, God, how I love this woman.

He jumped out and swept her into his arms, then looked over at Aaron and felt the worry that was on his face. He let go of Julie and asked, "Any word on Lana?"

"No," Julie replied, "just that she landed safely in New York, made it to the hotel, and planned to go to the Javits Center in Manhattan. Sorry, that's the best I have."

Devon looked at Julie and telegraphed with his eyes for her to say nothing more as he saw Aaron walk away to grab their gear from the SUV. When he was out of earshot, Devon said, "This is tearing him up. I don't know why she doesn't call him back."

"All she told me was that she was worried that somehow it would hamper Aaron's performance on your mission, and she doesn't want him to get hurt or worse. I have no reason not to believe her."

"Maybe, but I can tell you that the opposite may also be true. Julie, don't—"

"Don't say it," she said, cutting him off. "The CRRC boat is fully packed. Enough camping and provisions for two nights are loaded. I know you said only one, but I added another night, just in case."

"Julie, listen," he paused; he was tired and didn't want to hurt her feelings. "Honey, speed is critical..."

She leaned in and kissed his lips, cutting him off. Devon sagged; he knew he was beaten and there was no use arguing. He pulled his head back and said, "What about the armaments?"

"Two ARs and two thousand rounds. You've still got the two you took to Valdez?"

"Roger that."

"Two Glocks, five hundred rounds each, as requested."

"Did you load the blasters?"

"Yes."

"You are a sweetheart."

"Aren't you going to ask about food?"

"Not really. I assume its stowed right under my Dr. Dentins."

"Don't be a smart-ass."

"I love you…more than you know."

"I love you too. Devon, please take care of Aaron."

"Priority one—come on, rev this baby up and fly us out. We gotta go. Oh, and by the way, who's going to take care of me?"

She smiled and answered, "That would be me—but only when you get back."

***

Dae Dong knew that time had run out. The only chance for him and his men was to get to Chitina on the Copper River and get there fast. The truck that had hauled them down from PS11 was gassed up and waiting. He looked at his watch. The explosives that he had set at the oil storage facility at the port of Valdez were set to go off in five minutes. He knew the explosions would draw most, if not all of the National Guard away from the Richardson Highway. He had staggered four explosive devices, each with a delay of one hour and a location designed to draw the Guard further west with each blast. For the most part, the highway was cut along a narrow gorge, giving them maximum cover from drones and aircraft.

As they sat huddled in the back of the storage truck, Dae Dong sat by himself while his men huddled and groused over their failure to have inflicted any mortal blow on an enemy they had sworn to deliver a crushing defeat. His men wanted to go back to PS11 and make sure the valve had been destroyed, along with a large section of the pipeline.

Dae Dong's choice was simple: Make an all-out attempt to destroy the pump or accept defeat, then making a hundred-mile dash south to the Gulf of Alaska, hoping his submarine would still be waiting. Either way, he could not lose one man; not one single North Korean soldier could be blamed in an international incident of terrorism. He and his men were all willing to die, if it came to that, of that he was sure. The dilemma was how to dispose of the bodies—every scrap of evidence, including himself.

Their complaining continued until the sudden sound of a cough caused them to fall into total silence. The North Koreans looked up to see their captain standing over them, slapping a stick into his gloved hand. He stared down at them, as if he could read their inner, devious thoughts, shaming them. They looked away to the floor of the truck.

"I have come to a painful decision. Our mission has failed. It is not your fault. It is mine, and mine alone. It was I who decided to attack the control center in Valdez. It was a grave error—my error. Now we must retreat; we must leave this den of evil and return home to Korea. It is essential that we are not captured on American soil. When we return home, I alone will be court-martialed and face the penalty for my crime. That is all. We leave as soon as we arrive at Chitina."

An immediate murmur broke out through the crew. Kwon jumped to his feet.

"That is enough!" Kwon said. "I will not tolerate insubordination. Our journey home will take great strength and stamina. We have one hundred miles of treacherous water to traverse and we will have drones overhead searching for us. If I hear one word of complaint, I will consider it mutiny. That man will be shot on the spot and buried—no questions asked. Have I made myself clear?"

***

When they cleared the No Wake Zone, Devon opened up the throttle of the outboard motor and the Zodiac FC 470 responded in kind. The pounding of the craft above sixteen knots was brutal and they hung on for dear life. He had decided to ease off a bit so Aaron might get some shut-eye. He looked down and saw that he wasn't sleeping. Instead, his eyes were locked on Devon.

"You really need to try and catch some sleep, Aaron. We've got a way to go before catching up to them, so I don't need an extra pair of eyes right now. I know it's hard, bro, but you've got to try. Otherwise, you're not going to be able to help me when I need you."

Devon saw him nod, then tuck in his arms, and roll over into a fetal position.

When he felt Aaron had finally nodded off, he pushed the throttle further down and opened the Zodiac up. Again, the craft responded. It rose up and slammed hard across the crests of the waves. The wind and water pummeled his face—the hunt was on.

CHAPTER 74

LANA SAT IN THE BACKSEAT OF THE TAXI, STARING IN DIS-
belief at the packet that rested in her hands. She felt as if her blood had
been drained out of her body and the weight of the world had been
placed square on her shoulders. Even her breathing had slowed as she
came to understand exactly what Arkady Banketik's message, "Blow a
hole in the Chateau d'Arbonne," meant. But she also understood it was
far more than that.

This isn't about greedy power hungry families and their quest to
manipulate the world's flow of money and capital, she thought. No, this
ultimately leads to raw, total power—the power to commit genocide—to
turn entire peoples into mindless automatons. As she slid the papers
back into the envelope, the name Convent of St. Mary Magdalene struck
her as rather odd, an oxymoron, because her humanitarian side recognized that what she held was so catastrophic that it should never see the
light of day.

She also realized that the sound of rustling papers had caught the
attention of the driver. She looked up into the cabbie's rearview mirror
and caught his eyes as he asked in a stern voice that echoed his fatigue,
"Please, where to, madam?"

"The airport—"

In a horrific explosion of sound and light, a large SUV plowed into
the driver's side of the taxi. Coupled with the slamming of her body
and head against the passenger door, Lana's consciousness was thrown
into a swirling void. Her world went black. The taxi spun around three
hundred degrees, hit the curb, went airborne, and rolled over onto its
roof, slamming into a brownstone porch. Bystanders began screaming,
"Call 911! Call the police! Call an ambulance!" Lights from apartment
windows turned on everywhere. Within minutes, red flashing lights and

the sounds of sirens could be seen and heard in the distance. Flashlights began swirling around the taxi. Steam was coming out from under its crumpled hood.

Someone yelled out, "Stand back! There's smoke! I think it's going to blow!"

"Who's inside? Get them out!"

"I saw a truck hit the taxi!" said one.

"No. It was an SUV," said another.

"Where's the car that hit the taxi?"

"It took off—that way."

***

The paramedics were the first to arrive. A crowd of bystanders peeled back as sirens and flashing lights from the ambulance opened a path to the curb. It didn't take long for them to assess that the jaws of life was needed to open the driver's door. Once he was able to reach in, the lead paramedic yelled out, "He's dead—there's what looks to be a bullet hole in his forehead."

"Is anyone else in there? Did he have a passenger?" asked the other paramedic.

"No. Only the driver's inside. This looks like a crime scene...we better wait until the blues get here and tape the area off for the coroner."

***

CIA HEADQUARTERS
LANGLEY, VIRGINIA

Hatcher was beside himself. The call had come from the last conscious agent sent to guard Lana Gorenkov. "What the hell are you telling me, Keagan? Curtis and Johnson are dead?"

"Yes, sir, and Agent Anders is in critical care at Yonkers General. He took two hits; one to the chest, one to the gut. The surgeon is not a hundred percent sure, but he thinks Anders will make it, sir."

"What about Gorenkov? Is she all right? Where is she?"

"I don't know, sir. We lost her."

"What the hell do you mean, 'you don't know?' I sent four of our best agents, and you're telling me that you couldn't protect one woman for one day in Manhattan?"

"Sir, I swear, everything seemed as if it were a trap; almost like we were set up—"

Hatcher cut the agent off. "I want a full report on my desk in one hour."

He slammed the phone down and walked over to his window. The sun had set and the sky seemed at peace. As he stared blankly into the night sky, an ever-so-faint trail of a shooting star blazed its way across a sea of endless stars, belying the turmoil that ran heavy through his heart.

Two dead, he thought, one critical, and one missing—dear God, I hate this job! What the hell am I going to say to those families? What the hell am I going to say to Cohen?

Hatcher had a grown family, one that included a daughter and a son. He also had a career as a naval intelligence officer and then served as a four-term congressman. The sad fact was that his family had taken a backseat to his career. Although his children loved him, it was from a distance and expressed only at Christmas and Easter, and every other year at that, due to shared time with his ex-wife.

Then along came Svetlana Gorenkov. She had only been in his life for a brief period, but she reminded him of how he was in his younger days, so he took her in mentally as an adopted daughter; perhaps the relationship he never had, but desperately sought.

He reached up and rubbed his neck, trying to massage away the knot that was throbbing, and whispered, "She's gone. Killed? Kidnapped by the Russians? Why? What did she know?"

Continuing to stare, he stood for a few minutes, but his mind was empty. This was Hatcher's way of decompressing. He truly thought of nothing—he just stared into a void.

When he finally turned to face his desk, he wiped his eyes with his index finger and turned to the door that separated his office from his secretary, Helen. His glare turned cold.

If you had anything to do with this, I'm going to flush you out, Spider Lady, and then I'm going to flatten you with my boot, he thought.

CHAPTER 75

XO RYU WAS AT THE HELM OF THE NORTH KOREAN SANG-O minisub. Time was running out on the mission of Dae Dong's saboteurs. His captain had taken ill and had confined himself to his quarters. He said over and over it was nothing serious, but he hadn't eaten a thing in a day and a half. Because the minisub was on a special mission, they couldn't accommodate a ship's surgeon and barely had room for a designated medic, so Ryu had to take the captain's word that it was only an intestinal bug and would soon pass.

His crew had long surpassed the limits of tolerance waiting for Dae Dong to return. They had been cooped up with no proper exercise or fresh air since the exit of the commandos. The captain had run his ship by the book and had stayed submersed, but the tension among the men had grown to hostility. When the captain took ill, Ryu surfaced the boat and allowed his men to rotate topside for fresh air—it wasn't much, but he needed to do something, anything to ease the open grumbling.

Ryu was now measuring the time left against his fuel, calculating what was needed for the trip back to Korea. Both were reaching critical levels. Near as he could determine, Dae Dong had a little over fifty-two hours to reach their rendezvous. If he didn't appear on time, they would have to leave. Ryu remembered Dae Dong's harsh treatment of him before they collected their gear and left the submarine. He didn't wish him well—worse, he hoped he would be killed. He also remembered Dae Dong's searing hatred of the United States and willingness to have his entire crew commit suicide for his cause. I wonder, Ryu thought, if his death wish is about to come true.

***

COPPER RIVER, ALASKA

Dae Dong woke his men. It was time to move out. They needed to make

— 232 —

their last maximum push under the cover of darkness. His men were slow to move. The mission had failed; his men were crack soldiers, but now they were in full retreat, running under the cover of darkness. Their humiliation showed in their eyes.

"Attention, men. We should make good time tonight. The weather favors us, and if we are not detected by any of their guardsmen, we will have this last hard push through the delta where the river is difficult to navigate. I promise you: Once we are close to the sub, we will kill any American we find along this river, whether it is night or day; we will drink their blood."

With that, they began singing Kim Jong Un's patriotic song of unification, "Onwards Toward the Final Victory." When they finished, they collectively spat on the Alaskan soil and shoved off into the icy water. Dae Dong knew his words of killing Americans were a lie, for there should be no people in the delta area.

The night's voyage ran without incident. The boat held up, the outboard motor ran smooth, and the Copper River was remarkably free of floating debris.

***

Aaron pulled their boat off the banks of the Copper River. He had slept miserably, if one wanted to call it sleep. Turning every half hour, either from thoughts of Lana, pain, cold, bouncing, it didn't matter; he was sleep deprived. He looked over at Devon and was amazed at the stamina the man seemed to have. Maybe it was all those years in the—his cell phone ring broke his thought.

"Hello?"

"Aaron, this is Hatcher."

"Yes, sir."

"Aaron..." There was a long pause. "Aaron, Lana is missing."

"What do you mean, 'missing?'"

"I'm sorry, son, but two of the four agents that were guarding her are dead, the third is critical, and the fourth's alive. But we...we don't know where Lana is. She was in a taxi that was broadsided; the driver was killed and Lana is missing. We simply have not been able to find her."

Aaron screamed into the phone, "You *promised* me she would be okay! That's what you said! I'm doing this shit for you, and you couldn't even protect her?" Aaron rang off and put the boat in neutral. Looking around at nothing, he slid down and wept.

Devon jumped up from his seat in the stern, came forward, and put his arm around Aaron's shoulder. He waited...holding his friend firm, he asked, "Is Lana alive?"

Aaron remained silent for what seemed an eternity. Finally, he looked up and said in broken words, "I don't know. She...she was in... an accident. But she's missing. The...the agents...that were guarding her—they're dead, Devon, they're dead. What does that mean?"

"I don't know."

"It's those Russians, Devon. She went to see that Russian connection of hers, damn it! I wanted her to let those bastards from her past go. Why wouldn't she do it?"

"I don't have any answers, Aaron. Just know that Lana has convictions, man. And I mean that in the present tense. Did Hatcher actually tell you she was dead?"

"No, but—"

"No buts, bro. As long as she can't be found, then there's a thread of hope that she's alive. They killed my first wife and that was final. You still have a chance. You and me and Julie, we *are* going to find her, Aaron, as soon as we finish with these NK dogs."

Aaron stood and then watched as Devon pulled his knife from his ankle sheath. He made a tiny stab in his palm and then grabbed Aaron's wrist, forcing his palm upward. He made a similar stab, drawing a small droplet of blood. Devon clasped their bloodied palms together, simultaneously drawing Aaron to him in a bear hug with his other arm, and said, "We *are* going to find her—on my life, I swear to you."

CHAPTER 76

CIA HEADQUARTERS
LANGLEY, VIRGINIA

DIRECTOR HATCHER HAD HIS STRATEGY LAID OUT FOR catching the fox in the henhouse. He strolled to Helen's desk as if nothing had happened or was even suspected. "Helen, please come in and help me with some special arrangements for the families of Agents Curtis and Johnson."

"Right away, sir."

When she seated herself, Hatcher began by coyly referencing the bios on the two agents' families. "I believe they each have one child, both of who are about to enter college."

"Well, not quite, but you are close. Agent Curtis had a son who is a sophomore and Johnson had a daughter who is a freshman—both in high school."

"Okay, next I want you to find one of our black op money holes and arrange for funds to be transferred to set up a trust for the education of their children. Talk to the widows, find out the details, and get it going."

"Sir?"

"Helen, we hide billions—well, never mind. Just get me the details and have it on my desk by this evening. Oh, and did I mention Agent Anders?"

"No, sir, you didn't."

"Well, he's still in recovery...and it looks like he'll make it. Good man, that Anders...it seems he took down one of the Russian assailants...made him talk before he killed him. The Russian told him it was a set-up—even where the leak came from. Problem is, we got only partial info from Anders before he went into surgery, after which they had to induce a coma to try and save his life."

Shifting in her chair, Helen's whole demeanor changed in an instant.

Hatcher took it all in, analyzing the nuances of her facial expressions and body language. She cleared her throat and asked, "Should I get information on his children?"

"No, I think we'll wait until he recovers. That may be as early as this afternoon—who knows?"

"Uh, I'll get right on this," said Helen, as she rose and exited his office.

I have no doubts you will, thought Hatcher, like a fly on a cow pie on a hot summer day.

***

Helen fidgeted through most of the morning as she kept busy with her tasks from Hatcher, keeping a fretful eye on the clock. When lunch time came, she was the first to leave. Even though she was confident that she was under no cloud of suspicion, Helen decided to play it safe and chose a route to her rendezvous with her Russian contact that allowed for several stops. Each stop gave her time to sweep her perimeter, making doubly sure she wasn't being followed—or so she thought. She didn't know that Hatcher had a micro tracking device hidden in her security ID.

Helen had parked her car near the Jefferson Memorial and was eating her sandwich on a park bench overlooking the basin. When she finished, she got up, disposed of her brown trash bag in the steel waste receptacle next to her, and moved on, as if it were any ordinary day, back to work.

Ten minutes later, a park attendant, in proper uniform, came by in a park utility vehicle and emptied the receptacle into a larger, empty bin he carried behind. He drove off, ignoring the other trash receptacles along the route. Within minutes, he was apprehended by two men in black suits.

***

Helen was back at her desk when Agent Keagan came through the office door with another agent in tow. Keagan proceeded through toward Hatcher's door, while the other agent stopped next to Helen's desk. He looked down with his arms folded in front of him.

"Excuse me," said Helen, rising from her seat, "I'll see if the director has time to see you, Agent Keagan."

"Oh, I don't think that will be necessary. You see, he's been expecting me. You might want to have a seat."

Keagan reached into his suit jacket and pulled out a folded, hand-written piece of paper and held it up for Helen to see. She looked over and saw the other agent move over to block the door to her office. With a heavy sigh and shaky legs, Helen sat back down.

Keagan moved on, knocked on Hatcher's door, and entered. Moments later he reappeared and said, "The director will see you now, Helen. I trust your lunch was enjoyable?"

CHAPTER 77

COPPER RIVER, ALASKA

AARON WAS AGAIN STEERING THE ZODIAC. THE SPRAY FROM the river had soaked him through. Devon had spelled him for a short while, but searching for the North Koreans wasn't enough to keep Aaron's mind off Svetlana, so they had switched. He glanced over at Devon who scanned back and forth across the river with his binoculars; however, the width of his scan from side to side was getting wider by the hour. They were simply running out of normal river and going further into an ever widening delta.

"What do you think?" Aaron asked.

"It's not looking good, bro. I'm not sure how much confined river bank is left, and then we'll be guessing which pathway they took to the coast. Trouble is, there hasn't been one single sign of them anywhere. I don't know…maybe I *have* made a mistake."

"Hey! Knock it off! Don't start second-guessing yourself."

"Seriously, this delta is probably the most massive in North America; this is going to be like finding a needle in a haystack."

"This is your country, Devon, I'm just a city slicker, remember?" Aaron joked. "Come on—put yourself in their shoes. What's your move?"

Devon paused, looked pensive for a moment, and said, "Alright, I would go balls out for the Gulf, and then I would make a run east under the cover of dark, which then leads me south to Kayak Island, then to the sub."

Aaron looked at Devon, cracked another smile, and said, "Have you got an algorithm to back that up?"

Devon threw an arm around Aaron's head and faked a pounding. "Hit it, you pencil-pushing geek—south, southeast."

***

Dae Dong woke his men for what he hoped was the last stretch before boarding the minisub and heading back home. They had found no one to vent their anger upon along the river, but his men trudged on. They had reached the Gulf of Alaska and hidden their gear for the night; now they had to get to the furthest point out on Kayak Island and paddle a grueling twelve miles out to rendezvous with the sub in international waters. Twelve miles…he wasn't sure his men were up to the superhuman task that lay in front of them. They had been pushed too hard for too long.

He wasn't even sure that the sub would be waiting for them; yet somehow, he had gotten them here and on schedule. Protocol called for him to wait until the last minute before contacting the sub; however, he would pull out all stops to pressure the captain to encroach the twelve-mile limit to shorten the distance his men must paddle.

"Arise men, arise…this is our final leg. Our mission is almost over; one last effort, men…one last push."

CHAPTER 78

IT WAS NOT A REGULARLY SCHEDULED MEETING, NOR WERE the members of the families in a mood to be assuaged with small talk. They were nervous and wanted the meeting to begin without further delay.

"I wish that I could bring you better news, but I'm afraid there is none," said the senior member. "As you all know, we were successful in our endeavor in the Gulf of Mexico; however, we were not able to follow up with success in Alaska." He paused and shrugged his shoulders. Wincing, he said, "We…failed to cripple the oil pipeline in any way, shape, or form."

Grumbling among the occupants overtook the room until the din made it impossible to hear across the long table.

"Please! Please!" The senior family member called for order. "I will not continue unless I am able to have quiet."

The room fell to silence.

"Thank you. Now, as I was saying…our North Korean saboteurs failed to take out the two main valves that would have caused not only calamitous disruptions to the pipeline, but horrific environmental repercussions that would have sent a paralytic shockwave to the price of oil, thus collapsing the U.S. dollar. Alas, that did not happen."

"Who is at fault for this fiasco?" asked a second family member.

"Apparently the captain of the saboteurs, Dae Dong…on his own decided to attack the Operations Control Center in Valdez."

"So, because of one rogue decision, our whole mission was lost?"

"Unfortunately, that is true, but there will be other opportunities. There always are."

"Is any of this traceable to us?"

"So far, the Americans have only found the al-Qaeda hostages. As always, they are taking the political path of least resistance. They could have discovered something through the disappearance of the Federal Reserve's Van Leuwen, but that connection has been closed—permanently."

"When you say there will be other opportunities in the future…what do you mean?"

"I am referring to a rumor that has been circulating in Russia for some time now."

"Is this the old Nazi Germany virus rumor?"

"Yes, but we don't perceive it as a rumor any longer."

"But it has never been found. They say that if it ever existed, it was destroyed—back when Poland freed itself from the old Soviet Union."

"I understand, but remember, a virus never dies; it lays dormant, waiting for a host cell."

A third member added, "It lays dormant, yes, but only if it has never been destroyed. All the evidence we have ever seen is that the facility that housed the so-called Nazi virus was completely destroyed. Nothing was left but rubble."

The members all began talking again, some in agreement, some not.

"Please!" The senior family member again called for order. "There are those who were present at the time of the explosion. They witnessed people running away from the facility the moment it blew up. That has never been explained."

Another member laughed and said, "Too much vodka explains a lot."

"Nonetheless, we are following the lead, and we think it may be solid."

A member who had remained silent for all prior meetings appeared deeply disturbed. He unfolded his arms and raised his hand to be heard. When he was acknowledged, he said in a voice that echoed the tone of a schoolmaster, "Is this the level to which our circle of family members has descended? Have we sunk so low that we are considering employing Nazi tactics to achieve our ends? Did I hear the word virus used? This virus is a WMD! That can mean only one thing—that we are willing to infect people to achieve monetarist goals. Am I wrong?"

The first member became agitated and pounded his fist on the table to reign in order. "Please! I will not be made to feel as if I am on trial. Let me be perfectly clear. From what we are told, this is not a virus that kills, it is a virus that controls populations—specific populations. Right now, this is only a lead—nothing more! We cannot be sure of its veracity. But know this…if it exists, sooner or later, someone will gain access to it and will exploit its use. Would it not be better in our benevolent hands?"

More arguing ensued among the members. "Please! Please!" cried out the senior member. "Sometimes drastic measures must be taken. Look around you. The world is awash in chaos. The old world order has collapsed. New, fresh thinking is needed, and it is needed now. Our people tell us that this lead may have traction. If it is real, we certainly don't want it to fall into the hands of a terrorist organization like ISIS or Hamas, or God forbid fall in the hands of a terrorist state like Iran."

Amidst the rounds of agreement, no one heard the dissenting member say, "Or God forbid we find it and become a terrorist organization ourselves."

CHAPTER 79

DAE DONG HELD HIS SMALL FLASHLIGHT DOWNWARD between his teeth while fighting to hold his map open against the wind. Having a GPS locator didn't require an old paper map, but Dae Dong was old-school and wasn't going to take any chances at this point in the mission. As near as his GPS showed, Kanak Island was no more than thirty minutes away, where they would finally break out into the open water of the Gulf of Alaska. That would be their most vulnerable point; they would veer east and hug the coast until they reached Kanak Island, then onward to Kayak Island, where they would ditch the power boat in favor of the inflatables. There they would contact the Sang-O minisub and paddle the last twelve miles to safety.

He looked over the bow of his craft through his night vision binoculars—nothing was visible but the flat, marshy-looking delta riverbed that defined the Copper River. He listened—nothing was audible but the purring sound of his outboard motor as it churned through the calm waters. He looked up at the sky—the clouds were heavy and the moon was not a factor. Perfect for our breakout into the Gulf, he thought.

He looked again at his men; even in the dark, he could read the anger and resentment on their faces. They were loyal, but they were tired, and he knew they felt betrayed. Dae Dong knew why. He had played the last day of the mission out in his mind many times since leaving Valdez. His hatred of the Americans as well as his own arrogance had cost the success of the mission. A small spray of water to his face brought him back to the reality of what they faced in the moment.

***

Safely reaching the southern tip of Kayak Island, Dae Dong raised his flashlight and motioned for the men to pull the boat onto shore. Once there, they deflated its gunnels and buried its remains deep inland. When they accomplished this, they ate their last meal on American soil, inflated the rafts, and shoved off to what they hoped would be their rendezvous.

Having to fight a strong tide and six hours out, the men were struggling. Dae Dong knew the sub must come within the twelve-mile limit or they would never make it. The protocol would have to be breached.

***

Aaron and Devon had taken turns steering the Zodiac. They had agreed that in order to gain time, one would try to sleep for twenty minutes, then get up and either help navigate or search for the saboteurs. When nighttime fell, the catnaps were off and the night vision goggles were on.

"I don't know, Devon," said Aaron, his voice hoarse from yelling over the wind. "Number one, now I'm starting to wonder if they even came this way. Number two, if they did, I'm not sure we can catch them. Remember, they had a pretty good head start."

"Understood, but I still have to go with what my gut tells me, and it tells me this is right. So keep scanning forward and to the east because we're about to break out into the Gulf of Alaska."

"Then what?" asked Aaron.

"Then I'm going to cut a diagonal path straight across to the southernmost tip of Kayak Island."

Aaron frowned and asked, "What about that Kanak Island you mentioned before?"

"Nope. That's the long way where he'll seek cover. Then he'll drop down on the other side of Kayak. Us? We're going straight to where he wants to end up. You see, we don't need to hide."

Aaron smiled and said, "Ah so, Obe Wan. That is why you are paid the big bucks, no?"

"Yeah, right!"

***

First light was barely coming up over the horizon as Devon pulled the Zodiac onto the tip of Kayak Island. He pulled his flashlight out of the cargo pocket on his pants and began checking the surf for any signs that someone had been on the beach. Within minutes, the crisscrossing motion of his light ferreted out tracks in the sand that had not been washed away by the tide. "Aaron, take a look over here!"

When Aaron came near, Devon had already made up his mind. "There you go, bro. Proof positive that my gut was right. See how these drag marks were brushed over by what looks to be a bush?" Devon looked left, then right. "Over there!" he said as he pointed with his flashlight. "See where that branch was thrown in the water, but instead it washed up onshore? That's it. If we wanted to take the time, we'd find their boat buried somewhere inland—guaranteed."

Aaron was somewhat skeptical. "Okay, now what?"

"They probably took off in two small rafts and are paddling their asses out to meet their submarine at the twelve-mile limit."

"But where?"

Devon stretched his arms straight out and met his hands together in front of his face and said, "My guess—due south. Let's go!"

They hopped back into the boat and Aaron looked at the instrument panel. "Do we have enough gas?"

"We have extra in the other tank, we've got the fire power and we've got the guts."

***

TWELVE-MILE LIMIT
GULF OF ALASKA

XO Ryu was at the con when the protocol was first breached by Captain Dong's call for help.

"This is Distant Tiger. Need emergency assistance. Request break-in limit. Repeat; request break-in limit. Circumstance dire; cannot continue. Over."

Ryu froze. He hated the man that now needed his help. Crossing the territorial limit of the United States could provoke an international crisis, especially in light of what had recently occurred in Valdez, which had not yet been tied to North Korea. His captain was sick, and as of this morning, was not able to make any decisions, but he would try to talk to him one more time.

Ryu stood at the edge of his captain's bed. "Captain...Captain..." The man continued to lie in a state that was near delirium. His sheets were soaked. Ryu gently tapped his cheek, but to no avail. His condition hadn't changed in over three days. The XO left and went back to the con.

Ryu stared into space. It wasn't just one man that needed to be saved; it was many. His decision might have been easier if it were only the surly leader that would certainly abandon him if circumstances were reversed. Besides, Captain Dong now outranked him. He picked up his transmitter and paused. The thought of Dae Dong's propensity for mass suicide flashed though his mind. He replied, "Distant Tiger—will engage."

***

The Zodiac and its occupants had taken an absolute pounding on the open waters of the Gulf of Alaska. The sun had risen and although the day was overcast, visibility was good. Devon had correctly assessed that the North Koreans would head south. About eight miles out, Devon saw the outline of the North Korean minisub break the horizon. Through his binoculars, he saw men scrambling from rubber rafts to climb aboard. One by one, they went down a hatch until they were all on board.

Devon was sick. His heart sank. He handed the binoculars to Aaron, who in turn saw the same thing.

"Shit!" Devon blurted out. "The rafts are empty. The bastards have gotten away!" He sank down onto one of the gunnels and pounded the floor.

Aaron slowed the Zodiac to a standstill in the water. He also sat down. "At least you were right, Devon."

"Being right doesn't help, bro."

"Let's not forget what we stopped. After all—"

Aaron's words stopped in midsentence as a periscope, then a conning tower, and finally the full body of a United States submarine appeared behind the minisub. Ever so faintly they heard, "Stand down and prepare to be boarded."

Within minutes, the minisub submerged. The American submarine followed course. All that remained were two rubber rafts that drifted aimlessly about. Then, a massive explosion hurled the water upward, sending enormous waves onto their boat, nearly capsizing them.

"Whoa! What the hell was that?" asked Devon. Aaron's eyes nearly bugged out of his head in awe.

As the waters settled, the American warship rose out of the water.

A crew left the boat long enough to pick up the remains of the rubber rafts and return. The submarine then vanished below the surface. Its log showed that no torpedo was ever fired.

Devon looked over at Aaron and gave him a peculiar stare. "Did you...I mean...?

"You should've gone to CalSci, bro."

Devon gave him another one of those looks and said, "Nah, you... you mean you knew all along?"

Aaron smiled and said, "Remember your buddy, Hatcher?"

Devon stared in disbelief.

EPILOGUE

FAIRBANKS, ALASKA

WITH STEAM RISING FROM THE MUG OF COFFEE IN HIS hand, Aaron Cohen stood on the dew-covered deck facing the morning's sunrise. Its rays had broken the crisp, deep green of the pine forest that surrounded the McKenzie compound. He had been out there in heavy contemplation long before the sun began to rise. The sleepless night had given him no solace. There had been no word from Lana since she had gone missing in New York. In spite of Hatcher ordering up all the resources of the CIA, no leads had yielded results. Svetlana Gorenkov had gone dark.

Standing inside were Devon and Julie; it broke their hearts as they felt the enormity of his pain. Julie was the first to speak.

"We're going to have to do something, Devon. What if the three of us went back to the chateau? Do you think we could get in this time?"

"They will have that place so well patrolled, a rat couldn't sneak in. Besides, it's Lana we want; I doubt she's being held captive there. We've talked about this a hundred times."

"I know, but he can't go on like this, day after—"

"Shhh!" Devon said. "What is that pinging sound?"

"It sounds like it's coming from Aaron's computer."

Julie ran over to Aaron's desk and looked at his computer screen. "Oh my God, get Aaron!"

In the lower right hand corner was an icon of a Russian bear.

www.ingramcontent.com/pod-product-compliance
Lightning Source LLC
Chambersburg PA
CBHW061611170626
46811CB00001B/396